cocoa beach
Cabana

SWEENEY HOUSE
BOOK 6

CECELIA
SCOTT

Cecelia Scott

Sweeney House Book 6

Cocoa Beach Cabana

Copyright © 2023 Cecelia Scott

Cover designed by Sarah Brown (http://www.sarahdesigns.co/)

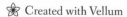 Created with Vellum

Introduction To Sweeney House

The Sweeney House is a landmark inn on the shores of Cocoa Beach, built and owned by the same family for decades. After the unexpected passing of their beloved patriarch, Jay, this family must come together like never before. They may have lost their leader, but the Sweeneys are made of strong stuff. Together on the island paradise where they grew up, this family meets every challenge with hope, humor, and heart, bathed in sunshine and the unconditional love they learned from their father.

For RELEASE DATES, preorder alerts, updates and more, sign up for my newsletter! Or go to www.ceceliascott.com and follow me on Facebook!

Chapter One

Sam

Samantha Sweeney had always been a big believer in New Year's resolutions, and this particular January 1st felt like an especially good time for some fresh starts, new habits, and a juicy list of goals.

Embarking on her first year as a divorced, single, completely independent woman, Sam had weathered the winds of change that had blown through her life, and felt ready for whatever was in store for her moving forward.

With optimism surging in her heart, Sam settled into the rocking loveseat on the back deck of the Sweeney family cottage, her fingers wrapped around a hot cup of coffee, and considered what should be Resolution Number 1.

Dottie peeked her head out through the open sliders, smiling at Sam. "Happy New Year, my darling daughter."

"Good morning!" Sam gestured for her mother to sit next to her. "Happy New Year, Mom."

Dottie raised her own mug in a mock toast, her blue eyes as bright as the morning sky over Cocoa Beach.

Ever since Sam had moved back to this beachside cottage—her childhood home—at the beginning of the previous summer, this back deck had become a place of support, fun, sisterhood, and great ideas, and she welcomed the prospect of a million more mornings like that with open arms.

"So, did you make it to midnight?" Dottie asked as she sat down, blowing softly on the steam coming from her coffee mug. "See the ol' ball drop?"

Sam shook her head with a soft laugh. "I'm the worst. I was out by ten-thirty."

"I got you beat. I believe there was still a nine on the clock when I drifted off." Dottie chuckled and sipped her coffee. "We sure aren't night owls."

"No, we're early birds. Which I prefer, because we never miss a glorious sunrise." Sam looked out at the breathtaking Atlantic Ocean, the sky above it streaked with orange and pink as the soft clouds glowed in the light of the rising sun.

"Ah, yes." Dottie sighed with contentment. "And here? They never disappoint."

Sam jutted her chin toward the adjacent beach, where Lori was hosting her sunrise yoga class on the sand behind the Sweeney House Inn.

"Looks like Lori's classes are going well," Sam said. "Did she tell you one of the big hotels down in Melbourne Beach contacted her to do these classes for them?"

Dottie's jaw loosened. "No. Is she going to?"

"Nope. She's building a real loyal following here, I'm happy to say. And she's considering adding more classes throughout the day when we reopen the inn." Sam leaned a little closer. "Her yoga-therapy mix will be a secret weapon for the inn when we reopen, Mom. No one else can offer that to guests."

Ever since Sam's newly-discovered half-sister spontaneously showed up in Cocoa Beach with her pregnant daughter looking to get to know the family she never thought she'd have, Lori Caparelli had become more and more integrated into the Sweeneys and the town, starting with her staple sunrise yoga class.

"It is," Dottie agreed. "Look, there are five people there on New Year's morning. How wonderful."

"It is. She said she prefers small classes like that. I'm sure she's teaching today with the theme of new beginnings or resolutions, instilling a feeling that's peaceful and hopeful in the way that only a retired therapist can." Sam smiled, reflecting on how close she and Lori had become over the last couple of months, and feeling so thankful for that bond.

They sat in quiet peace for a few moments, then Sam asked, "So, do you have any New Year's resolutions?"

"Hmm." Dottie drew back, considering the question. "I suppose I haven't really given it much thought this year. We've been so wrapped up with the inn renovation and the family and the holiday season, I've hardly had time to reflect."

Sam nodded. "I know Dad was a big resolution guy. I think he imbued that in all of us, because every single year, I find myself making a list."

"Oh, was he ever." Dottie chuckled at the memory. "With monthly check-ins on your goals."

"Please." Sam pressed her hands to her chest,

warmed by the memory of something that was so truly Jay Sweeney, it almost hurt to think about it. "Of course, Erica the Overachiever was at the head of that line every month."

Dottie laughed. "With your firstborn brother not far behind."

"Dad was always about self-improvement, always wanted us to be the best versions of ourselves in every way." Sam sighed. "I love him for that."

Dottie looked at Sam wistfully, giving her hand a loving squeeze. "He'd be so proud of you. Of all of you."

"I know." Sam smiled.

"So, to answer your question..." Dottie took a drink of coffee and held up a finger. "I'll get back to you on my resolutions."

"Please." Sam flicked her hand. "You don't need to change a thing, Mom. Your life is beautiful."

"As is yours." Dottie leaned forward to get a better look at Lori's setup, but squinted as the sun hit her eyes. "Eesh, I don't know how she does it out there when the sun gets over the horizon. Even in January, it's blinding."

The air of Cocoa Beach's winter, if one could even call it that, was still warm and smelled of salt. The occasional cool breeze was the only real indicator of the season, but Sam didn't mind the endless summer sun of her home.

"You can't escape the sunshine here," Sam agreed.

"Although it looks like Lori is trying to do just that." Dottie pointed at the four large beach umbrellas that Lori had set up on the sand in an attempt to make some shade for her yoga students.

It appeared to be a bit in vain, as the umbrellas were one strong wind away from toppling. One already had, and the rest weren't providing much in the way of relief.

Watching, Sam wrinkled her nose. "There's got to be a better way for her to do the class on the beach without everyone getting sunburned."

"And if she adds those classes throughout the day, it'll be unbearable without shade," Dottie said.

"We should think of something," Sam said, an idea sparking in her mind as she turned to Mom. "We should figure out a way for her to do the classes behind Sweeney House without having that crazy direct sun blasting all her yoga students."

Dottie sat up, brightening. "That's a wonderful idea, Sam. Like a...tent, or an overhang, or a—"

"Cabana!" they said in unison, making them both laugh.

Sam groaned a little. "Do we really need another renovation at this place, Mom? I feel like we've been at this improvement for a long time."

"We have, but this is brilliant! We need a beautiful cabana on the sand. Guests could use it as a relaxation spot, and Lori could teach her classes in it in the morning."

"So true," Sam agreed. "Plus, since her teaching style is so personal, it wouldn't have to be too big but it would mean she could practice in rain or blaring sun."

"It should be a decent size, though," Dottie countered, studying the space where Lori was finishing up her class, giving each of the women a heated, scented wash-cloth as they lay in their final resting pose. "So five or six people could have room to spread out."

"Yes, definitely." Sam nodded. "It's very doable, and would be an awesome addition to our new and wildly improved Sweeney House."

"Ah, the quest to improve..." Dottie shook her head, glancing wistfully at the ocean. "It never does stop, does it? Jay is up there smiling."

"I guess we've added another resolution to our list. Cabana." Sam held a finger up and made a checkmark in the air. "Now, the question becomes, who can build it and how much will it cost."

Dottie slid her a look. "I bet Ethan could build it," she suggested gently, clearly trying to tiptoe around Sam's heart, which was still bruised after their difficult breakup before Thanksgiving.

"I don't..." Sam swallowed, the wound fresher than she'd like it to be. "I don't know, Mom."

She'd been managing since they said goodbye, keeping herself distracted, busy, and focused on the soon-to-be-completed renovation of Sweeney House. That didn't give Sam much time to wallow in her sadness over losing a man as special as Ethan Price.

Instead of being his girlfriend, she stayed focused on being Taylor's mom, Annie's best friend, Dottie's busi-ness partner and daughter, Lori's closest confidante, Erica, John, and Julie's sister, and an aunt to a whole lot of nieces and nephews.

Sam loved her newfound role in the center of this family, especially after having spent her entire twenty-five-year marriage being pulled away from them. As exciting and hopeful as the short-lived romance with Ethan had been, there was no time for regret.

Although she got kicked by remorse frequently enough. She should have left well enough alone, believed him when he told her the truth, and trusted the man she'd been falling in love with.

She'd done none of those things, so...now, the very thought of seeing Ethan Price building a cabana for Sweeney House made her throat tight and her heart ache.

"Oh, honey." Dottie reached over and gave Sam's hand a loving squeeze. "I'm sorry. We'll hire someone else, of course. I know you're still hurting."

"He'd do the best job," Sam said softly, knowing it was true. "He'd do it, and he'd pour so much love into that cabana that every single person who sat underneath it or walked past it would know how special it is."

Dottie let out a slow breath, wisely not arguing with that. Ethan had restored, repurposed, and revitalized enough of Dottie and Jay's precious antiques that she was fully aware of his invaluable skills and talent with wood-working and furniture.

"I can talk to him," Sam said reluctantly.

"No, Sam. Please." Dottie shook her head, pressing her lips together. "You need to heal. That split was rough on you, and I don't want this to set you back and bring up any pain."

"I can handle it."

But her mother just shook her head again, with certainty this time. "Nope. I will look into other options."

Sam leaned back into the cushion of the loveseat, watching the waves lapping onto the shore as the sun rose higher in the clear blue sky.

"Unless you think there's a chance..." Dottie turned to her, brow arched. "That you two might, you know...rekindle."

Sam shut her eyes, trying to tamp down the swell of hope that formed in her chest at the thought.

"It is a new year, after all." Dottie sighed. "New beginnings are afoot."

Sam couldn't get her hopes up for that. Ethan had been pretty darn clear that their relationship, as intoxicating and wonderful and serious as it had been, was over.

Sam had overstepped her bounds trying to discover why he was so closed off about his past, and confronting him with a news article headline she'd found online was definitely not the best way to go about things.

She couldn't dwell on the regret, and had to remind herself that she hadn't been able to fully fall in love with him until she knew about his past, and his divorce. And, he didn't want to talk about it, which had terrified her. So, she'd...dug. And when she saw the snippets online about him having had a relationship with one of his students at his old high school, yes, she'd gone to him, completely freaked out.

But by the time Ethan was able to explain that the whole thing was a false rumor made up by a lovesick teenager, he felt his trust had been betrayed and that Sam didn't respect him enough to leave it alone.

And...that was that. Boom. Done. Over.

"I don't know if I can add 'get back with Ethan' to my list of goals this year, Mom." Sam sipped her coffee and crossed her ankles on the table in front of them.

"I understand. I just wish you two could have worked it out. You were so happy together."

"Maybe I'm just not meant to find love again," she mused, secretly hoping that wasn't true. "Maybe I'm meant to be a lot of other, different things. I have so much in my life that makes me happy now. This family, the renovation, you..." She smiled widely. "I'm okay, Mom. Really. Lori and I have gotten close, too, and that's been wonderful. I guess one of my resolutions would be to continue to grow that bond with her and help her find her new direction."

"That's a wonderful resolution, Sam."

Something nagged in the back of Sam's head, though. Something she'd been holding onto for nearly six weeks now, since the night she and Ethan broke up. But it wasn't about Ethan.

Her mother turned to her. "What's on your mind?"

She gave a soft laugh, not surprised that her mother could sense something was wrong. With a sigh, Sam leaned back, thinking of how to respond.

She couldn't tell Dottie what she'd overheard between Lori and her daughter, Amber, that night she'd broken up with Ethan. She couldn't tell a soul, at least not until she addressed it with Lori first. But she'd put off that conversation since then, and deep inside, Sam knew she couldn't do that much longer.

She had to talk to Lori. She had to come clean. And what better time than January 1st?

Sam looked out toward the beach behind Sweeney House—the future spot of a fabulous cabana—to see Lori packing up her yoga mat, portable speaker, and bag of supplies.

Her students had all left, and she was alone.

"I'm going to go talk to her," Sam said.

No surprise, Dottie didn't offer to come along or be part of the conversation, and Sam was grateful her mother was so intuitive.

Sam had to have this talk alone. It was time for Lori to be aware that she knew the truth, and time for a fresh, clean, honest start to the new year.

A FEW MINUTES LATER, Sam jogged down the beach. "Good class this morning?" she called to Lori, who was just twisting her long blond hair up into a knot on top of her head as she fanned her face with her other hand.

"Oh, it was magnificent. Just...wow. A little hot. Are we absolutely sure it's January?"

"Welcome to Florida." Sam held her hands out.

"Well, I don't actually mind it, it just makes for a sunny class. But I'm a bit worried what my business will look like come summertime." Lori reached down to slide a water bottle into a canvas tote bag. "If this is, you know, 'winter.'" She added joking air quotes.

"Actually, my mom and I were just talking about that very thing when we saw you teaching out here."

"Really?"

"Yes, and we think we may have a good solution. We think we should build a cabana. Well, *we* wouldn't build it," Sam added with a chuckle. "We want to have a cabana built. For your yoga."

Lori froze in place as she wedged a towel into the bag, slowly lifting her gaze to Sam's, her eyes wide with surprise. "You guys...you want to do that...for me?"

"Yep," Sam assured her. "You bring a true value-added amenity to this operation, Lori. And we think a beautiful cabana that shades and protects your students will be nice—necessary, actually—for your classes." She pointed her finger with a smile. "We can't let some other hotel lure you away."

"Sam." Lori stood up, instantly reaching her arms out for a hug. "I'm so touched. That's...that's incredible. Thank you."

Sam embraced her sister, then pulled back and smiled. "You're family, Lori. It's what we do for each other."

"And what a family it is," Lori proclaimed. "I'm still getting used to this gang, but wow. I like being part of it. It's kind of amazing, to be honest."

"Well, speaking of being honest..." Sam took a deep breath, digging her toes into the sand as she tried to find the right words to tell Lori what she knew about Amber's pregnancy. "There's actually something else I want to talk to you about."

"Oh?" Lori glanced out at the ocean. "Want to go for a walk?"

"Yes, let's do it."

They headed down to the shore and walked side by side along the ocean, letting the gentle waves splash up around their ankles with every step.

"Okay..." Sam drew the word out slowly, hoping Lori didn't think she was snooping or eavesdropping that night. "I have to tell you that I overheard...something."

Lori turned to her, her eyebrows pulled together in confusion. "You did?"

"Yes." Sam cleared her throat. "Almost two months ago, actually. The night Ethan ended things with me."

"Oh." Lori looked at Sam. "That was a while ago. What happened? What did you overhear?"

"Well, I came home that night and saw you and Amber sitting on the front porch of the cottage. It was late, and I was, well, moments after a breakup, so I wanted to be alone. I wasn't ready to talk about it, so I parked at the inn to avoid seeing you guys. No offense," she added.

"Totally understandable. None taken," Lori said, clearly having no idea where this story was going.

"Anyway, I stayed in my car for a bit, cried, wallowed, eventually pulled it together and walked over to the cottage. I headed around the house to slip in through the back door—"

"To avoid me," Lori teased.

"Obviously," Sam said playfully. "But that's when I heard you and Amber talking."

"Oh. *Oh.*" Lori's face fell and her pace slowed to a near stop, obviously remembering the conversation. "So you..." She swallowed, locking eyes with Sam. "So you know."

"All I know," Sam said on a deep breath. "Is that the congressman Amber had been working for is the father of her baby, not a one-night stand. And that he's...married. Unless I misheard."

Lori shook her head, brushing a strand of hair back into her knotted bun. "You didn't mishear."

"Lori..." Sam breathed her name. "I'm so sorry it happened this way. I promise I wasn't trying to eavesdrop or snoop. Amber was just really upset and I heard your voices, and—"

Lori placed her hand on Sam's arm, turning them to face each other. "Can I be honest?"

Sam nodded. "Please."

"I'm so relieved you know."

"You are?"

"Oh my gosh," Lori groaned. "You have no idea. I desperately need someone to talk to about this. Carrying it around all by myself has been exhausting. There've been many times you and I have been talking about our daughters and I've wanted to tell you so badly, but..." She shook her head. "I couldn't do that to Amber. She was adamant that it remain a secret. I'm sure you can understand why."

Sam? The woman who'd been cheated on by her

husband and had her whole family ripped apart because of it? Yes, she could certainly understand why Amber would feel shame in that situation.

But she didn't want to judge Amber. Not until she knew everything. "Of course I understand, but... Can you tell me what happened?"

Lori nodded, gathering her thoughts for a moment, then said, "Well, as you know, Amber was a junior campaign manager for Congressman Michael Garrison of North Carolina."

"Right. He was running last fall."

"Yes. And in full fairness to Amber, he and his wife were completely and officially separated, with divorce papers filed but not finalized. It was understood by everyone at the office and on the campaign that they were getting a divorce, so you could hardly call it an 'affair.' He swore he was done with the marriage, basically just waiting to sign the papers."

Well, that was certainly different from what had happened to Sam, which was a relief.

"Everything changed when Amber got pregnant," Lori continued, her eyelids shuttering as she said the words. "Michael all but begged her not to keep the baby."

Sam gave a grunt, hurting for Amber. "That's rough."

"It was horrible," Lori said. "All he cared about was his reputation. He didn't want it getting out that he was having a relationship with a younger woman, and a campaign staffer to boot. Men in far higher positions had been toppled for that, so he knew a scandal could cost him his high-flying and quickly growing career in politics."

"But she didn't end the pregnancy, so what happened?" Sam asked.

"Michael Garrison, scum of the earth that he is, did what any sleazy, selfish, heartless politician would do."

She shook her head, waiting to hear the conclusion.

"He got back with his wife. Broken marriages don't get votes, he decided. The baby was some sort of wake-up call to him, and he realized he'd been playing with fire. He relinquished his parental rights and basically told Amber goodbye and good luck, and please stay away forever."

"Holy...wow. That is horrible."

"She had no problem saying goodbye to him, since she knew his true colors. And he did offer her money, but she turned it down because she felt he was buying her silence."

"Would she go public with this?" Sam asked.

"Never. Amber isn't vindictive and vengeful." Lori shook her head. "She made a mistake in judgment, but she wants the baby. I guess she'll have to figure out what to tell her little girl when she gets older, but for now, all Amber is thinking about is the daunting task of being a single mother."

"With all of us and you to help," Sam added warmly.

"Of course." Lori sighed. "That's a huge benefit of living here, but it has still been a very emotional and, honestly, scary time for her. She's introverted, as you know, and has held a lot of this in while she adjusts to a very different life than what she expected."

Sam processed this, thinking of how she would feel if it had been Taylor who'd been through the experience of being lied to and manipulated by a married man—especially one with status and money and power. And to carry his baby and raise it alone? No wonder Amber seemed jaded and withdrawn. Poor girl.

"I am so sorry that she had to go through all of that." Sam put a loving hand on Lori's shoulder as they walked down the beach, heading back toward the cottage and the inn. "Men can be such unfathomable jerks."

Lori snorted. "No kidding. And, as her mother, I don't know how to help her, you know? She can't get a job doing what she loved because he won't give her a reference or recommendation, even though she's amazing at campaign management."

"So that's why she quit to be a waitress," Sam said slowly.

Lori nodded. "She had to get out of that office, and I don't blame her. And then, I told her about you and Julie showing up and telling me about the Sweeneys and Cocoa Beach and the magic, and she was basically packed by the next day."

"Really?"

"Oh, yes." Lori laughed at the memory. "Amber was desperate for an escape, a way to get out of that city and to somewhere you didn't see Michael Garrison's lying mug everywhere on a billboard or yard sign."

Sam shuddered. "Of course. That's terrible."

"So, in the interest of us both needing fresh starts and new beginnings and every other cliché you and Julie fired off at that coffee shop that day..." She gave a teasing wink. "We headed down here. And that is the real truth. Wow, it feels good to get that out there."

"I can imagine. You two have been holding onto that secret since you arrived."

"We have. And, please, don't tell anyone else. I'd really like to just keep this between us, for Amber's sake. We really don't want it getting out. Plus, obviously, she feels horrible."

"Well, she shouldn't feel horrible, but I promise I won't tell a soul." Sam held her hand to her chest. "It's Amber's story, and it's not my place to tell it."

"Thank you." Lori leaned her head onto Sam's shoulder as they strolled down the beach. "What made you decide to bring this up now? You've just been sitting on this information for six weeks, and only just now decided to talk to me about it? It must have been driving you crazy!"

"I just felt like it wasn't my place. I heard something I shouldn't have." Sam shrugged. "But my Mom and I were talking about New Year's resolutions and the idea of a fresh start and I figured it was time to bring it up."

"Oh, I *love* resolutions."

Sam laughed. "See? You really are a Sweeney."

"I just really love the idea that you have this whole, brand new year ahead of you. It can be anything you want it to be. There's no better time to try and change something, or fix something, or start something new."

"I couldn't agree more. I'm so glad I talked to you. I feel like a huge weight's been lifted off my chest."

"Me, too." Lori tilted her head toward the sky. "I think we should tell Amber. Together."

"Together?" Sam drew back, surprised.

"Yes. I think we should go over there now, and talk to her. Tell her that you know the truth, and assure her that no one else will, at least until she's ready. I think she could use another voice of guidance and support on this—not that she would ever admit that. But I can sense it."

"Okay." Sam pushed a strand of hair out of her eyes as they reached the back deck of the cottage and headed up the sand-covered wooden stairs. "I would love to be that for her."

As they brushed the sand off their feet and got their shoes on, Lori glanced over at Sam. "No word from...*you know who?*"

"Oh, I know who," Sam joked. "I haven't talked to Ethan more than a cursory hello when he happened to be at the inn over the holidays."

"So I guess he won't be the one building the cabana, then?"

She sighed. "You've been spending too much time with my mother. She had the same thought."

"Well, he's just done so much for the inn, I figured..." Lori shrugged. "But I know you two aren't together anymore."

"I know he'd do an amazing job, but no." Sam swallowed. "Not after the way things ended. We've been cordial in passing a couple of times, but...even 'cordial' is a stretch. Ice cold is more like it."

"That's so hard. Ben isn't in his class anymore, though, right?"

"No, Ben moves to Calc 2 this semester, so with work wrapping on the inn, I suppose I'll be seeing less and less of Ethan." The thought was so sad, she almost couldn't bear it.

Was it really the end?

"What about *your* 'you know who?'" Sam asked, angling her head as she slid on a pair of white sneakers. "Rick?"

Lori's face fell at the mention of her soon-to-be ex-husband, who Sam knew she was most definitely not over. Lori had confided that she had abundant regrets about how their marriage had ended.

But they were separated, heading toward divorce, and with no change in that status, Sam knew it made Lori blue.

"No updates, really."

"All right, sister." Sam wrapped her arm around Lori as they headed out to the driveway to go to Lori's town-house and talk to Amber. "One emotional roller coaster at a time. Let's go ride the Amber train first."

Lori just laughed. "That should be...fun."

Chapter Two

Amber

Amber Kittle stared at the calendar on her computer screen, her eyes firmly locked on one little square. May 10th was highlighted and circled and colored in every imaginable way, leaving Amber to wonder if it was going to be the best or worst day of her life.

She had one hundred and thirty one days—give or take—until she had to push an entire human being out of her body, and then spend the rest of her life loving it, raising it, and, hopefully, not royally screwing it up.

"One thirty one," she whispered to herself, flopping back onto the pile of pillows at the top of her unmade bed.

She squeezed her eyes shut and held one hand on the small bump on her tummy, waiting to feel some sort of connection for the tiny person growing inside.

But all Amber felt was sadness and fear.

"What are we gonna do, Kidney Bean?" She glanced down at her baby bump, who she'd affectionately nick-named Kidney Bean after seeing the image on her last ultrasound.

That was also the day she found out Kidney Bean

was a girl, which somehow made this whole thing that much more real.

Amber sighed, picking up her phone and scrolling through her messages and call history. She let out an audible whimper of sadness when she realized she hadn't spoken to her father in nearly three weeks.

Their conversations since she and Mom had moved down to Florida had been few and far between. The ones she had managed had been very, very tense and surface level. It hurt Amber like a stab wound to push away and isolate her father like this, but it would hurt a lot more to tell him the truth.

Disappointing Dad, the man who'd been her biggest cheerleader in life and a true friend, was a purely wretched thought.

Yes, Amber had her mom, and they'd gotten very close during this ordeal of an unplanned pregnancy and the move to Florida. But Lori's career had been insanely demanding and time-consuming for all of Amber's childhood, so her father, beloved Rick Kittle, talented photographer, at-home chef, and all around awesome man had been the hands-on parent.

He took her to her soccer games and helped her with her homework. He even put his whole photography business on hold for the first ten years of Amber's life so he could be a full-time parent to her.

The two had been true buds, making Amber a certified Daddy's girl. But ever since Kidney Bean came into the picture, she could hardly hear her father's voice on

the phone or read a text from him without being overwhelmed by shame.

At first, he'd been worried and concerned when
Amber started to pull away—asking what was wrong,
calling Lori to find out if something was going on, sending
Amber texts and telling her how much he missed her.
Then he started to seem hurt and confused.

Who could blame him?

Now, he seemed to accept that they'd grown apart, no
doubt blaming it on the divorce.

She flipped through the pictures on her phone,
finding old shots of them together. Touring college
campuses, smiling at graduation. Her gaze landed on a
photo taken during the first campaign she'd ever worked
on, for a county commissioner's seat. Her candidate had
won, and she was over the moon.

Dad had been so proud of her. He'd stood in the auditorium where the election results had been announced,
arm around her, beaming with joy.

He wouldn't be proud now, she thought. He'd be
horrified. He'd be furious. He might never be able to look
at Amber the same way again.

"I'm so sorry, Daddy," she whispered, closing her eyes
again, wishing she could disappear.

Hurting her father had to be without a doubt the
worst byproduct of this whole mess, but the way Amber
saw it, she didn't have a choice. He couldn't find out. Not
yet, anyway.

Keeping the identity of the baby's father a secret was

one of the main reasons she'd been so eager to leave North Carolina. If she didn't see Dad very often, she could delay coming clean. She could wait. But until when?

The clock was ticking. That calendar was moving. And her once rock-solid, unbreakable bond with her father might just be shattered for good in a matter of months.

"Amber, honey, you here?" Mom's voice echoed through the townhouse.

"In my room," Amber called back, knowing her mom would probably urge her to make her bed, open her blinds, throw in a load of laundry and 'set herself up for a good day.'

She could hear the cheerful enthusiasm that Lori Caparelli never seemed to lose. Amber, on the other hand, could do without the cheer.

"Hey, Amber." Lori peeked her head in and knocked on the bedroom door softly, like she was waking a bear from hibernation. "So dark in here."

"Mmm," Amber grunted.

Lori floated over to the window and, predictably, opened the curtains, letting in an ungodly amount of sunlight.

Wasn't it winter?

"So, listen." She sat down on the edge of the bed, picking up some clothes and unconsciously folding and smoothing them while she talked. "Sam is with me right now. She's in the living room."

Great. Company.

Sam, like all the other Sweeneys, was nice and kind

and came from a good place. Amber knew that. But some-times, it didn't matter. Sometimes it felt like no one on the planet would ever understand how she felt, and what she was going through. And trying to connect with people and bring them into her life only made her feel more alone. Especially because she was lying to all of them, saying she'd just had a one night stand.

"Okay," Amber mumbled, rubbing her eyes.

"Listen, I need to tell you something," her mother said, her voice even more tender than usual. "You're going to want to pay attention."

Amber sat up a little, propping her back on her pillows and headboard. "What is it?"

"Sam knows. The truth."

"She *what*?" Amber sat straight up now, the shock of her mother's words reverberating through her chest. "You told her? Mom, you swore! You promised me that you wouldn't tell—"

"Honey, stop." Lori placed a hand on Amber's leg through the thick comforter. "I didn't tell her. She over-heard us talking about it."

Amber frowned. "When?"

"Many weeks ago, actually. Before Thanksgiving. You and I were talking on the front porch at the cottage. Sam was coming back from Ethan's place and she over-heard our conversation."

Amber felt her shoulders sink as she let out a breath, knowing she'd have to accept that the truth was out, and there was nothing she could do about it. "Great. Sam knows. Sam, the woman whose husband cheated on her with a younger woman at work. And he, too, got his mistress pregnant, right?" Amber flopped back into the pillows and buried her face. "Oh, God, she's gonna think I'm as bad as her husband's sleazy girlfriend."

"No, no, she's not. She's not judging you." Lori gently tugged the pillow off Amber's face. "Besides, I explained everything. About Michael, how he lied to you, how he went back on his word and manipulated you. She understands what it's like to be lied to and played by someone you think you can trust."

Amber brushed some knotted hair out of her face and considered that.

"Look, A. Sam has been the dearest friend and sister to me since we've moved here, and she will not do anything to hurt either of us. I promise. I think we should all just talk, okay?"

Amber sniffed, not entirely sure what that talk was meant to accomplish, but what choice did she have? "Okay."

"Come on." Lori stood up and patted Amber's leg, nodding toward the door. "I'll have a cup of decaf waiting."

Amber rolled her eyes, knowing the real coffee she craved was off the pregnancy table.

After a few minutes of gathering herself, tying up her mess of hair, and brushing her teeth, Amber slid her feet into her fuzzy leopard-print slippers and shuffled out into the living room of the townhouse.

The room, of course, was flooded with warmth and

sunlight, since Mom had some sort of personal vendetta against blinds or curtains.

"Hey, Amber." Sam smiled and scooted over on the L-shaped sectional, making room for her to sit between the two of them. "Cute slippers. Taylor would covet."

Amber managed a laugh. "Thanks. I'll send her a link, they're so comfy."

She sat down and sipped the coffee her mom handed her, letting it warm her throat and chest, which was all decaf was really good for.

"So..." She turned to Sam, tucking a strand of hair behind her ear. "You know my story, huh?"

Sam nodded. "I do. And, first of all, I want to assure you that I haven't told a soul and don't plan to."

Amber lifted her brows. "Really?"

"Of course. It's not my place."

"I just..." Amber shrugged. "I guess I assumed the Sweeneys have an open-door, no-secrets policy."

"We also have a protect and respect each other policy," Sam said. "Fun secrets get shared. Secrets that matter and affect someone's life? No. I won't go running my mouth, I promise."

"Thank you." Amber locked eyes with her, already feeling more at ease. "I really appreciate that. I'm sure my mom explained to you that it wasn't like, an *affair*, or something like that. They were separated, and he told me—"

"I know," Sam cut her off, giving her a gentle and sympathetic smile. "Please. You do not have to justify what it's like to be lied to by a powerful, high-status man who swept you off your feet. I've got a stack of divorce papers and lengthy list of regrets to prove it."

Amber snorted softly, glancing at her mom, who smiled. "Thanks, Sam. I actually was most worried about you finding out. I didn't want you to think I was like... whatever her name is."

"Kayla," Sam said, curling her lip humorously at the mention of the woman who broke up her family and marriage and life. "Amber, listen to me. You are nothing like that. And frankly? I don't even have ill will toward her. The person in the wrong was my husband. Just like, in your case, the person in the wrong was that slimeball Michael Garrison."

"Slimeball is the perfect word," Lori added, shaking her head in disgust.

"That makes me feel better." Amber took another sip from her coffee mug and held a throw pillow against her baby bump.

"Good. That's the goal here, A." Lori smoothed Amber's hair on the top of her head. "We want you to feel better."

"We do," Sam agreed. "And I know you've got your awesome mom, but if I can offer any support at all, I'm more than willing to do so." She leaned in close and winked dramatically. "Everyone needs a fun aunt in their life."

Amber laughed, a bubbly, real, genuine laugh that felt better than she could have expected. "I've never had a fun aunt."

"This is why we're here." Lori beamed, nodding slowly. "Family is everything. I'm learning that."

"It is. And, for the record," Sam added, "you have nothing to be ashamed of."

Amber wasn't entirely convinced of that yet, but it still felt nice to hear it from someone other than her mom, who Amber always felt had to say that stuff out of obligation.

"You can tell Taylor, by the way." Amber lifted a shoulder. "I know how close you two are, and I trust her not to go spreading it around. Besides, I like her. It'd be nice to not have to keep lying to her."

"Only if you're completely comfortable." Sam raised her brows. "I'll fill her in. But don't worry about her. She's still in far too much of a love bubble with Andre to really see past that."

Amber smiled. "Good for her. I want to hear about the love bubble. Maybe I'll meet up with Taylor sometime this week. I could even tell her the truth myself."

Her mother's eyes widened with hope, which was probably warranted, considering that was about the most enthusiasm and normalcy Amber had shown in months.

Maybe they were right. Maybe this visit with Sam was just what she needed.

"I never thought I'd say this..." Amber twisted a loose strand of hair. "But it's weirdly comforting for someone else to know the truth. With just the two of us knowing," she gestured at Lori. "It felt so isolating all the time. Like we had to live in our own world with all these walls up."

Lori shut her eyes and breathed a visible sigh of

relief. "I'm so glad to hear you say that, A. I felt exactly the same way."

Amber looked back and forth between the two women, sitting on either side of her, holding her up like pillars of support that she hadn't known she needed until right now.

"In the spirit of telling people and starting fresh and perhaps the fact that it's New Year's Day..." Lori said slowly and gently, wiggling a brow at Amber.

"Oh, God." Amber groaned playfully. "Please, no resolutions."

Sam cracked up.

But Lori's expression remained serious. "Have you thought about when you're going to tell your father?"

Oh, man. Amber had known this was coming. Clearly, she hadn't been the only one that morning who felt the weight of Dad not knowing the truth.

"I mean, Amber, he doesn't even know he's going to be a grandfather in four months."

Amber gulped. Somehow, four months sounded like a lot less time than one hundred and thirty one days. "I know," she said weakly.

"Are you just going to tell him you're pregnant? Or tell him...everything?" Sam asked, taking a sip of coffee.

"That's the thing." Amber huffed out a sigh, adjusting the pillow that was against her tummy and tucking her legs underneath her. "I can't lie to him. I just...I can't."

Sam nodded in understanding. "Your mom told me how close you two are."

"How close we *used* to be," Amber corrected. "Now he thinks I want nothing to do with him and he doesn't even know why." Her throat tightened with emotion unexpectedly. "It's breaking my heart. I can't lie to him, but I can't tell him the truth, either."

A single tear slid down Amber's cheek and she wiped it away quickly, drawing in a deep, shuddering breath to center herself.

Her mom looked as sad and broken as Amber felt, because there was nothing Lori Caparelli hated more than being helpless, and not being able to instantly solve a problem. But in this situation, there was nothing Lori could do. Or Sam.

The only person who could deal with it was Amber, and maybe January 1st was a darn good time to start... dealing with it.

"Look." Sam leveled her gaze, giving Amber a stern yet comforting expression. "Take it from someone who wishes more than anything in the world that she could have one more conversation with her father: tell him."

Amber felt her heart fold at the thought of never being able to talk to her dad again. She got the impression that Jay Sweeney, who was her biological grandfather, was one heck of a dad to all his kids. And Rick Kittle was one heck of a dad, too.

"He doesn't deserve the way I've been treating him." Amber sniffled. "I know that. And...you're right." She turned to look at Lori, then back at Sam. "You both are. I need to tell him about the baby, and...I need to tell him the truth."

Lori placed a hand on top of Amber's, squeezing it. "Your father loves you unconditionally, just like I do. He is not going to judge you or hate you or think any less of you, I promise."

Sam nodded. "She's right. Parental love is truly and profoundly unconditional."

Amber slowly lowered her gaze, looking down at the little bump where Kidney Bean was residing.

Would her love for this little girl be unconditional? What if she wasn't capable of that because of who the baby's father was?

No, Amber couldn't go there. Not yet. She had one hundred and thirty one days to mentally prepare for becoming a mother. And one thing was clearer than ever.

"I need my dad," she stated simply. "I'm going to call him."

Lori smiled widely with relief, relaxing back onto the couch cushions. "Oh, Amber. I am so happy to hear you say that."

She leaned against her mom, affectionately resting her head on her shoulder. For all of Lori's cheerful, mental health-oriented, natural light-obsessed guidance, her therapist mother meant well, and Amber was forever grateful for her and her unconditional love.

And now there was Sam. The fun aunt that Amber never thought she'd have.

She sat up and gently touched Sam's arm, smiling. "Thank you for coming here and being so kind to me. I...I thought you'd have a much different reaction if you ever found out."

"Nah." Sam flicked her fingers dismissively. "I'm here for you. Seriously."

"I guess I have a phone call to make. I'm not ready yet, though. I think I'm going to give it a week or so to think through what I'm going to say and mentally prepare."

"That's perfectly fine," Lori said.

"Of course," Sam chimed in. "Take all the time you need. I think what matters is that you've decided to do it, and the sooner you do, the sooner you can heal your relationship with your dad. Remember..." She glanced at Lori. "One roller coaster at a time."

Amber stood up, stretching and taking a deep breath before placing a hand on her belly, which seemed to grow a tiny bit every day. "You know, Sam, I'm starting to think that maybe Cocoa Beach isn't magic."

"What do you mean?" Sam asked.

"It's you," Amber said, jutting her chin. "You're the magic."

Sam just smiled, clearly touched by the comment.

Chapter Three

Julie

As much as Julie Sweeney completely adored the hip, bohemian, and totally quirky apartment that she and Bliss had moved into, she seriously missed waking up at the cottage every day.

Thankfully, their new pad was only ten minutes from her beloved childhood home, which was always harboring some amount of family members. Whenever Julie wasn't teaching a guitar lesson, hanging with her daughter, or playing a gig, she was here at the cottage, soaking up every drop of family time she'd spent years missing out on.

Despite the fact that Bliss was sixteen and a junior, today was her first day of what she called "real" school. That meant sitting in a public school classroom with other kids instead of doing virtual learning in the backseat of a tour van, like she had been accustomed to her whole life.

After dropping her off this morning, Julie felt a bit silly for being reflective and melancholy, considering her daughter was a teenager, not a five-year-old headed to kindergarten. Nonetheless, the two had been inseparable for Bliss's entire life, so sending her off to school was a big moment.

That left Julie on her own for the day, five days into a new year, and entirely unsure what this year might have in store.

It didn't matter. Bliss was healthy. That's what mattered, and that was something that Julie Sweeney would spend every moment of her life being grateful for.

"Hey, it's me!" Julie called into the cottage as she let herself through the front door and beelined for the kitchen, which would reliably be stocked with a delicious assortment of breakfast foods and K-cups.

No one responded, so Julie figured Taylor must be at work, and Sam and Dottie were likely next door at the inn getting an early start on their never-ending renovation.

With a fresh cup of coffee and a blueberry muffin, Julie headed out to the back deck for some air.

It was remarkable how much her heart and soul had changed since she showed up on the doorstep of this cottage a few months ago, begging for someone to give Bliss a kidney. Prior to that surprise visit and insane request, Julie had been solely focused on her dreams as a musician, spending her days traveling the country in a van, playing gigs every chance she got.

But once she came home and her sweet saint of a mother donated a kidney to save Bliss, Julie realized that the grounding and support of this family was something she now never wanted to be more than ten minutes away from.

"It's completely infuriating!" The faint sound of Sam's voice echoed through the cottage, startling Julie as she heard the front door shut and footsteps approaching.

"Ridiculous, is what it is," Dottie said, clearly as irritated as Sam was. "Utterly ridiculous."

"Hey, you two." Julie stood up and waved to them through the open sliders, holding up her coffee mug. "What's got your collective panties in a bunch?"

"Ugh." Sam marched right out to the deck, slumping down in a chair across from the loveseat where Julie was perched. "Mom and I are at a complete standstill with our latest project, and it's really frustrating."

"Beyond frustrating," Dottie agreed with a huff, joining them on the patio. "Oh, good, you're having a muffin."

"I couldn't resist," Julie admitted, tearing a bite off the top of the sweet blueberry cake. "So what's the problem? Anything I can help with?" Julie asked.

"I don't think so." Sam shrugged, crossing her arms over her chest. "We've been battling with the City of Cocoa Beach Property Laws all morning. All week now, in fact."

"Property laws?" Julie frowned, shaking her head in confusion. "Is this about getting approval to add a restaurant in Sweeney House? Because I thought you already went to the city council and fought your way through that one."

"No, it's not about the restaurant," Dottie answered, her tone defeated. "About a week ago, Sam and I were sitting out here, watching Lori's yoga class and the magnificent sunrise, and we decided we wanted to have a big, beautiful cabana put in behind the inn."

"Right on the beach." Sam pointed to the backyard of Sweeney House, which was a vast open area of white sand and blue sea. "Wouldn't that be awesome?"

"That sounds amazing." Julie brushed some hair away from her eyes and sipped her coffee. "What's the issue? It's your property. Surely you can put whatever you want on it."

"*That's* the issue." Sam held up a finger. "Sweeney House and the land on which it sits is our property. The beach, technically speaking, is public property and cannot be owned or purchased privately in the state of Florida."

Julie scrunched up her face and took another bite of muffin. "Seriously? I didn't realize that."

"Oh, yes." Dottie nodded. "All beaches in Florida are public. That's fine. All it means is that you have to get special permitting from the city in order to build a structure of a certain size on any beach area."

"Okay..." Julie glanced back and forth between Sam and Mom. "So, why can't you just get the permitting? People who have beach houses put big decks and stuff behind their homes all the time. I'm sure the process is relatively simple."

"Well, it would be..." Sam's brows knitted together. "Except that there's no mayor right now, and the mayor has to sign off on this particular permit before we can start planning construction."

Julie drew back, swirling her coffee as she propped

her feet up on the table in front of her. "What do you mean, there's no mayor right now? What about Lonnie or whatever his name is?"

Sam snorted and almost smiled. "Linus Pemberton, you mean. His term is up, and the election for a new mayor isn't until early February. So they're in major limbo right now."

"Can't Linus just sign the papers?" Julie asked. "Isn't he still technically the mayor until the new person gets elected?"

"That's the other problem," Dottie said with a deflated sigh. "Linus stepped down before the new year, and the council couldn't find a replacement for such a short time."

"Not to mention," Sam added. "There's only one guy running for mayor and he's a complete jerk."

Julie drew back. "Really?"

"Oh, yes." Dottie shook her head, her eyes shut dramatically. "Horrific man. Truly."

"Eesh." Julie wrinkled her nose. "That's awful."

"Trent Braddock." Sam rolled her eyes, her face a picture of disgust. "I already tried to talk to him to see if I could get on his calendar for as soon as he's in office, since he's running unopposed. But he told me that he doesn't believe in 'obstructing the beaches.'" Sam held up her fingers and made air quotes and rolled her eyes, rightfully so. "And basically told me to get lost."

"Seriously?" Now Julie was annoyed. "That's unfair. You're not putting it on the surf, for crying out loud. This would be nothing more than an extension of the inn, which is a landmark and has followed every rule this town has."

"Exactly." Dottie clicked her tongue. "We're just at a loss."

"And we were so excited about the cabana," Sam said glumly. "It was going to be an amazing addition to the inn, and now, because of the mayoral gridlock and the raging jerk known as Trent Braddock, we can't do it. And since he's running unopposed, it looks like it'll never be happening, since I doubt he'll sign a permit for it even once he's elected."

Julie leaned back, watching the calm waves on the shore as she pondered their dilemma. "It seems so unjust that he can ruin that for you."

Dottie shook her head and threw her hands up in defeat. "It's the way of the world with small-town politics, I'm afraid. Your father and I battled at so many city council meetings when we were first building Sweeney House, you wouldn't believe it."

"This Trent guy," Julie glanced at Sam, angling her head. "You said he's running unopposed?"

"Unfortunately." Sam curled her lip and raised her coffee mug to her mouth.

"Huh." Julie scratched her head and leaned back.

"What is it?" Dottie asked.

Julie's mind started to move, working its way through a wild and crazy idea that might just be the most impulsive and ridiculous thing she'd ever thought of. And for Julianna Sweeney, that was saying a lot.

"What if I ran against him?" she blurted out, staring at her mom and sister's stunned and speechless reactions.

Sam laughed and rolled her eyes playfully. "Ha-ha. Very funny, Jules."

"I'm serious." Julie inched forward to the edge of the loveseat, getting more and more thrilled by the prospect of this every second. "I don't have any kind of steady job, and I'm teaching less now that kids are back in school. Plus, this is the first time in my life where Bliss isn't at my side twenty-four-seven. I could use some purpose and passion and work."

"Well," Dottie raised a shoulder. "You *were* born and raised here. And, despite the fact that you left for twenty-plus years, you did come back. That says something about your love for the town."

Julie felt a familiar splash of guilt for leaving her family for all of that time, but what was done was done. All that mattered now was the future, and Julie had a bright, shiny new vision of that future rapidly taking hold in her mind.

"You? Mayor of Cocoa Beach?" Sam raised her brows as her jaw fell slack. "Jules, please don't take this the wrong way, but up until last September, you couldn't physically stay in one place for more than a couple of weeks. Are you sure you'd want to do this?"

"Well, yeah, I mean...why not?" Julie shrugged. "I love it here now. I've been all over the country and I've never felt more at home than I do in this little beachside sanctuary. I couldn't find another place I wanted to plant even the tiniest seed, and here I've got deep roots. This could really be a chance for me to make a difference and give back to this community that has given me so much."

"Oh, Jules." Dottie placed a hand on her chest, smiling as she was clearly touched by Julie's words. "I think it's a wonderful idea. You'd be a brilliant mayor."

"This town rallied around me when I needed it the most." She thought of all the people who'd helped her through Bliss's sickness. The doctors and nurses, the local business owners, the people who gave her gigs to play and students to teach.

"Cocoa Beach welcomed me back with open arms, and I'd really like to return the favor." She stood up, letting the ocean breeze blow her long black hair as she pumped a victorious fist in the air, electricity zipping through her as she fell in love with the idea.

"It's decided. I'm running for mayor!"

"Who's running for mayor?" Lori's voice caught all of their attention, and the women turned around to see Lori and Amber standing in the cottage living room behind the deck. "There's no way I just heard what I think I heard." Lori smiled.

She and Amber walked out to the back deck to join them, sharing a big chair in the corner by the railing.

"You heard correctly." Julie straightened her back, feeling proud and excited for her new endeavor. "I've decided to run for mayor and beat the jerk named Trent Braddock. I think I can do a lot of good for this town, and now that I'm settled here and putting down roots, why not?"

"Woohoo!" Lori gave an impulsive clap. "I love your

spirit and spontaneity, Jules. Go get 'em, Tiger!"

"Hear me roar!" Julie joked.

"We stopped by to see if there were any updates on the cabana," Lori said.

"Actually..." Sam twisted her lips up. "That's sort of what prompted Julie's sudden interest in small-town politics."

Sam and Dottie filled them in on the whole saga about Linus Pemberton, the permitting issues, and Trent running unopposed.

"And that's how I came up with the idea." Julie grinned and finished off her muffin with a satisfied nod.

"Wait—you decided this *just* now?" Lori asked, shaking her head with a chuckle.

"Yeah, when I heard about how unfair it was that they couldn't put a cabana behind Sweeney House, I feel like something must be done. Even if it's a conflict of interest for me to do it, because I'm family, I would delegate it, right?"

Dottie nodded. "Exactly."

"And if not me, then who?"

"I imagine you've got your work cut out for you," Lori said. "That's no small undertaking. Especially if this Trent guy has already been campaigning for months."

Yes, she was not wrong. Julie knew that her sudden idea for a fun life plot twist was going to require a metric ton of work, research, knowledge, and figuring out.

But it was Cocoa Beach. The Sweeney family had roots here deeper than oak trees, and Julie was supremely good at adapting and learning on the fly.

How hard could it be?

"Well, okay." Julie held her hands up. "Admittedly, this all happened very fast and I'm a little overwhelmed. I don't know the first thing about local politics. But, I don't know, I feel like—"

"I'll run your campaign."

All eyes turned to Amber, who had been silent up to this point.

She gave the other women a half smile and pushed some auburn hair out of her face, looking a little shocked as they stared at her.

"I was a junior campaign manager in Raleigh," she added softly.

Julie's eyes lit up and she felt even more enthusiasm zing through her. This was all falling right into place. "For the mayor?" she asked.

"For a...congressman," Amber said, biting her lip. "I just haven't mentioned it, but..." She glanced at her mother, who looked a little surprised, but happy.

"Amber has actually been involved in several campaigns on the local level," she said. "She's organized, understands the polls, knows how to deal with the press, and has several victories under her belt."

"Ooh, even better." Julie pumped a fist. "You know what you're doing, girl. You are hired!"

"How wonderful!" Dottie clasped her hands together and took long looks at each of the women, adoring them one at a time. "A family affair. I am so excited for you both. This is going to be fantastic."

Sam lifted her coffee mug. "We are here to help. And

when I say 'we,' I'm speaking for all the Sweeneys. This *is* a family affair, and we are getting Jules in the mayor's office."

Julie let out a cheer and blew kisses to her sweet sister.

"We'll definitely need all hands on deck," Amber chimed in, becoming more animated and lively by the second.

It sure was a change, Julie thought. She hadn't seen the girl show much interest in anything since Lori and her daughter had arrived, and it was nice to see Amber start to come to life. Who would have thought it would take a spontaneous mayoral campaign to bring her out of her shell?

"Absolutely," Julie agreed. "Sweeneys come in numbers, so we'll have no shortage."

"You need to turn in a candidate's application very quickly, Julie," Amber told her, moving to the edge of her seat. "I'd like to research the competition, review recent polls and local newspaper articles, find the town hot-buttons and key topics, and start our messaging strategy immediately."

Julie made a face. "I'm going to have a messaging strategy?"

"If you want to win," Amber replied.

"Oh, honey," Lori whispered, leaning close to her daughter. "Are you sure you feel up to this? You want to do this?"

"More than anything, Mom. This is where I thrive. I

need this. So...thank you for the opportunity, Julie. I won't let you down."

"Oh, honey." Julie laughed, shaking her head. "I hope I don't let *you* down. I have absolutely no clue what I'm getting myself into."

"That's okay," Amber said. "Enthusiasm is about ninety percent of the game."

"What's the other ten?" Julie asked.

"A great campaign manager," she replied on a laugh.

"Well, thank you for stepping in to save my butt and actually give us a chance at winning."

"We don't have a chance at winning," Amber said, her eyes fiery now.

"We don't?" Julie frowned. "But..."

"We're *going* to win. No chance about it." Amber stood up, looking down at her mother and nodding toward the front door of the cottage. "Mom, can you drive me home? I want to get to work. We've got a lot to catch up on."

Lori shot up, sharing a look with Sam and Julie of pure joy and disbelief. "Of course, sweetie. Let's go now."

As they went off, Julie dropped back in her seat with a sigh of wonder and disbelief.

"I'm not sure what just happened," she said on a laugh. "That girl just transformed before our eyes."

"Little miracles," Dottie said, pushing up. "New Year's miracles."

"And that," Julie said, "is what makes this place so special."

They laughed and clinked coffee mugs, all excited for the thrill of change on the horizon.

Chapter Four

Lori

"**M**om, please don't get all sappy and emotional on me." Amber shot her a look through her thick lashes as they drove back to the townhouse.

"I am neither sappy nor emotional." Lori held up her hand as if she were swearing. "But can I please just be a mom for a minute?"

Amber sighed and laughed a little. "Fine. Be a mom. I'll cringe, but you're going to do it anyway."

"I'm proud of you, honey." Lori smiled, already feeling tears stinging behind her eyes. The good ones, for once.

Happy tears were a rare occurrence these days, but seeing Amber volunteer to run Julie's campaign for mayor gave Lori the first glimpse at joy and normalcy in her daughter in what felt like ages.

This was old Amber. Real Amber. Amber before everything spiraled and she shut down. She was excited about this campaign, and ready to give it her all.

"Thank you, Mom." Amber nudged her arm playfully and smiled. "I'm looking forward to it, actually. I need something to keep me busy, and I don't think I could physically stand another waitressing job."

"Well, even if you wanted to, it would be too much time on your feet anyway." Lori made a face. "Sorry, being a mom again."

They both laughed and Amber gently placed her hand on her baby bump, rubbing it softly.

Lori was dying to ask Amber when she planned to talk to Rick and tell him the truth about everything, but she decided this rare moment of joy and normalcy was too big of a victory to jeopardize by bringing up a sore subject.

As she drove down A1A toward the quaint little neighborhood where they were renting, the sun shone down brightly and the soft breeze swayed the palm fronds. Bunches of sea grapes spilled on the east side of the road, hiding rows of gorgeous beachfront bungalows.

"I love it here more every day," Lori said as she made the turn into Dolphin Point, their complex of townhouses.

"I'm starting to love it, too." Amber looked at her mother. "I don't think I've said this to you enough, but... thank you."

Lori pulled into the drive and shifted the car into Park, turning to Amber feeling surprise and a wave of emotion. "For what?"

"For coming here with me. You picked up your life, left the job that defined you for decades, said goodbye to everything you knew and loved, and came here with me. I needed to escape and you...you saved me."

Lori's eyes misted again, but she didn't try to hide it. "Oh, A." She placed a hand on her daughter's slender fingers, and gave them a squeeze. "Sam and Julie saved both of us by showing up on my office doorstep and suggesting I move to some random town called Cocoa Beach."

Amber snorted.

"Although you were definitely the reason I actually decided to move." She reached out and stroked Amber's cheek, which was smooth and glowing. "I just wanted to protect you. I wanted so badly for you to be happy again, and I would have done anything on Earth to make that happen. Plus, I needed the fresh start, too. Badly."

Amber nodded, leaning over to rest her head on Lori's shoulder. "We both did. But you really put me first, and I appreciate it. I'm sorry I've been so...cranky."

Lori laughed tearfully, drawing back to give her daughter a look. "Honey, I love you to pieces, but 'cranky' is the understatement of the century."

Amber shook her head. "I'm doing better, now."

"I can tell. And nothing makes this mamma happier."

They got out of the car and headed into the townhouse. Lori felt a spring in her step, and noticed a hint of one in Amber's.

"You know, I was thinking," Lori said as she hung her keys and purse on a hook by the door. "My little sunrise yoga practice is starting to gain some traction."

"I know it is." Amber went right to the kitchen. "You told me about that hotel contacting you. Word's getting out that you're very good." Standing at the pantry, no doubt looking for a Rice Krispie treat, she glanced over her shoulder. "You're Lori Caparelli.

Everything you touch turns into ambition-fueled, money-making gold."

Warmed by the compliment, Lori smiled. "Well, thank you, A. You know, one of my students is a nurse and she suggested I do my yoga therapy at her hospital."

"Wow. People are going to discover how good you are, Mom. And that's not that far out of your element." Amber slathered peanut butter onto the beloved Rice Krispie treat, completing her current craving. "Although you might be the most Type A yoga teacher of all time."

Lori laughed. "That's why I started practicing in the first place, to relax. But I love it. Especially with these small, intimate class sizes, I'm able to really use some of my background and professional experience to help people, in some cases even more than formal therapy, but just in a much more zen and comfortable way than traditional psychotherapy and analysis."

"I think it's awesome, Mom." Amber smiled through bites of her bizarre treat, and the glimmer in her eyes made it genuine. "I'm really happy for you."

"Thanks, hon. Anyway, I was thinking since the little business is growing a decent bit, maybe I should set up a website?"

"You definitely should." Amber nodded. "Maybe get some marketing going, too. I bet Taylor could help you."

"That's a great idea!" Lori grabbed a glass of water, leaning against the countertop as she sipped it and thought about this. "Now that I have some semblance of credibility in the community, I could really try to get the word out and build a little bit of a brand around this whole thing."

"Uh, heck yeah." Amber pushed some hair behind her ears. "Do you think you'll go back to being a therapist? Open another practice or something?" Amber asked, grabbing a paper towel to wipe her mouth.

"Honestly, I still don't feel like I could do that. The last thing I want right now is to sit on that couch and tell people how to fix their broken marriages and families. I'm not qualified."

Amber scoffed. "You are beyond qualified."

"Your father left me. What do I know?"

Amber pressed her lips together, her eyes flashing with darkness. "You know a ton. But for the record, I think the yoga practice is awesome. And if you never want to be a formal therapist again, I fully support that."

"I never want to let work swallow up my entire life again, that much I know for sure."

And she didn't. Lori's workaholic tendencies and years of demanding clients led her to stay so deeply immersed in her job that it cost her a wonderful marriage —a regret that still burned like a raw wound in her heart.

But Lori was here to heal that wound, she reminded herself. And, slowly but surely, the pain was beginning to ease.

A sudden knock at the front door startled them both. Amber gave Lori a quizzical frown as she tossed her wrapper into the trash. "Who's here?"

"No clue." Lori shrugged, walking out of the bright, corner kitchen to the front door of the townhouse.

Figuring it was either Sam or Julie or some other Sweeney, she swung the front door wide open without checking the peephole.

And that was when Lori felt every ounce of blood drain from her face and her heart almost leap out of her chest.

"Rick..." She breathed her husband's name, feeling her voice shake as she inched closer, not believing her eyes. "What are you...how did you...you're here."

"Hey, Lor." Rick stepped forward, holding his arms out for a hug. "I had to come. I had to see you."

"Oh my goodness, I..." She hugged him tightly, shutting her eyes for a few seconds and just savoring the moment, the comfort of him. "I can't believe you're here right now."

Richard Kittle. Her Rick. The only man Lori had ever loved, the father of her child, the person who adored her and supported her and gave up everything so that she could have her dream career. The husband who...gave up on their marriage.

She pulled back, leaning away and taking a second to study the man who was somehow her closest friend and a complete stranger at the same time.

He looked the same, classically handsome, with tanned skin and those thick, dark curls that he'd passed on to Amber. His high cheekbones and strong nose were punctuated by his deep, brown eyes that, despite having a few more creases around them than when he and Lori were young and in love, still made her melt.

Part of her wanted to cry tears of joy and kiss him, and another part wanted to yell at him for walking away from her. But mostly she was completely conflicted and confused.

"Rick." Lori moved out onto the front steps, softly shutting the door behind her and wondering if Amber was listening or had any idea her father was here.

And...oh, God. She couldn't hide her secret anymore, that was for sure.

"I had to see you," Rick said, running a hand through his hair and angling his head low. "I've been so worried, Lor. Amber hardly talks to me anymore. I've asked her what's wrong and if she's upset with me, but she never gives me a real answer. And you, I..." He shook his head, his eyes darkening. "I miss you. I miss both of you. I couldn't take it anymore. You're my family and I feel so far away and shut out from everything, it's been eating me alive. I need to know that you and Amber are doing okay."

"Oh." Lori sighed and pressed a palm to her forehead, truly not having the slightest clue where to begin.

Of course he felt cut off. Of course he felt isolated from his family. But he'd walked out on her.

"You said you wanted a separation." Lori swallowed, leaning back against the door. She sure as heck couldn't invite him inside until she briefed Amber.

"I know I did, and..." Rick sucked in a breath. "I've made a lot of mistakes, Lor. I've hurt you and I've hurt our daughter and I really, really would like a chance to make it right."

Lori was speechless. Any words that came to her mind got stuck in her throat.

What did he mean, "make it right"? Was he saying he wanted to get back together? But then there was the issue of Amber and her pregnancy, which had to be firmly at the top of the priority list before Lori could think about her own feelings or relationship with her almost ex-husband.

"Rick, I..." She let out a breath, dropping her head into her hands. "It's been hard. I'm hurt. I'm broken, actually, and only just now starting to put the pieces of my life back together."

"I'm so sorry, Lori. I just...I had to walk away. I was so empty, I was so alone—"

"Please." She held up a hand, blinking back tears. "I don't want to hear about how terrible of a wife I was right now. There's too much going on already."

"You were not a terrible wife," he said softly, his gaze fixed downward onto the pavement. "I just missed you. I wanted my best friend back, and I couldn't get to you. It destroyed me."

"Well, you destroyed me when you walked out of that house." Lori's throat tightened and she clenched her jaw, shaking her head. "I can't get into this right now, Rick. There are much bigger things going on and—"

"What do you mean?" He frowned. "What's really going on here, Lor?"

She took in a slow, shaky breath, meeting his gaze.

"Is it Amber?" Rick asked, concern and fear woven into his voice. "Is she okay? She hardly talks to me anymore, Lori. I know I drove the separation of our marriage, but does she really have to hate me for it?"

"She doesn't hate you for it, Rick." Lori pressed her lips together. "I promise, she doesn't."

"Then why has she almost completely cut me off? Amber and I were always so close, and now it's like I hardly know her. I get that this has been tough on her, but what happened?"

Lori stayed quiet. The only sound she could hear was her heart thumping in her chest, echoing through her eardrums.

It wasn't her place to tell him about the baby, or the circumstances that led to the baby. This was between Amber and her father, and Lori had to respect and protect their relationship in this moment.

"Lori?" Rick pressed. "Are you just not going to tell me what's happening here? I know we're separated but you're still my wife. You and A are still my family."

"Just..." She shut her eyes and held up a finger. "Just let me go inside and talk to Amber for one second. Don't move."

"Okay." He stepped away, leaning against one of the square columns that framed the doorstep. "I'll be right here."

Lori slipped into the townhouse, gently shut the door, and took a deep breath. "Amber."

"Yeah?"

"Your dad is here."

She paled, and for a moment, Lori thought she might faint.

Chapter Five

Amber

Well, this was it. Amber could attempt to hide a lot of things from a lot of people, but her five-months-pregnant belly was not one of those things. She'd always been thin, and her stomach was quickly starting to look like a basketball on her tiny, five-foot-two frame. Even in the baggiest of sweatshirts, hiding was no longer an option.

Amber took about thirty seconds to gather herself after the first wave of panic was washed away by embarrassment and regret. She couldn't run from this conversation anymore. She couldn't hide from her sweet, wonderful Dad, keeping him at arm's length and all but ignoring him to avoid telling him the truth.

There was no more procrastinating and putting it off. He was here, on their front doorstep, and everything that Amber dreaded and feared was about to happen, and there was nothing she could do to stop it.

She wrapped her fingers around the handle of the front door, shut her eyes, and swung it open, the words "unconditional love" echoing through her mind over and over.

"Hi, Daddy."

"Amber, hi—"

He froze. It was as if he was staring at a ghost or a zombie or something so incomprehensibly shocking that his face went white and his jaw fell slack. He didn't move or speak for a few beats, and Amber held her breath.

"Amber." Rick repeated her name, but this time it was soft and stunned, dripping with astonishment and worry and...did she sense a hint of disappointment?

Amber placed a shaking hand on top of her belly. "I was going to tell you, I just—"

"You're...*pregnant?*" He breathed the question, his eyebrows knitting together as he drew back, still visibly in shock. "Honey, why didn't you say anything? How could I not know about this?"

Amber shook her head, stepping to the side as she gestured toward the living room of their townhouse. "Want to come in?"

"Sure." Rick swallowed and nodded, clearly working hard to gather his bearings.

Amber couldn't blame him.

Lori walked into the room, tying her hair into a ponytail and glancing back and forth between Rick and Amber. "I'm going to step out for a walk so you two can...catch up."

Amber shot her a silent look of gratitude. Of course Lori, the world class family therapist, would know without a doubt that this was a conversation that needed to be had one on one.

Between father and daughter. Two best friends, two

peas in a pod that had now grown to be distant and awkward and far apart.

It killed Amber that her secret had done that to their precious relationship.

Maybe it could be repaired. He was here, after all.

"Here, Dad." Amber sat down on the couch and patted the spot next to her.

Rick walked over, still moving slow with wide eyes and a permanent look of shock plastered onto his face. "Amber... How could you keep this from me?"

"Look..." She clasped her hands together. "I was going to tell you, I really was. It's just been...a lot."

"How did this happen?" He glanced at her baby bump.

"Well, you know..." Amber lifted a shoulder, feeling her cheeks burn. "The normal way, I suppose."

Rick shot her a glare. "I know *how* it happened, Amber. I mean...with who? And you left Raleigh... Was he—"

"Not in the picture," she said. "He's not going to be in the picture."

"At all?"

"At all." Amber nodded.

This was it. This was the instant where she had to decide if she was going to tell her father the shameful and embarrassing truth about Michael Garrison, or if she was going to give him the same one-night stand story that everyone else got.

She took a moment, studying her dad, remembering all of those homework sessions and trips to Blockbuster after school. Never complete without a 7-Eleven Slurpee, of course. He was a saint, the textbook definition of the world's greatest dad.

He, Amber decided, deserved the truth.

"Sit down." Amber nodded to the place next to her. "I'll tell you everything."

"A." He scratched the back of his neck, clearly reeling from the shock of seeing his completely single daughter pregnant. "Before you dive into the story, I need to know. Are you okay? Are you handling this all right? Did something bad happen?"

"I'm okay, Dad." Emotion rose in her throat. She hated how much she'd hurt him and pushed him away. "Something sort of crappy happened, yes. But I'm doing better now. I was planning on telling you really soon. I was going to call."

"I couldn't stand the silence anymore, Amber." He shook his head, his eyes flashing. "I had no idea what was going on with you. I'm almost relieved that there actually *was* a secret, because I had myself convinced you just flat-out hated me for separating from Mom."

Amber shuddered. "I could never hate you."

"Good." He breathed a sigh, nodding slowly. "Okay, I'm ready. Tell me everything. I'm here for you."

Amber clenched her jaw and dove right in. "Obviously, you're familiar with Michael Garrison, the congressman I was working for."

"Of course. You were his junior campaign manager and, in my opinion, the sole reason he got elected."

Amber laughed at Rick's fatherly pride that never

seemed to fade, even under the toughest circumstances. "Well, he and I had...a relationship."

"Oh." His jaw fell slack again.

"Yeah, I know—bad idea. But it just sort of happened. He was completely, and publicly, separated from his wife at the time, so it wasn't an 'affair' or anything like that. At least...it didn't feel like one."

Rick just listened, his eyes kind and loving. "But he was still legally married, right? I mean, he's married?"

"Yes," Amber whispered the word on a soft shiver. "He's married. He swore to me that he was getting a divorce, that after the election we were going to be together for real. He convinced me that he loved me and I loved him back. Hard. I loved him so much I quit the campaign so I could be with him once his divorce was final."

Rick's eyes widened as he drew back with surprise. "That's why you quit? I thought you said it was a toxic work environment and they weren't paying you fairly and..."

Amber shook her head. "The work environment was fine, and the compensation was great. I actually loved my job on his campaign team. But...I loved him more. Big mistake, I know."

Rick let out a sigh.

"When I got pregnant, of course it was, well, a major accident. But I thought we loved each other, and we had all these plans to be together once he was divorced, so I figured it would be okay. But...it wasn't. The baby changed everything. First, he wanted me to..." Amber dropped her gaze to the couch, staring downward. "Seriously consider other options."

"I'm so glad you didn't," he said simply.

"I didn't want to give up this baby." She lifted her eyes and met his again, feeling the nerves and tension dissipating a bit more with each passing second. "And when I told him that was out of the question, something shifted in him. He went cold and mean and basically iced me out, before formally announcing that he was back together with his wife, happy and forever."

"Oh, Amber." He reached out and placed a supportive hand on her arm. "You must have been so heartbroken. I can't believe this was all going on under my nose and I had no idea."

"Don't feel bad." Amber shook her head. "I went out of my way to make sure you stayed in the dark. I was so embarrassed, Dad. I thought you'd be ashamed of me. I really let you down, and—"

"Amber Kittle, you could never let me down." He looked at her with certainty and sincerity and...unconditional love. "I am not ashamed of you. I'm ashamed that there's a man out there who thinks he can treat you that way. It's unthinkable. But you? Honey, I know you and your heart. I know you didn't mean for it to happen that way."

Amber felt herself breathe out with relief. "It was just such a hot mess. All I wanted to do was get away. When Mom told me about Sam and Julie, her secret half-sisters that showed up and begged her to move to Cocoa Beach, she said they were nuts. I said they just might be our saving grace."

"I can see how that sounded like an appealing escape."

Amber scoffed. "When I couldn't drive two blocks without seeing Michael Garrison's face on a yard sign in Raleigh? Yes, it was."

Rick shook his head in sympathy.

"So, we came here. And I guess I've been...hiding." She tucked her legs underneath her and twisted a strand of hair in her fingers. "From you and from the world. I thought it would make me feel better to disappear, but it's only made everything worse." Amber leaned forward, holding her arms out to hug her dad. "I'm so sorry I pushed you away."

"Amber, please." He hugged her back, tightly, and she let herself fall into the embrace of her first real protector, her safe space, her best friend. "Don't apologize to me anymore, okay? I'm just glad you're all right."

"Thank you." She felt her eyes close as she pulled away from Dad, realizing just how massive the weight on her shoulders had been. It was gone now. He knew, and he still loved her, and he always would.

"And you!" He shifted his gaze down toward Amber's belly, a smile lighting up his face and making her feel even more at ease. "I'm going to be a grandfather." He laughed, lifting his eyes back up and shaking his head with the realization. "It didn't hit me until just now."

"Grandpa Rick." Amber nudged him playfully as

laughter bubbled in her chest. "This little gal lucked out in the grandparent department, that's for sure."

"Wait a second. Did you say 'gal'?" Rick leaned away.

"Oh, yeah." Amber touched her stomach gently. "It's a girl. I just found out last week."

"A girl." Her father laughed with disbelief, and Amber realized that this was the first time she'd seen someone react with genuine excitement for her pregnancy. "Have you picked a name?"

"I can't! Maybe you can help me, Dad. I just call her Kidney Bean now."

He snorted. "Kidney Kittle. Has a nice ring to it, A."

She laughed, joy surging through her for the first time in so long. Not only was she relieved to have told him, she was thrilled by his response.

Her friends had all asked what she was going to do and seemed scared for her, even though she told them the one-night stand story and insisted she was fine. No one knew the truth. Except Mom, of course, who cried and held her and tried to make a gameplan.

But Dad? Dad was obviously over the moon and would be the world's greatest grandfather. He'd just proved it—he knew the truth now, he'd heard the story, and not only did his love for Amber not waver, but he was brimming with excitement about the baby.

It was pure joy.

"A granddaughter." He laughed, his eyes a bit misty with joy. "I'm going to have a granddaughter. Wow. This is incredible."

Amber sighed, leaning her head against the couch

cushion. "I have to admit, it hasn't always felt so incredible to me."

His smile faded and he gave her a sympathetic look. "I'm sorry, honey. The circumstances were terrible, and so unfair to you. I don't mean to diminish that by being excited, I just..."

"No, Dad, it's okay." She smiled. "You're not diminishing anything. In fact, it's really nice to see someone who is genuinely elated about this news. It's sort of felt like everyone just feels sorry for me."

"I feel sorry for how Michael Garrison treated you." He frowned, his eyes darkening. "But this kid is going to be a blessing, Amber. You watch. You're going to love her like you've never loved anyone or anything before. You're going to love her so much, you would do anything for her. And, believe me, you will be so glad she's yours."

Amber leaned forward and rested her head onto her dad's chest, just like she always used to do as a little girl. "I hope she and I will be best friends. Like we were."

"Were?" Rick pulled away and made a mock offended face.

"Still are," Amber corrected with a chuckle. "It's good to have you back, Daddy-o."

They sat in silence for a few minutes, just Amber and her father, as she processed the unexpected craziness of life's events. She felt significantly more optimistic about everything now that she had Dad back in her circle.

Amber had no idea what his dynamic with Mom was going to be like, but so far every aspect of their separation had seemed amicable, at least as amicable as a couple ending their marriage could possibly be.

She was certain they would handle everything with maturity and love and grace, for each other and for Amber. And, of course, for Kidney Bean Kittle.

The topic of her parents' separation was something that Amber had hardly given any thought or attention to, as it got completely overshadowed in her life by the six-month storm that was her relationship with Michael.

Of course, she'd been heartbroken when Dad left Mom, but she had been so wrapped up in that romance and then the pregnancy and the heartbreak, that Amber wasn't sure she ever entirely processed or had come to terms with the fact that her parents would never be together again.

They'd never be a family again.

Suddenly, out of nowhere, that thought made her want to weep.

"Dad," she said, looking up at Rick.

"Yes, honey?"

"What's your plan now? Like, are you gonna stay here for a little bit, or..."

He sighed, locking his hands behind his neck and looking out the main window of the townhouse. "You know, A, I'm not sure. I miss you like crazy, and I miss your mom, too."

"You do?"

"Of course I do. She and I spent over thirty years together. I felt so cut off from both of you and, clearly, I was pretty out of the loop." He arched a brow in the direction of Amber's stomach.

She gave a sheepish laugh. "Sorry again."

He waved it off. "So, I'm not sure. I guess I'm going to talk to your mother and figure out what I want to do. I'm not exactly in a big hurry to get back to Raleigh. Feels like it's more important for me to be here. I've got flexibility with my business, so, I can hang around for a bit."

"Well…" Amber inched closer, grinning. "I, for one, am very glad you're here. And I'm sure Mom is, too."

Rick clenched his jaw and glanced off. "I'm not too certain about that, but we'll figure everything out, okay?"

Amber nodded. "We always do."

And, for the first time since that day when she sat on the bathroom floor and sobbed over two pink lines on a pee stick, Amber actually felt like she just might have a shot at figuring everything out.

Chapter Six

Sam

"So, sixteen feet wide?" Sam shielded her eyes from the blistering sun as she and Dottie ran measuring tape along the sand to plot the area for the cabana. "That seems like a good size."

No, they didn't have the necessary permitting yet, or even any real hope of getting said permitting anytime soon. But Sam and Dottie Sweeney were not to be stopped when they wanted something. They had decided that nothing was going to get in the way of their cabana. The last piece of the Sweeney House renovation puzzle.

With the new hope of Julie running for mayor, it made sense to just draw out dimensions and get some plans in place so that the second those papers were signed, they could get to work.

"Rectangular shape will be nice." Dottie placed her hands on her hips, the breeze blowing her white linen pants around her thin legs. "Lori's students can line up and all have a sunrise view while they do yoga."

"Awesome." Sam clasped her hands together. "Tall, with billowing sheer curtains all around it, hanging from all sides."

"Beautiful." Dottie smiled. "Just beautiful. You have

such a vision for these types of things, Sam. It's very inspiring."

"Really?" Sam lifted a shoulder. "Thank you. I sort of just go with my imagination. I bet we could even fit a half bathroom in the corner, on the side of the wall of shelving and built ins."

"Wow, this cabana is going to be a work of art. Assuming we can get the approval from the mayor's office."

"Mom." Sam walked over to her mother, snapping the measuring tape back into its case and tucking it into the pocket of her loose-fitting jeans. "Are you doubting Julianna Grace Sweeney and her ability to get elected as mayor?"

"I most certainly am not." Dottie shot Sam a look. "I'm just worried she might be in a bit over her head. Yes, it's a small town, but there is a lot to winning this election. I mean, Trent Braddock and his family have deep, deep roots here. There's more at play than just good intentions and a fiery spirit. Plus, he's very well-liked. Lord knows not by me, but he is."

Sam cocked her head. "Julie's family has deep roots here, too." She nudged Dottie and gestured back at the beautiful, historic Sweeney House Inn.

"Well, yes, but...I don't know, Sam. I don't want her to end up disappointed. She's so excited about this. And I do believe she can do it, but you know Jules. She has a hard time focusing on any one thing for too long."

"I think she's changed a lot." Sam brushed some hair out of her eyes. "Ever since Bliss got sick and then recovered, Julie's focus and attention hasn't wavered. She was reckless and impulsive for a lot of years, but it's different now. She's settled, and running for mayor."

Dottie nodded, smiling at the idea. "That is certainly true. I just hope she wins, Sam. She's been through so much, and she deserves a new purpose in life. I know she has her music, and that'll always be her passion, but she was so excited about this. I'm just praying it works out."

Sam reached over and squeezed Dottie's hand. "It will. With our family behind her? She can't lose."

"All right then." Dottie glanced down at her delicate gold watch and her eyes popped wide. "Oh, boy! I'd better be going."

"Where are you off to?"

"I've got a follow-up with the surgeon who did the kidney swap." Dottie flicked her hand. "They are still demanding to see me in there every thirty days since the procedure, even though not a single thing has been wrong. Something about..." she lowered her voice and arched a brow. "Me being an 'older patient.' I do believe the word geriatric was uttered more than a few times."

Sam rolled her eyes and smiled. "They're just looking out for your health, Mom. It's a good thing."

"Well, I'm as healthy as can be, but I do relish the chance to brag about that, so off I go." She leaned in and kissed Sam on the cheek. "Oh, I forgot to mention..."

Sam frowned. "What?"

Dottie winced, hesitating like she really didn't want to say whatever was coming next. "Ethan is, uh, stopping by in a few minutes."

Sam felt her heart kick. "Oh."

"He's dropping off that dresser for the upstairs. You know, the one Jada wanted painted blue with clouds on it."

Sam shook her head at the memory. "I can't believe he actually did that." She added a soft laugh, as if her heart wasn't slamming at the thought of a painfully awkward one-on-one encounter with Ethan. "I am excited to see it."

"And him?"

"Oh... Whatever."

"I'm sorry, Sam." Dottie pressed her lips together, clearly not falling for Sam's fake nonchalance. "I told him to stop by today and the doctor's appointment completely slipped my mind."

"It's okay, Mom." Sam waved a hand. "Seriously. I'm almost forty-four years old. I can handle a slightly awkward conversation with my ex-boyfriend."

Dottie angled her head, lifting a shoulder. "Have you two spoken at all since you broke up in November? He's been primarily communicating with me regarding the furniture and antiques. I figured that's for the best while things are still, you know, fresh."

"Yeah, I know." Sam let out a sigh and glanced out at the ocean. "I've seen him in passing a couple of times when he's come to drop something off or whatever, but no. We haven't really spoken. Not more than an awkward hello before I ducked out to hide and avoid him."

Dottie sighed and shook her head. "I'm sorry to be leaving you in a weird position."

"Oh, please, Mom. It's fine. Like I said, I'm a grown woman, and I can deal with seeing my ex-boyfriend. This town is too small, and our lives are too intertwined for us to not eventually break the ice and get over it. It's a good thing."

Sam, of course, was desperately trying to convince herself of that.

"All right." Dottie placed a hand on Sam's shoulder. "I'm off, then. Best of luck."

"I don't need luck, Mom. It's no big deal, seriously."

Dottie nodded walked away, leaving Sam alone on the beach with her thoughts.

She took a deep breath, gathered herself, and headed back up to the inn. There, she slipped into the bathroom of one of the downstairs suites and looked at herself in the mirror.

Not bad for nearly forty-four, she thought.

Sam certainly didn't have the smooth, porcelain skin she did fifteen years ago, but her eyes were bright and she looked tan and glowing and happy. Her light brown hair was shiny and wavy around her shoulders, and she felt proud enough to carry herself well.

Had she known she'd be seeing Ethan Price today, she might have opted for something other than a white T-shirt and some ratty-looking jeans.

But whatever.

She barely had a chance to smooth some flyaway hairs before she heard the chimes on the front door ring through the inn.

Sam walked out with her head held high, and tried

her very best to swallow the nerves and anxiety that rose with a lump in her throat.

Ethan slowly walked into the lobby, glancing around before his eyes landed on Sam and widened. "Oh. Hey. I was, uh, looking for Dottie."

"I know." Sam forced a smile as she got closer. "She had to run out to a doctor's appointment, so..." She shrugged and gave an awkward laugh. "Guess you're stuck with me."

Ethan's ocean-blue gaze lingered on her for a long time, and he opened his mouth like he wanted to say something, paused, then changed his mind.

"You've got a dresser for us?" Sam asked, craning her neck to peek at his truck parked in the driveway through the front window of the lobby.

Wow, this was bad. She needed to speed up time, like, now. Just standing in his presence felt cold and awkward, as if the air between them was filled with the things that should have been said but never were.

One big 'what if.' That's what Sam saw when she looked at Ethan Price.

What if it had worked out? What if he had been her second chance at love? What if they were made for each other but her nosiness and his stubbornness got in the way?

"Yeah, for upstairs." He ran a hand through his sandy blond hair and glanced in the direction of the driveway. "Blue with clouds."

"Yes, I heard." Sam laughed softly, tucking her hair

behind her ears. "I commend you for actually painting it as described by my eleven-year-old niece."

Ethan shrugged, his shoulders broad. "Well, Dottie said it was important to follow through on that. Something about Jada feeling like she's officially part of the family."

She smiled. "Yes, well, I don't think little Jada has any trouble feeling that way now, but still. It was cool of you, and I'm sure she's going to flip out when she sees it."

"Awesome, good." Ethan held his hands behind his back and swallowed, keeping the world's most awkward eye contact with Sam.

"Yeah, it is." She pressed her lips together, her mind flooded with the million things she wanted to say to him and ask. "So, should we..." She gestured toward the truck parked in the driveway.

"Yes, right." Ethan pulled his keys out of his pocket and laughed nervously. "I'll go get the dresser. You've just got to tell me where you want it."

Sam gave a thumbs-up as she swung open the glass front door of the inn. "Can do."

God, this was like pulling teeth.

Ethan hoisted the dresser, which was covered in a sheet, onto a dolly and rolled it up the driveway and into the lobby of Sweeney House.

Sam inched to the side to let him pass her as she held the door open. "Sorry," she said quietly when he brushed against her, reminding her of all their stolen kisses and secret moments and every second with him that just felt a little too good to be true.

And, evidently, it had been.

Sam led him into the elevator and pressed the button to go upstairs, barely able to breathe through the tension in the small space.

"So..." She smiled, turning to him and deciding this ridiculous weirdness was completely unnecessary.

They were adults. They were exes, but they didn't need to act like strangers.

"Look, Ethan." Sam shook her head as the elevator rose. "I know this is awkward—"

"So awkward," he interjected.

"But I would really like it if we could get past the weirdness and just be...I don't know. Friends?" She sighed. "It's impossible for us to avoid seeing each other."

"Despite our best efforts," he teased, flicking his brow and easing a tiny bit of the stiffness. "But, yes, Sam, I'd like that, too. I know things are...uncomfortable right now."

"To say the least," she retorted as the elevator doors glided open and they stepped out into the upstairs hallway.

They walked all the way to the end of the hall into the last suite, where the blue dresser was meant to go under the window, just like Jada wanted.

"Right in here." Sam unlocked the door and held the door again as he rolled the dolly into the room.

"Wow." He glanced around at the fresh lavender paint and the white board and batten accent wall behind the bed. "This place is really shaping up."

"Thanks." Sam held her chin high, feeling proud.

"We've tried to make each room have a slightly different vibe. I love how this suite came out."

He nodded. "And what better way to complete it than with..." Ethan yanked the sheet off of the dresser. "A sky dresser."

"Oh." Sam held her hands to her chest. "It's perfect."

The six-drawer chest had been completely redesigned, and painted a soft sky blue, with fluffy white clouds all over the drawers and sides. "Came out pretty cute, didn't it?"

"Beyond." Sam shook her head with admiration.

"You got it." Ethan slid the dresser to its spot under the window and positioned it in the center of the wall. "What do we think?"

"Hang on." Sam pulled out her phone and snapped a photo. "I'm sending a picture to Erica so she can show Jada. They're gonna die." She sent the photo and tucked her phone back in her pocket, returning her gaze to him. "Thank you, Ethan. Seriously."

"Of course." He shrugged and patted the top of the dresser. "I actually had a lot of fun with this one. I don't generally paint like that, mostly just wood staining. So this was cool."

"Well, you crushed it." She resisted the urge to reach out and touch his arm, a gesture that would have been second nature a couple of months ago. It also would have been followed by a kiss and a laugh and none of this strange discomfort hanging between them.

"So." He brushed some imaginary dirt off of the front of his jeans and gave a smile. "I guess I'll head out then."

Sam nodded, surprised by the thud of disappointment in her stomach. Shouldn't she want this encounter
to be over?

"Right. I'll walk you."

They headed back down the hallway and into the
elevator, where Ethan turned to her and held out his
hand. "Friends?"

Sam smiled, shaking his hand and lifting her eyes to
meet his. "Friends."

After an awkward goodbye, Sam shut the front door
of Sweeney House and leaned her back against it,
groaning audibly to herself.

Why did it still hurt so much? Why did it feel like
there were mountains of unfinished business between the
two of them?

Memories they'd never have, moments they'd never
experience, possibly a lifelong romance that would never
come true because of a stupid disagreement.

Sam knew she had to focus on the good in her life,
and move forward. After all, she'd come to Cocoa Beach
to get away from a man, not find a new one.

Still, she ached.

THAT EVENING, Sam didn't have much of a chance to sit
around and overthink her breakup or her weird interaction with Ethan. Taylor had called for an impromptu girls
night at Sharky's with whoever in the family was
available.

Even though Taylor was still living in the cottage, Sam had hardly seen her daughter the past several weeks. Ever since her big, romantic airport moment, she and her new beau, Andre Everett, had been practically inseparable.

Of course, Sam missed having her best friend hanging around the house all the time, but it was physically impossible to be anything but over-the-moon thrilled for Taylor, who visibly glowed with love and happiness.

After she dabbed on some lip gloss and fixed her hair in her little car mirror, Sam climbed out of the driver's seat and headed up to their favorite local spot. She walked straight around the side of the restaurant and onto the back deck, where she spotted Taylor, Annie, and Erica already seated around a high top sipping frozen cocktails.

"There you are!" Taylor lit up and hopped off her barstool, rushing over to give Sam a big hug. "Hi, Mommy."

Sam laughed at the childish name she treasured. "Hi, hon." Drawing back, she paused to admire her girl, who wore white jeans and a pink tank top with buttons. Her dark hair fell in thick, shiny waves around her shoulders, and Sam couldn't help but marvel at how her little girl was, well, a woman.

"Hey, you!" Annie blew Sam a kiss.

"Join us, sister." Erica patted the open stool on the last edge of the table and Sam plopped down and smiled at the girls.

"No Julie?"

Erica shook her head. "Busy with campaign stuff already."

"Makes sense," Annie added. "I can't believe she's really going for it."

"It's awesome." Taylor sipped her pina colada. "Do you guys really think she has a shot, though? I mean, Aunt Julie is amazing, and I think she'd be a fantastic mayor. But pretty much the entire town thinks Trent Braddock is a total shoo-in."

Sam shrugged. "Not necessarily. I mean, he was a shoo-in when he was running unopposed, but you never know. Trent is well-known and generally well-liked, but he's no Julie. She's so fun and endearing, the contrast alone could win her votes."

"Let's hope." Taylor smiled. "It would be so cool to have a Sweeney as the mayor."

"I imagine they'll need fundraising for the campaign." Annie raised her brows. "If it's a bake sale, count me in. In fact, no matter what it is, count me in. And Trevor and Riley, too."

Sam's heart warmed at the mention of Annie's growing romance with the single father who owned the gym next door to her new bakery.

"Annie, fill us in," she demanded. "We know the grand opening of The Cupcake Queen after the fire was a smashing success, but how is everything going with Trevor?"

Annie clasped her hands together and beamed with joy and pride. "The opening was awesome, and I know it's only been a couple of weeks that the bakery's been up and running, but...I've just never been happier."

"No more electrical problems, right?" Erica raised a brow and pointed a warning finger at Annie.

"None, I swear." Annie held up her hands. "And as for Trevor..." She glanced down and her cheeks turned visibly more rosy than usual. "It's going really, really well. We're actually going away for the weekend together, up to Savannah. Riley is going to stay with her grandparents in Tampa and we're taking our first little getaway as a couple. My assistant, Jackie, is going to run things at the bakery for a couple of days.

"Annie!" Taylor exclaimed, reaching over to give her an affectionate shove. "That's so exciting!"

"It really is." Sam agreed, smiling at Annie.

She was truly filled with joy and happiness for her dear friend, but she couldn't ignore that tiny green splash of envy that hit her chest.

As much as she wanted it to work out with Ethan, it hadn't. That wasn't her journey. As she looked around the table, she thought about the love that each of these women had in their lives.

Erica, of course, had Will Armstrong—her absolute dream of a capable and steady husband who worshipped her.

Then there was Tay, who was radiant with the high of a new and young love. She just might have found the man she was going to spend the rest of her life with.

And Annie, who was embarking on a new romance of

her own, and becoming a mother figure to an adorable little girl in the process.

And Sam was...alone. She had her family, and dear friends, and no shortage of people who loved her and cared about her. Why couldn't she just be grateful for that instead of focusing on what she was missing?

"What's up, Mom?" Taylor asked, bringing Sam back into the moment. "You look distracted."

"Oh, nothing." Sam sipped a Bahama Mama that the server had brought her and flicked her fingers. "I just...I had to see Ethan today, and it was super weird."

"Oh, Sam." Annie placed a hand on her arm. "I'm so sorry."

"That has to be hard." Erica shook her head. "And, I mean, it's not like you can really escape the guy."

"I can't," Sam agreed. "Ben isn't in his calc class anymore, so I don't have to worry about too much school-related stuff, but he's still working on a ton of antiques and furniture pieces for the inn. He's really skilled, and Mom and I love his work so much, we've even hired him to construct built-ins in a couple of the rooms." She clicked her tongue. "I've got a lot more Ethan Price in my future, just not in the way I would have wanted him to be."

Taylor gave a sympathetic pout. "Mom."

"It's fine, you guys." Sam shook her head and smiled. "It's all good. I've got my girls and the inn. We've got Julie's campaign to think about. There's a ton of good in my life. And best of all, there's no Max Parker."

"Cheers to that!" Taylor laughed and held up her drink, and the four of them clinked glasses together.

"Oh, one more thing about Ethan." Erica lifted her finger. "Sorry."

Sam shrugged. "What is it?"

"Jada completely flipped out over the sky dresser." She laughed. "When I told Mom how much she loved it, she offered to let us take it home and put it in Jada's room."

"You should!" Sam exclaimed. "It was her idea. She should have it."

Erica shook her head. "Jada said no. She wanted it to stay at the inn, so that Sweeney House will always have a piece of her. I think it makes her feel like she's truly part of this family."

"She is!" Taylor flipped some hair behind her shoulders. "I can't even remember life without Jada around, which is crazy, because you only adopted her, what? Seven, eight months ago?"

Erica nodded. "Right before Julie and Bliss came back. But I can't imagine my life without her, either."

"It's amazing, Erica." Annie pressed her hands to her heart. "Your family is a testament to the beauty and importance of adoption."

"Thank you, Annie. We're so blessed." She turned her attention to Taylor. "And you, Miss Lovebird? How's Andre?"

"Amazing. Incredible. Perfect." Taylor jokingly pulled out her phone. "Should I just pull up a thesaurus? Because I could go for hours."

Sam rested her chin in her hand and sighed as she grinned at her daughter. "I'm just so beyond happy for you, Taylor. You and Andre are perfection."

And she meant it. Sam had been Team Andre in Taylor's love triangle ever since he'd come to her privately to ask for advice and express how much he cared for Taylor. Sam was thrilled with the way everything was shaping up for her daughter, who deserved nothing but the best.

Taylor smiled and glanced around the table. "I also have a little news I'd like to share."

"Let's hear it." Annie lifted a shoulder.

"I..." Taylor locked eyes with Sam and paused before finishing her sentence slowly. "Found an apartment."

"What?" Erica exclaimed, nudging Taylor's arm. "That's awesome, girl!"

"Very exciting." Annie smiled.

"Mom." Taylor leveled her gaze with Sam. "Don't be sad."

"Sad?" Sam raised her hands defensively. "I am not sad."

All three of the other women gave her a 'get real' glare.

"Okay I'm a little sad," Sam admitted quickly on a soft laugh. "But I think it's wonderful, Tay. You don't want to live in your grandmother's cottage forever. You're almost twenty-five, and you've got a serious boyfriend. Not to mention the absolutely killer career you're building for yourself in marketing. It's natural that you would get your own place, and I'm thrilled for you."

"Okay." Taylor let out a breath. "Good. Because I'm stoked."

"One condition, though." Sam raised an eyebrow.

"Anything."

"You must let me help decorate."

They all laughed at that.

"Where's the apartment?" Erica asked.

"Near Cocoa Village, a bit inland, across 520. I'll only be ten minutes from the cottage and about fifteen from work, so it's all good."

"And about thirty seconds from Andre," Annie added with a teasing wink.

Taylor's cheeks flushed and she gave a coy shrug. "Okay, it might be a bit closer to him, which is one of the many reasons I love the place I found. Here." She pulled out her phone and tapped the screen. "Check out some pictures."

They passed around the phone and admired the bright apartment in a new building that featured shiny white countertops and big, screened in balconies.

Sam could already picture Taylor filling it up with laughter and cats and all things Tay, and the thought made her heart swell with joy.

As they chatted on about Jada and the bakery and Julie's mayoral campaign, Sam felt her phone buzz in her pocket and pulled it out to read a text from Lori.

You're never going to believe this, but Rick is here. He showed up this morning. I've been trying to spend the day gathering myself and meditating on it before telling anyone, but I needed someone to know.

Sam's jaw nearly fell open, but she decided this wasn't the time to tell the other women. Lori's life wasn't gossip.

She typed out a quick response, stunned by the fact that Lori's soon-to-be ex-husband had shown up here unannounced. So, he must know about Amber's baby.

Would he and Lori reconcile? Get back together?

Sam had no idea what was in store for her newest sister and niece, but she knew she had to be there for them.

And she had to be there for Julie and her campaign. And Dottie with the inn. Of course, she also had to be there for Taylor, growing up and moving into her own place.

It was a good thing that she wasn't distracted or preoccupied with Ethan and love and a relationship. It was more important that she be able to support everyone around her.

That was Sam's new role in life, and she was determined to find complete joy and fulfillment in it.

Chapter Seven

Julie

"Okay. I got this. I can do this," Julie whispered to herself as she rifled through the stack of papers she picked up at City Hall, the first one titled, "City of Cocoa Beach Mayoral Candidate Registration."

The packet was due back to City Hall by the end of the day, and Julie had barely made a dent in it.

Evidently, she was already late, because the applications were supposed to be filed sixty days prior to the election. But since the only current candidate was running unopposed, the city council had extended the deadline to encourage someone else to start a campaign.

And that someone was a retired rock musician with zero political experience—or work experience in general.

But Julie cared about Cocoa Beach, deeply. Since making the decision to run, she'd been driving around, looking closely at the town, and really envisioning herself as the mayor.

The role felt good. It felt right. And this decision was about so much more than just getting Sam and Mom their cabana. This was about finding a new purpose in life and dedicating herself to helping the town that welcomed her back with open arms. She'd fallen in love with Cocoa Beach in a way she never thought possible. What better way to express it?

She had assumed the application to run would consist of some basic questions, proof of residency, maybe a fun little essay question and, boom, done. But this was not that simple.

She worked her way through each question, many of them requiring research or digging to be certain she was answering them correctly.

"They're not messing around with this," she mused quietly as she stapled the scanned printouts to the back of the packet and slumped down at her kitchen table, lifting her eyes to take a break from the paperwork and admire her surroundings.

She and Bliss had found a fabulous two-bedroom loft near the beach, and Julie could not be happier with her sweet new home. From the exposed brick wall in the living room to the guitars hanging on racks everywhere the eye could see, this place was home.

Bliss had decked it out with old vinyl records and tapestries, and the whole place just suited them so well.

Occasionally, Julie still braced for the day she'd wake up with that familiar feeling. The tingling in her fingertips and tightness in her chest and voice in her head saying, *"It's time to leave. On to the next adventure."*

But with every passing day, she just felt happier and happier in her forever home.

This, Julie thought as she turned her attention back

down to her now nearly completed application, *is my next adventure.*

A knock on the door caught her attention. Julie hopped up to go answer it, smiling when she found her new campaign manager on the other side.

"Amber!" She smiled and swung the door wide open as she welcomed her pregnant niece into the apartment. "Thank God you're here."

"You ready to get started?" Amber smiled, and a sparkle that Julie had certainly never seen before flickered in her eyes.

Granted, she hadn't spent too much time with Amber since she and Lori had arrived in Cocoa Beach a couple of months ago, but the girl seemed noticeably brighter.

"You come prepared." Julie nodded at the books and laptop in Amber's arms.

"Absolutely." Amber tipped her head. "This is kind of my thing."

"Good." Julie laughed softly with relief and gestured for Amber to sit across from her at the tiny kitchen table for two. "Because I am just about the furthest thing from prepared that you could possibly imagine."

"That's okay." Amber set her stuff on the table and flipped the laptop open. "You're running a grassroots campaign. It's going to rely heavily on appealing to voters' emotions. The most important thing in your case is going to be showing your heart, goodness, and passion to the public."

"I can do that." Julie nodded. "I mean, I used to get

entire concert halls on their feet singing along and clapping with my music."

"See?" Amber shrugged, leaning back in the seat. "You can command an audience. That's going to work in your favor in the mayoral debate."

"The de— *What*?" Oh. Oh, boy. Of course there would be a debate. Julie hadn't quite thought that far ahead.

"Don't panic." Amber held up a hand. "Like I said, you're comfortable in front of an audience. It'll be a piece of cake for you."

"I don't know." Julie pressed her lips together. "I'm comfortable singing soft rock and playing the guitar, not arguing with the opposition about street parking and trash collection issues."

"It's okay." Amber clasped her hands together, straightening her back. "We have time to prepare. Not too much, though."

Julie couldn't help but take another moment to marvel at the shocking change in Amber just since she'd last seen her. She was fiery and ready to jump into this campaign.

Was this bright-eyed and engaged girl the same creature who sulked at Sweeney family gatherings with her hair over her face? How could it be?

She had purpose, that's how. And so did Julie. In fact, with this new and alive version of Amber, she might have a real chance at winning this thing.

Curiosity and their family ties made Julie want to ask Amber about her personal life and note that she seemed so much happier than before, but she decided to keep things focused on the campaign.

Clearly, this election was a sweet spot for Amber, and Julie felt like they could both really use it to help each other.

"Before we start thinking about debates..." Amber looked up over the laptop screen and arched a brow at Julie. "We should really nail down your platform."

"My platform." Julie nodded, leaning back in the chair as she thought about what kind of political platform she could run on.

Certainly not a dilemma she'd ever thought she'd have, but life was funny that way.

"Well, obviously, having a daughter, I care a lot about education."

"Definitely." Amber started typing rapidly, her eyes glued to her computer screen.

"I would love to put money and resources into the public school system. Want to know what's crazy? Bliss was home schooled, er, should I say *van* schooled, her entire life up until this month, and she's actually *ahead* of her classmates."

Amber drew back. "Wait, seriously?"

"Yup." Julie nodded. "That girl did online school in the back of a touring van and is several chapters ahead of Florida public schools in math and science. She also has already read most of the books that are required reading for juniors."

"That's stunning." Amber shook her head.

"I know, right?" Julie lifted a shoulder. "Selfishly, I

was kind of relieved. I mean, I was always so worried she wasn't getting a real education online while we toured and travelled. Now I know that I at least did something right."

She smiled. "I haven't gotten to chat much with Bliss, but she seems like a great girl. I'm sure you did a lot right."

Julie noticed something flash in Amber's expression, and it didn't take a trained psychologist to deduce that the prospect of motherhood was haunting this girl.

"Anyway." Amber shook her head and tapped the wooden surface of the table. "Education. Funding the city and county's school systems is a great platform, especially since you currently have a daughter transitioning into the public schools here now. That'll help us a lot with the mom votes."

"Mom votes." Julie nodded, leaning back in her chair.

"Parents, specifically women, will be a major part of your target demographic for sure." Amber typed for a bit on the laptop, making notes. "They'll connect with you. What other demographic do you think we could really reach? People you imagine your work as mayor could really help?"

"Well, of course, I've been through the medical system here." Julie pressed her lips together. "I don't know how much the mayor's office has to do with the hospitals or healthcare systems, but I would really love to find a way to give back to the doctors and nurses that saved Bliss's life. And my mom's."

"That's awesome." A smile pulled at Amber's pretty

face as she typed furiously, clearly enjoying this new undertaking as much as Julie was.

"Healthcare...workers...and first responders would fall into that area, too." Amber mused softly as she typed, then finished with a big smack on the Enter key before looking back up at Julie. "Now, what we want to do is narrow down your key messages."

"Right." Julie swallowed, letting out a long exhale. "My key messages." She wrinkled her nose. "Is that like a campaign slogan? Julie for Justice or Sweeney is...Sweet?"

Amber gave a soft snort. "Not exactly. We need to nail down the most important phrases, and issues, that you want to drive home. Like funding for education and support for teachers for that portion of your platform. Maybe increased support for the fire department, education programs for first responders. Specific things you want to do. These are the promises that will resonate with people, and give voters a way to visualize the changes and improvements you are going to make as mayor of Cocoa Beach."

"Okay." Julie got out of the chair to pace around, wandering over to the fridge in their small, corner kitchen. "Let me think on that. You want something to drink? A Coke? Oh, I used to love an afternoon Coke when I was pregnant with Bliss. Not diet, but the real sweet stuff. Probably not the pinnacle of prenatal nutrition, but I don't think it hurt anyone."

"Actually..." Amber angled her head. "A Coke sounds amazing."

"I got you, girl." Julie swung open their refrigerator door—a light green, 1950s-style fridge that Dottie had acquired through her network of antique lovers and surprised Julie and Bliss with as a housewarming gift.

Bliss had declared it "total vintage perfection," and Julie smiled every single time she yanked the horizontal silver handle.

"Here." Julie snapped the tabs on two bright red cans of ice-cold Coca-Cola, sliding one over to Amber as she sat back down at the table.

"Thank you." Amber took a deep drink of the soda and closed her eyes. "You're right, this is heavenly."

"See?" Julie laughed. "Okay, platform. Let's think."

"Think about the things that would drive your decision-making as mayor. Your values, your goals, your passions."

Julie racked her brain and chewed on her lip.

"You know, we could consider something like—oh." Amber drew back, placing a hand on her small baby bump as her eyes grew wide with surprise and possibly panic.

"What is it?" Julie asked, concern rising her voice. "Are you okay?"

"Yeah, yeah." Amber kept her hand fixed on her stomach and stared straight ahead. "I'm good, I just...I think I might have just felt my baby move."

Julie gasped softly, her hands flying to her mouth. "The first kick."

"It didn't..." Amber shook her head, clearly rattled by the first indication of the miniature human living inside her. "It didn't feel like a full-on kick, just a...almost like a tickle."

"Yup." Julie nodded and smiled at her, recalling her pregnancy with Bliss. Despite the fact that she was on the road and still playing gigs and sort of roughing it at the time, pregnancy had been, well, *bliss*. Julie loved every second of creating her sweet daughter. "The early ones aren't, like, full on soccer kicks."

"It was like a little swipe from inside my belly." Amber pointed to the side of her bump. "Right here. Do you think that's what it was?"

Julie nodded. "Definitely."

Instinctively, she stood up to come around the table and give Amber a hug. Amber didn't come off as a particularly affectionate person, but this was a big moment, and it called for a hug.

"Come on." Julie held her arms out and smiled. "I'm your wacky aunt now, and I just watched you feel your baby for the first time."

"I seem to gain a new wacky aunt every day." Amber glanced up at her and laughed softly, her face a bit flushed as her eyes shone. She stood up and wrapped her arms around Julie, holding her much tighter than Julie expected. "Thank you," Amber whispered.

"Of course." She pulled away and noticed Amber's glow was even brighter. "I'm so glad you're here."

Amber pushed some hair behind her ears. "In your apartment or in Cocoa Beach?" she joked.

"Both," Julie said.

Amber walked around the small apartment, still

holding her stomach with her right hand as she studied the décor and furniture before walking over to the green velvet sofa and plopping down. "I'm sorry. I just...need a minute."

"Absolutely," Julie said. "Can I join?"

Amber patted the spot next to her on the sofa. "We can get back to your campaign in a second, I just... Wow. I know I shouldn't be so taken aback. I mean, the baby is inside me. Obviously, I knew I was eventually going to feel it move. It's just getting so real, I'm gonna be a mom. And I don't even know where to begin."

"Well," Julie said softly. "You could start by not referring to your baby as 'it.'"

Amber cracked up. "Her," she corrected. "It's a girl. *She's* a girl."

"A girl." Julie's heart warmed. "Congratulations."

"Thank you," Amber said sheepishly. "I'm in a bit over my head with the whole thing, if you can't tell."

"Honey, no one is ever really prepared to become a mom. Even the most prepared people in the world aren't prepared."

"Yeah." Amber huffed out a breath and hugged a colorful bohemian throw pillow to her chest. "I get that, I just...I feel so alone in this, you know? My friends who have had babies are all married. And when my mom and dad had me, they were obviously married and totally in love and stable and...it made sense. I'm on my own with it, and it feels like no one can really relate to that."

"Umm..." Julie wiggled her eyebrows and pointed both of her thumbs back toward her own chest. "Hello?

I've been running the unconventional single mom game for sixteen and a half years."

"Wait, really?" Amber furrowed her brow and blinked with surprise. "You raised Bliss completely by yourself? For some reason I thought her father had been in the picture. I guess I haven't really had a chance to hear the full story."

Julie sipped her soda and set it back down on the coffee table. "In and out of the picture would be the best way to describe it. Roman is...unreliable, to say the least. Loved himself an adventure and a bottle of whiskey even more. He'd be with us here and there, you know, a couple of months, a dozen gigs or so. And then he'd...disappear. Doing God knows what."

Julie shuddered at the memories of some very dark nights she'd spent waiting for him to come back to the van or motel or call or text or *anything*. "Bliss and I would go weeks and weeks without hearing from him. Then, suddenly, he'd show up and spend some time and travel around with us. But we were never what he wanted. Even on the road, touring all the time, he couldn't stand the pressures and commitments that come with a family."

"Oh." Amber shook her head, processing Julie's story. "Wow. That had to have been so hard on both of you."

"It was," Julie admitted. "Don't get me wrong, we had tough times. I sometimes even wondered if it would have been better if he had just stayed out of the picture completely, you know?"

"Right." Amber nodded in understanding. "Instead

of just popping in and out of your lives. That would drive me absolutely insane."

"It was tough. But I did what I could to give her a wonderful childhood, and, honestly? Looking back, I wouldn't have had it any other way."

"Really?"

"Heck, yeah. Are you kidding?" Julie gestured around the apartment, a place that truly only two rock-and-roll hippie girls could live in. "That girl is my best friend on the planet. She's my world. I may not have had the traditional white-picket-fence house—*cough, John, cough,*" she joked. "But I got something beautiful and special and uniquely mine."

Amber's eyes filled with tears, which she quickly wiped away, giving an embarrassed laugh. "Sorry. Hormones and...stuff."

"Oh, Amber." Julie smiled. "Don't apologize."

"It's just that you're the first single mom I've really talked to about this. And you're really giving me a lot of hope. Hope that I can make something...uniquely mine."

"You can. And you will."

Amber bit her lip. "I guess I just feel like not having a partner is going to make it so tough on me."

"It wasn't easy. But like I said, I wouldn't change it."

"Is he still around at all?" Amber asked carefully, clearly not wanting to pry.

Julie hoped that by now Amber knew she was a totally open book.

"No, he isn't. When she got sick last year, he disappeared entirely. That, he could not handle."

Amber pressed a hand to her chest. "That's why you came back here," she said softly, putting together the puzzle pieces of Julie's life.

"Exactly. I could handle a lot on my own, but not that." Julie let out a breath. "I needed my family. They say it takes a village, and when Bliss got sick, I understood why. I needed my village. And, as it turns out, my mother's kidney. When I realized how loved and supported and stable Bliss and I both felt here, I never wanted to leave."

Amber nodded, considering this as she took a sip of her Coke. "It takes a village," she whispered to herself. "I've heard that."

"And Cocoa Beach is one hell of a village." Julie smiled, glancing out the big window of their living room, which overlooked a grassy, swampy area that was about a mile from the beach.

She turned her attention back to Amber, gently placing a hand on her arm. "You know, you've got the village behind you now, too."

"Yeah." Amber let out a sigh and scratched her head. "I just still feel weird asking for help or support."

"Well, don't," Julie said point-blank, then laughed at her own stern tone.

Amber softly ran a hand over her baby bump and smiled, glancing down, then bringing her focus back up to Julie. "Thank you. I think I'm starting to actually warm up to the whole 'village' concept. It's foreign to me."

"Oh, honey." Julie snorted. "I ran away from it when I was barely an adult. I didn't think I wanted anything to do with the small-town, big family, slow-paced beach life. I wanted to get far away and fast. And I adored my family. It was nothing against them. I just thought I needed so much more than this town, but..."

"Now you're running for mayor."

"Yes." Julie laughed, shaking her head at the whole thing. "For my village. For everything they did for me. Not just the Sweeneys, but the entire town."

"I think that's awesome."

She studied Amber's troubled expression. "Seriously, though. You have the village now. You were brought into this family for a reason. They'll help you. They'll support you. We all will. That's what this place means."

Amber nodded, her eyes misty with emotion.

Julie gave her a kind smile. "I know it feels like you're on your own. Believe me, I'm familiar with that feeling. But you're not."

"I've got the village," Amber whispered, her features softening. "And I think we may have just come up with your campaign platform."

Julie gasped excitedly. "We did?"

"It takes a village." Amber grinned. "It's a starting point, but a great foundation."

"I love it," Julie said, closing her eyes and thinking about the words. "It takes a town?" she suggested. "Sorry, my songwriting self wants alliteration. Plus, I think 'it takes a village' was used by another politician. But I love the concept. You, Amber Kittle, are a brilliant campaign manager and I'm so glad I hired you."

Amber laughed heartily. "Wasn't I your only option?"

Julie chuckled. "I'll have you know, I had campaign managers lining up to be a part of this historic run."

"Well then, I feel very lucky," Amber said. Her tone made it seem like she was teasing, but Julie detected some sincerity in that voice.

She smiled. "I do, too."

Chapter Eight

Lori

Lori didn't schedule a yoga class today, but she was up at five a.m. on the dot regardless.

She paced around the living room, clutching her coffee mug like somebody might break in and steal it, her fuzzy robe flowing around her as she walked. And thought. And worried. And breathed. And tried to stop worrying.

It was still completely dark, but Lori drew all the blinds anyway, because she liked the moonlight, and the sun would be rising soon enough.

Rick had checked in to an Airbnb a few minutes away, and Lori had no idea how long he planned on staying in town. She couldn't help but wonder if he was awake right now, too, pacing around his rental condo, wondering what was to become of their lives.

Lori had always prided herself on not being a worrier. She thoughtfully planned, calculated and analyzed every aspect of her life that was within her control, and had learned to love and accept things that weren't. Which, admittedly, there never were a lot of until recently.

Ever since her life began to crumble several months ago when Rick asked for a separation, Lori had found herself losing her grasp on that precious control and spiraling into fears and doubts.

And just when she was finally starting to get the first glimpses of togetherness and control in her life, Rick showed up on her doorstep, sending everything into a tailspin.

At least things went well between him and Amber, she reminded herself, taking a deep drink of hot coffee and leaning against the kitchen counter. That was a huge win, and the weight lifted off of Amber's shoulders was visible and palpable, bringing Lori indescribable relief.

Of course Rick was going to love and accept Amber regardless of what happened. He was a deeply good man, and Lori knew that. But Amber had been so petrified of him finding out about her pregnancy, and now that it was out in the open between all three of them, the air felt a lot clearer.

Lori's heart and emotions, however, had never been muddier.

She'd only seen Rick for a handful of awkward minutes since he'd arrived two days ago, but in those little slices of time, she'd managed to feel pain, anger, regret, hurt, longing, and...love.

Maybe more love than she thought she'd feel. And maybe that love was why she'd tossed and turned all night, thinking the space next to her felt especially empty, knowing that her husband of thirty years was sleeping in a hotel down the street.

Or maybe she was just emotional and vulnerable and staring at a scary new chapter in life without him, and parts of her subconscious were aching for the comforts of a life that once was hers.

She let out a deep sigh and drank her coffee, and was startled when her phone buzzed with a text.

Who was up at this hour? Dottie, maybe, she guessed as she grabbed it and read the message on the screen.

Rick: *Hey, I know it's early, but do you want to grab a coffee? We haven't had a chance to really talk.*

Lori couldn't completely identify the little zing that went through her heart as she read the message. Surprise? Definitely. Worry? Yes. Excitement? Maybe.

She swallowed, tightening the tie of her robe and staring at the text, trying to decide how to respond.

Of course she wanted to have coffee with him. She'd missed him desperately for months, and seeing him show up at her door the other day had really thrown her.

She was still angry at him for walking out on their marriage, but at the same time, she completely understood. She might have advised a patient to do the same thing, had their spouse been as absent and preoccupied as Lori was.

She squeezed her eyes shut, thinking that no matter how hard she tried to move on and let go of her marriage, she couldn't bring herself to do it.

She typed a response.

Sure. There's a Starbucks on A1A that's open now. I can meet you in 15.

For a brief moment, Lori wondered if the text she'd just sent was too forward, but she realized there was no reason to play coy with her husband of thirty years. *Please*.

Lori brushed her teeth and threw on some leggings and a V-neck T-shirt, studying herself in the mirror. She added a couple of quick swipes of mascara and a dab of blush and called it a day.

This man had seen her at her worst, after all. Still, she couldn't help wanting to look at least...decent.

Before leaving, she peeked into Amber's room to see her sleeping soundly. The TV was on at a low volume, so Lori picked up the remote, clicked it off, and blew Amber a kiss before heading out the door.

As she drove down the beach road during the earliest hours of the day, she wondered what it was going to be like with Rick. How could this man—the man who had been her rock and partner and best friend for her entire adult life—feel like a stranger?

She couldn't help but compare her situation to everything she knew about what had happened between Sam and Max. But this was nothing like that.

There was no infidelity or dishonesty. There were things that could have been fixed. Maybe there was even...hope.

"Oh, boy," she whispered out loud to herself as she pulled into the parking lot of Starbucks. "Careful, Lori."

She took a breath and centered herself for a moment before getting out of the car and heading inside.

It wasn't even six yet, but the popular coffee chain was bustling with early risers.

Lori quickly spotted Rick, who was standing at the back of the three-person line at the order counter.

He gave an awkward wave and she walked to join him, swinging her purse over her shoulder.

"Hey." Lori smiled, trying not to look too long at the sadness in his eyes. She wondered if her eyes looked sad, too.

"Couldn't sleep either, huh?" He angled his head.

"Not really." She faced forward and pushed some hair behind her ears. "I'm used to getting up pretty early now, for my classes."

"Right, of course." He cleared his throat.

Painful tension filled the silence in the air, and Lori couldn't help but think that this might have been a bad idea.

What if there really was nothing left between them? What if he had brought her here to say he wanted to officially file for divorce?

She knew that was a very real possibility, but the thought made her queasy.

They quickly ordered coffees, and Lori handed her credit card to the barista to avoid any awkwardness. They still shared a bank account, after all.

But wow, right now? It didn't feel like they shared much of anything.

Rick walked over to a small table in the back near a window, taking the seat that faced the wall. He knew Lori always had to face the restaurant, never the wall.

The small gesture made her smile a bit.

"So." He tapped his fingers on the table, sipping his coffee. "That's going really well, then, yeah?"

"What is?"

"The yoga classes."

"Oh. Right." She wrapped her hands around the steaming cup, giving a nervous laugh. "Yes, it is, actually. It's sort of taking off. People have come from other hotels, and some locals, too. I'm surprised, really."

"I'm not." Rick leveled his deep brown eyes with hers, and Lori watched them form that familiar crinkle as he smiled. "It's your Midas touch. I knew it would turn to gold as soon as you told me you were doing it."

Lori leaned back, her face warmed by the compliment. "Really? Because I didn't. No one showed up for my first class, and I was pretty much certain it was going to be an epic failure."

"You could never fail, Lori Caparelli." He raised his brows. "It isn't in your DNA."

"I failed this marriage," she blurted out.

His face went stoic, and those familiar eyes flashed with a stormy darkness. "You didn't fail. It just...wasn't working."

"Right." She swallowed. "Because of me. I...failed."

"Lori." Rick shut his eyes. "Please stop being so hard on yourself. There were a lot of different reasons why I wanted to separate. It was a complicated issue, and..."

"Was it?" She frowned. "Because the day you left, it didn't sound complicated. It actually sounded very simple. I was married to my work, and you were married to me. I believe that was the exact phrasing you used."

He cleared his throat and glanced out the window beside them, where the sky was just beginning to fill with light from the sunrise. "Well, that was how I felt. I was at my breaking point, Lor. You have to know that."

"I do." Emotion tightened in her chest. She could hardly look at Rick without feeling like she was drowning in regrets and memories. "But you should know that, no matter what I accomplished in my career in psychology, or what I accomplish in the future, I will always live with the fact that I failed you." She stared at him, her heart pounding. "And I'm sorry."

"Hey." Rick reached across the table, taking her hand.

She let the weight of his hand press down on hers, savoring the comforting warmth and security. "Sorry to be so blunt, I just...want you to know. It's been hard for me."

"It's been hard for me, too." He gave her hand a squeeze, holding her fingers tightly in his for a few moments, long enough to send a jitter dancing up Lori's spine. "And...can we just talk about Amber for a second?"

Lori broke into a soft laugh. "We're going to be grand-parents."

"*Grandparents.*" Rick's eyes widened as a genuine smile pulled across his handsome face. "I mean, I know the circumstances are unusual, and I hate what that jerk did to Amber. But...I think there's so much to be excited about."

Lori leaned back in her seat and sipped her black coffee, studying Rick. Even at fifty-six years old, he still had that boyish charm she'd fallen so hard for in college.

The way he lit up talking about Amber's baby made her heart fill with affection.

"You know, it's funny." She shook her head. "In all of the stress and drama and worrying about Amber and her broken heart, I don't think I've really given myself the chance to be excited. Like, truly, genuinely excited."

"Well, get excited, Grandma," Rick teased.

"Oof." Lori wrinkled her nose. "Not quite ready for that title."

"May is coming sooner than you think."

"I know." She blew out a sigh. "It's right around the corner. I know Amber's never going to be fully ready, but I do hope that she starts to get excited, too."

"She will. And even if she doesn't, the second she holds that little girl, it's all over."

"Maybe she'll even decide on a name."

"Besides Kidney Bean," Rick joked. "I know she's just going to turn to mush before our very eyes."

Lori laughed. "She does have such a soft heart. She's going to be a wonderful mom."

Rick locked eyes with her. "We did all right, didn't we?"

She nodded, smiling as she glanced down at her coffee cup. "We did all right."

"So, your yoga stuff." He took a drink, clearly more comfortable now that the awkwardness of the initial meetup had faded away. "You said it's going really well. Are you happy?"

"Actually...yeah." She tucked some hair behind her ear and thought about the question. "I am happy, but not in the same way my therapy practice used to make me happy. This is a sort of peaceful happiness. A calm, comforting feeling. Much different from the never-ending busy schedule and patient visits and…yeah." She laughed softly. "You know what it was like."

"I certainly do." He raised a brow. "But it's good to hear you're enjoying work again. In a new way."

Lori nodded, lifting a shoulder. "The yoga thing does make me happy. You know, it's actually making me wonder if my old job truly made me happy, in the realest sense of the word. I wonder sometimes if it was more of an obsession with the success of my patients than a true source of joy and fulfillment for me."

"Wow." His eyes widened. "File that under things I never thought I'd hear you say."

Lori gave a mirthless laugh. "Things change, Rick. Anything can happen."

"Yes." He pressed his lips together, his gaze lingering on hers. "Anything can."

"And now I'm a sunrise yoga instructor with more free time than I physically know what to do with." She shook her head and chuckled. "But it is getting busier as the business takes off a bit. I might add more classes, since there seems to be a demand."

"How did that happen?" He leaned forward. "Are you doing marketing and advertising, or is it really all word of mouth around here?"

"Well, I started with some meager marketing efforts, but I honestly owe most of the success to Sam and Dottie. If the Sweeneys weren't so well-rooted in Cocoa

Beach, I don't think it would be blossoming nearly as much, or as quickly. With the connection to the inn and the fact that their family knows everyone in town, it's helped a lot."

"That's amazing." He scratched his head and searched her face. "I can't believe how well you two have integrated here. And Amber? Running a mayoral campaign? It's great."

"I was so glad when she jumped at that opportunity. She's been so down lately, she needed something to lift her up again." She looked at him for a long time and decided not to overthink what she said next. "I'm glad you're here, Rick."

His eyes flickered with surprise, but a smile pulled at his cheeks. "I'm glad, too, Lor. And, hey, if you did want to up your marketing game for the yoga classes, maybe get a website going...I might know a professional photographer who could help you out." Rick winked in a way that would have made her heart somersault back when they were dating.

It still kind of did.

"Actually..." She felt her lips lift. "That would be amazing. I haven't tackled the website beast yet, but professional photos are a must."

"It's settled, then." Rick placed his palms on the table. "I'll help you. God knows I could use something to do, too."

"So, you're...you're staying." She bit her lip. "For a while."

He inhaled and then paused for a moment. "If that's

okay. I don't want to intrude on you or Amber or the Sweeneys, I just...I missed you guys. I missed my family."

Lori swallowed, a lump rising in her throat. "I want you to stay."

"Good." He reached across the table and gently took her hand. "Like you said, anything can happen."

Chapter Nine

Sam

S am looked at everyone gathered around the white wooden dining table in the cottage and noticed how the number of seats seemed to keep expanding every couple of months.

Now, the ever-growing Sweeney family sat on mismatched chairs and a piano bench, filling the room with even more lively conversation and laughter. And they had set up a "kids" table in the living room, where everyone under sixteen could have their own dinner.

But Sam loved that—the "fun" table—as much as this one.

This particular dinner had been requested by Julie, who now needed all hands on deck for her campaign to be the next mayor of Cocoa Beach. In true Sweeney fashion, they showed up in large numbers with platters of food and minds full of ideas.

Amber, for the first time since her arrival, was engaged and present and even leading the conversation. As Julie's campaign manager, it made sense, but it was still surprising and wonderful to see the girl come alive, despite the recent struggles in her life.

Every few minutes, Sam snuck a glance at Lori, who

beamed with pride and visible relief as she watched her daughter become herself again.

"Okay." Julie looked at Amber for backup as the table went quiet to hear the future mayor speak. "The biggest hurdle right now is, obviously, we need money," she said bluntly. "And a lot of it. Trent Braddock comes from a stupidly wealthy family and has been fundraising donations for his mayoral campaign since he was in the womb, basically, so we've got some catching up to do."

"Everyone knows the Braddocks, it's true." John chuckled, raising his brows. "You need one heck of a fundraiser, and fast."

Julie pressed her lips together, turning to face her twin brother. "Any ideas?" She looked at Taylor, too. "Marketing geniuses?"

"Hmm." Taylor tore off a piece of a roll and popped it into her mouth, staring at the ceiling while she thought. "We can certainly get the word out to some of clients with local businesses, see what they can do to get your name out there. I'll talk to Andre, and—"

"Six," Sam interjected, quietly teasing Taylor with a wink.

"What?" Taylor asked.

"It took you six seconds to mention his name. That might be a new record."

Taylor cracked up and finished her roll. "Would you hush? The brewery could be a big source of young voters."

"You know I'm kidding." Sam smiled at her daughter. "The brewery is a great idea."

"We could probably have you come in for an event or something," Taylor suggested to Julie.

John nodded. "I'll talk to a couple of other local clients, see what they can come up with. I'm just not sure if we have the means to drum up the kind of money you need in such a short time."

Erica lifted a shoulder and chimed in. "I'll certainly put the word out at Jada's school, since I'm getting to know a lot of moms there."

"It's a good thought, Erica." Dottie nodded. "I'll tell the ladies at my book club brunch to vote and share the news. Mariam Wilkinson is in my group, and she simply cannot stand the Braddocks, so I'm sure she'll help the cause."

"Ah, yes." John said with a sigh. "The old Wilkinson-Braddock feud."

Imani turned to her husband, smiling with intrigue. "There's a town feud? I'm riveted."

Erica waved a hand. "It's not so much a feud as it is two Old Money families who sort of don't like each other. I don't think it runs deeper than that."

"Dang." Will, Erica's husband, ran a hand through his hair, laughing softly as he sipped his water. "I was hoping for some Hatfields and McCoys-level drama."

"Come on, my dear family." Julie snapped her fingers. "Stay focused. Fundraiser."

Ben, who had recently opted to leave the kids table and sit with the adults, lifted a hand. "What about a car wash? That's what the baseball team does every year and you'd be shocked how much money we bring in."

Sam wrinkled her nose. "I love the enthusiasm, bud, but I think we've got to be bigger than a car wash."

Amber held a finger up to talk. "Obviously, Julie's going to garner donations via her campaign website and a GoFundMe that can be accessed via the QR code on all of her promo materials. But we do need to think pretty big in terms of fundraising, simply to get the word out about her candidacy, if nothing else. I mean, I'm pretty sure ninety percent of Cocoa Beach probably still thinks Trent is running unopposed."

"And the ten percent that doesn't is sitting in this room," Julie cracked. "Plus, the whole town adores him."

"Oh!" Taylor blurted out. "I have an idea!"

All eyes turned to Tay, who had come so much into her own as a thriving twenty-five-year-old, Sam hardly recognized her girl sometimes.

"When I was in college, they put on this massive fundraiser every year for the children's hospital. Sometimes it raised a couple million dollars."

"Million?" Dottie gasped.

"Yes, it was huge. I'm not saying we could replicate it on that scale, but it's definitely something that could bring in the kind of fundraising Aunt Julie needs."

"What was it?" Dottie asked impatiently.

"This giant dance party. Dance Marathon. Once a year, a ton of students would gather in the basketball gym and dance for twenty-four straight hours. Donors would pledge a certain amount of money to the dancers, and the only rule was that you have to be on your feet for twenty-four hours. Everyone has a dance partner, and every hour the pairs stay standing, it's more money to the campaign from the donors."

"A dance marathon!" Imani lit up. "Brilliant! And so much fun."

"It is!" Taylor grinned.

"So, how would it work?" Lori asked. "Donors pledge money beforehand? Or during the event?"

"Both, I believe," Taylor explained. "All of the dancers will reach out to friends and family, social media, all of that before the fundraiser to get donations. I have a few contacts at *Florida Today* who will likely do a story about it. And during the actual dance marathon, people come and watch and pledge money for dance pairs with every passing hour. It can all be done on Venmo, so it's super easy. It gets pretty rowdy, but people love it."

"It sounds fantastic." Amber grinned at Taylor. "We can chat more later and figure out all the details."

"Definitely!" Taylor exclaimed. "I have a couple of friends who were super involved with it at UF. I'm gonna text them for insight."

Julie clasped her hands together. "This is awesome. And of course, since it's a dance marathon, we'll have to have some great music."

"You should play!" Dottie said excitedly, gesturing at Julie. "It would be so perfect, since it's your campaign."

Julie sucked in a breath. "For twenty-four straight hours?" She glanced over at Amber, who arched a brow.

"Do you want to raise a lot of money? Because people will eat that up," she said.

Julie cocked her head. "I better get my guitar back in tune."

"Just one last important question, of course." Amber looked around the table, leaning forward. "Who are the dancers going to be?"

Sam raised her eyebrows, gesturing an arm vaguely at the family. "I believe you're looking at them. And, of course, anyone else who wants to join us."

"Everyone needs a partner." Erica placed a hand on Will's arm. "And we better get on this, fast."

"ASAP," Lori agreed.

Sam sat back in her seat, taking a sip of iced tea and trying not to wish that a certain *someone* was her dance partner.

SAM HELD her breath before lifting her hand to knock on Ethan's front door, having to consciously remind herself that she was there for a reason, and that reason had nothing to do with their romance or breakup or feelings.

Ethan had a very specific set of skills, all of which had turned out to be shockingly useful in many facets of Sam's life, and, romance or not, she needed him.

Ethan opened the door, his eyes wide as he raised his hand to shield them from the morning sun. "Hey Samantha. What's going on?"

"Sorry I didn't call. I was just in your area and really needed to discuss something with you."

His eyes flickered with interest and surprise.

"It's not...personal." She bit her lip awkwardly, looking down at the brick doorstep.

"Come on in." He stepped away from the door and gestured toward the entryway. "I just brewed some coffee."

Sam walked into Ethan's house, which had started to feel familiar and homey during their time together. She'd grown fond of the faint smell of wood and had nearly memorized all of the different furniture pieces throughout the house, most of them lovingly built or restored by Ethan.

She followed him into the kitchen, remembering how she'd once sat at the countertop watching him make scrambled eggs in his pajama pants, and thought that she might spend the rest of her life with this man.

But...that was then. And now? They were barely weird and awkward friends, tiptoeing around each other and never saying what was on either of their minds.

It was sad, but it was what it was.

He poured her a cup. "Here you go."

"Thank you. Can I get a little bit of sugar and—"

"Half a tablespoon of cream," Ethan finished, a half-smile pulling at his cheek. "I remember."

A melancholy heaviness settled in Sam's chest, but she forced a smile and sat down on one of the barstools, taking the hot mug he handed her, which had the Surfside High logo on it.

"Thanks," she muttered.

"Of course." Ethan poured his own cup, leaning

against the countertop as he studied her. "So, to what do I owe this incredibly awkward surprise visit?"

Sam laughed, his comment easing some of her tension. "We're friends, remember?"

"I know, I know." He took a sip. "And let me guess... my friend needs me to start drawing up plans for a beach-front cabana, yes?"

Sam smiled. "Not quite yet."

"Still dealing with red tape, huh?"

"More like a red brick wall." Sam sipped her hot coffee and let it warm her belly as the steam hit her face. "Hopefully, we can get Julie elected and break ground on the cabana the moment that happens."

"Well, you know where to find me." The corners of his mouth lifted, and his eyes glimmered as he looked at Sam.

She had to look away. She couldn't still feel things for him, not after everything that happened.

"Anyway." She cleared her throat, gripping her mug with both hands. "Speaking of Julie's campaign, we're organizing a fundraiser to raise money and awareness to get her elected."

"Okay." He nodded. "Good idea. I'm happy to donate, if—"

"No, no." Sam lifted a hand. "I mean, that'd be awesome, but that's not why I'm here."

He searched her face, waiting for her to continue.

"We decided last night at a large family dinner that the fundraiser is going to be a dance marathon."

"Oh, nice." Ethan laughed, scratching his head.

"That's when people have to stay on their feet for a full day, right?"

"Exactly. I'll be one of those lucky people." She sucked in a breath. "Anyway, I was wondering if you'd be able to throw together a small wooden stage we can put up at the community center for the event. Julie's going to play music the whole time, so we need a platform for her. It doesn't have to be anything elaborate."

"Sure." Ethan shrugged. "And I'll do it gratis for the campaign, since I assume that's why you don't want to rent one."

Which would have been so easy, she thought, covering with a sip of coffee as she nodded. But then she wouldn't be sitting here at Ethan's kitchen counter, looking at a stack of graded calc quizzes and drinking his coffee and being with...him.

"A stage platform is easy," he said, letting her off the hook. "When's the big day?"

"A week from Saturday. We just booked the community center this morning, so we're all running around like chickens with our heads cut off trying to get everything ready."

He chuckled. "You Sweeneys are a special breed. I'm happy to build a stage and help out in any way I can."

"Well, we do need more dancers," Sam joked with a shrug.

"I can dance."

She stared at him. "I was kidding, Ethan. I would never expect you to subject yourself to that."

"What do you mean, *subject* me?" He waved a hand.

"It sounds like fun. Besides, being the Surfside calc teacher, I bet tons of my students, and their parents, would show up and pledge money just to watch me have to dance for twenty-four hours. I, uh, might make it worth extra credit. Those new calc kids are desperate for it."

Sam laughed at that, but couldn't argue with the logic.

"Well..." Sam gave a cheesy grin. "That would be completely awesome, if you're up for it."

"Definitely. I'm happy to support Julie's campaign, since I'm not a huge Trent Braddock fan, despite his glittering reputation."

"I don't know him personally, but evidently he's the pinnacle of charisma." Sam wrinkled her nose. "The only thing about the fundraiser is..." She lowered her gaze back down to her coffee for a second. "You need a dance partner."

Ethan hesitated and ran a hand through his light brown hair. "Something tells me you do, too, *friend*."

Sam tried to tamp down the jitters that zipped up her spine. "Are you sure that's a good idea?" she asked, her voice barely above a whisper.

"Yeah, why not?" He leaned over the counter, pinning her with his blue, blue gaze. "It's for a good cause, right?"

"Definitely." Sam swallowed, giving him a slightly nervous smile.

Why did it feel like he was...flirting with her? She wanted to remind him that he'd ended their relationship.

He was the one who said he felt betrayed by Sam sniffing around for details about his past.

Granted, she was the one who'd sniffed around. There was blame on both sides, but all of that seemed so distant now. It seemed like something that could maybe be...forgotten.

"Dance partners, then?" Ethan held out his hand, giving her a playful smile.

"Dance partners." She shook it and laughed softly.

And maybe, eventually, something more, Sam thought to herself.

She supposed there was a possibility that Annie and Taylor were right when they said Sam and Ethan might not be done for good. Maybe she was holding on to false hope.

But when she saw that glimmer in his eyes and watched him part his lips like he wanted to say so much, she felt like her hope was definitely not false.

Chapter Ten

Amber

"Honey, you almost ready?" Lori's voice reached Amber's room from down the hall. "There could be traffic on the way down to Melbourne."

"One second, Mom." Amber finished typing up an email to the caterer she'd lined up for the dance marathon asking about rates for a beverage package.

Once she finished that, she opened another tab to check on the status of Julie's candidacy, which had recently been approved, officially putting her name on the ballot. Then she navigated back to her campaign schedule, narrowing her eyes as she scanned the dates of upcoming events and debates.

They had a lot of work to do, but Amber was ready. Her vision was clear, and her heart was in this. In fact, her heart was more in this than it had been in anything for a long time. It felt so good to get out of her head, stop wallowing in self-pity, and climb back into the political saddle after everything had gone up in flames with Michael.

Plus, she believed in this campaign, she believed in Julie, and she was starting to care deeply about this town.

She'd always known local politics was like catnip to her and she just couldn't get enough.

"Come on, A." Lori leaned in the doorway of her room, arms folded. "I know you're busy, but this is an important appointment."

"Eighteen-week checkup, I know." Amber reluctantly closed her laptop and got up off of the bed. "Is it going to be any different than my last checkup?"

"They're probably going to do another ultrasound. You'll get an updated sonogram, and at this stage, little baby is going to be even more developed."

Amber sighed, a shiver of nerves fluttering through her as she slid on a pair of white sneakers and slung her purse over her shoulder. "All right, let's go."

Lori wrapped her arm around Amber as they walked through the hallway toward the front door of the townhouse.

Amber held a hand on her growing tummy, wondering if her little Kidney Bean was actually going to look different now.

"I'll drive." Lori flipped her keys in her hand as she opened the front door. "You just relax, put on some music, we can talk about the campaign, and—"

The two of them stopped in their tracks the second they stepped outside to see Rick standing in the driveway, closing his car door and giving the two women an awkward wave.

"Dad." Amber smiled, rushing over to give him a hug. "What are you doing here?"

"Hey, kiddo." He pulled back, glancing past her at Lori, who didn't seem too eager to run over and hug him. She didn't seem unhappy to see him, though, Amber noticed.

"Rick, hey." Lori joined them and brushed a strand of hair out of her eyes. "This is a surprise."

"Yeah, sorry to just drop in on you guys. I—"

"Dad." Amber gave him a playful elbow jab. "We're a family. You're not dropping in on us."

There was a beat or two of awkward tension after the "family" comment, but Amber didn't care. She was too overjoyed to have the weight of her secret off of her chest and her amazing dad back in her life.

"Well, you know." Rick waved a hand. "Anyway, I was just coming by to see if there was anything I could do to help out with the dance marathon. I know you said you were handling catering and all of that, A, but I'd be more than happy to take pictures and document the whole thing for the papers and local news, or whatever Julie needs."

"That would be great!" Amber exclaimed, glancing back and forth between her mother and father. "We could post all over about the huge success of the event, and how the community rallied together to support Julie. That content would help us reach more voters, especially with the surge of funding we're hoping to raise."

"I'd be happy to do it." Rick smiled. "If it's okay with you, of course," he said, turning his attention to Lori. "I don't mean to horn in."

"Rick, please." Lori gave a soft laugh. "You're not

horning in on anything. Photography would be awesome."

"Sweet." Amber clasped her hands together.

"But we do have to get going," Lori said. "Amber has her eighteen-week ultrasound down in Melbourne."

"Oh, right." Rick glanced at Amber, pressing his lips together. "Drive safe, and I'll talk to you—"

"Unless you'd like to come with us," Lori said, shocking Amber and, from the look on his face, shocking Rick even more. "To the appointment," she finished softly.

"Really?" He smiled widely, his eyes lighting up. "Amber, you don't mind?"

"Of course not." Amber felt her heart tug with joy at the prospect of having both of her favorite people at this appointment.

She wasn't entirely sure how much or how little they'd talked since Dad showed up, but her parents definitely seemed to be on good terms, all things considered.

"I'd love that," Amber clarified.

"Let's go then." Lori swung open the driver's side door of her car.

"I'll take the backseat, Dad." Amber climbed in. "I want to stretch my legs out."

"You sure, kid?"

"Yup."

The ride down to the doctor's office in Melbourne seemed to fly by and take way less time than the twenty-six minutes the GPS estimated.

The drive was spent talking mostly about the

campaign, with Amber filling her dad in on everything they'd been doing.

Lori chimed in, and as the minutes ticked by, the tension eased. By the time they got to the medical plaza in Melbourne, Amber could almost shut her eyes and pretend they were still a family.

"All right, you guys." Lori parked the car out front of the medical building where Amber had been going to see her OB-GYN, who she actually liked quite a bit.

As usual, Amber's heart started to race, and her mind began to fill with all of her typical thoughts and fears and regrets about her situation. In moments like these, her pregnancy felt so real, and there was nothing she could do to distract herself or push those feelings away.

She was used to it at this point, and as the three of them stepped into the elevator to go up to the fourth floor of the building, Amber braced for the usual wave of fear and sadness.

But this time, she was flanked by both of her parents, and the wave felt less like a tsunami and more like a little splash on the shore.

With Mom and Dad on either side of her, figuratively holding her up like pillars of support, Amber didn't feel so bad. For the first time in almost four months, her pregnancy wasn't instantly associated with dread and regret.

She felt...hopeful. She was happy. And at an OB-GYN appointment, that was a shocker.

"You okay?" Lori asked as the elevator slowed to a stop and the doors slid open.

"Yeah." Amber smiled, glancing at her dad then back at Mom. "I'm good. Really good, actually."

Lori shared a look with Rick that Amber couldn't quite identify.

"Awesome." Rick gave a thumbs-up.

It *was* awesome.

The three of them walked down the hallway into Dr. Angela Guittierez's waiting room and sat down after Amber signed in at the front.

She looked around the waiting room, her eyes landing on a woman who looked to be around her own age. She was clearly further along in her pregnancy, her belly about ready to pop. Next to her, a handsome man sat and held her hand, clinging to her and beaming as they whispered softly.

Amber waited for the green monster of envy to reach around her throat and choke her with jealousy and bitterness. But this time...it didn't come.

She felt so much more complete with both her mom and dad here. She might not have that life partner to do this journey with, but she had the two of them.

And maybe one day they could be a family again.

"Amber Kittle," a woman called. "Come on back."

She stood up and smiled at her. "Can I bring my parents?"

"Absolutely." The woman grinned, stepping aside for the three of them to walk through the doorway and down the hall. "I'll be your ultrasound tech today. My name is Kiara."

"Hi, Kiara. I'm Amber." She shook her hand. "These are my parents, Lori and Rick."

"Nice to meet you." Lori reached out and shook Kiara's hand, and Rick did the same.

They settled into a back room, where Amber took her place on a now familiar bed under the machine that would show a black and gray blob that looked more or less like a kidney bean.Mom and Dad sat side by side in the extra chairs in the corner of the room, sharing a smile.

"All right, ladies and gents." Amber rubbed her stomach, which seemed to feel bigger by the day. "We're going to get some pictures of the little dude today."

Rick grinned, pressing his palms onto the tops of his knees. "Awesome. Thanks so much for letting me come along. I'm really happy I get to be here and get a sneak peek at my granddaughter."

Lori and Amber both laughed at that.

"Of course," Lori said, turning to him and holding his gaze long enough for Amber to notice. "I'm glad you're here."

"I'm glad I'm here, too, Lor."

Suddenly, Amber felt like she was witnessing an exchange that was a bit more than just a pleasantry. Could there actually be hope for her parents yet?

Kiara flipped a couple of switches on her machine and yanked on some latex gloves. "You ready, girl?"

Amber nodded, sucking in a nervous breath through her teeth as she smiled. "I think so. I'm excited."

"Let's get into it then. This is going to be cold, so bear

with me." Kiara slid Amber's T-shirt higher to expose her stomach and rub some chilly gel over her baby bump.

"Wow." Amber flinched at the freezing sensation hitting her skin. "Like ice."

"Sorry," Kiara said sympathetically. "It'll warm up."

Amber nodded, catching the gaze of each of her parents and shooting them a smile. She had no idea she could feel this good and happy and peaceful at a baby appointment.

Maybe this whole thing wasn't going to be so bad after all.

"All right..." Kiara slowly ran the scanner probe over Amber's stomach, her head turned to face the screen on a table by the bed. "Hmm..."

"What is it?" Lori asked, nerves rising in her voice. "What's wrong?"

"It's okay, ma'am. I'm just trying to find the heartbeat. Sometimes it takes a couple of minutes."

Amber felt her own heart rate start to pick up as she swallowed a sudden lump of fear.

As the moments ticked by, the silence grew loud and suffocating.

Amber looked up at Kiara. "Where's the heartbeat?"

Kiara pressed her lips together and kept her attention focused on the ultrasound, slowly moving the probe over Amber's stomach. "Sometimes the baby can be in a weird position that doesn't allow us to hear the heartbeat."

"Sometimes but..." Amber felt a chill go up her spine. "What about other times?"

"Don't worry, Amber," Kiara said calmly. "I assure

you we will do everything in our power to make sure your baby is healthy and safe."

But how much was in their power? What if something had gone wrong?

Suddenly, Amber felt the sting of tears behind her eyes and the tightness of a sob in her throat. She looked at her parents, noticing fear in her mother's wide eyes and concern furrowing Dad's brow.

She could hear her pulse pounding in her head and she waited. And waited. And waited.

"I'm going to get Dr. Guittierez," Kiara explained, reattaching the probe to the ultrasound machine on the cart next to her. "We'll have her come in, take a look, make sure everything is all right."

"Is everything *not* all right?" Amber asked, panic edging her voice.

"Please." Kiara set a gentle hand on Amber's shoulder, then looked at her parents to make sure her words were heard by all of them. "Take some deep breaths. Everything is okay. I'm just going to have the doctor come in and take a look." She glanced at the ultrasound machine. "Sometimes these things can be wonky."

Amber thought, *And other times, the baby doesn't make it.*

Kiara headed out of the room, and the second the door shut, a hot tear slid down Amber's cheek.

"You guys." She looked at her parents, hearing her voice thick and wavering. "There's no heartbeat."

"That's not what she said," her father said in his most reasonable-sounding voice. "She just couldn't find it. The baby could be in a weird position. I'm sure that happens all the time."

Amber forced herself to nod, but she wasn't convinced.

Lori brushed the front of her white jeans, crossing one leg over the other and taking a deep breath before looking at Amber. "Let's just see what the doctor has to say before we go into panic mode, okay?"

Amber sucked in a ragged breath. "Okay."

"Like I always say," Lori continued. "Let's not worry until there is something to worry about."

But there is *something to worry about*, Amber wanted to scream. But she didn't. She knew her mother meant well and was just trying to keep Amber calm.

Amber leaned forward and looked down at her pregnant stomach. She watched it rise and fall with her rapid, shallow breaths and imagined what the tiny little person in there was going to be like.

She'd already felt the baby move! She knew it was a girl! She couldn't...

Suddenly, Amber realized her "unwanted" pregnancy was anything but. Yeah, this little dudette had derailed her life and isolated her and cost her a lot. Plus, motherhood terrified her.

But now, the thought of *not* having this baby was a thousand times more terrifying than being a single mom had ever been.

She looked at Lori and Rick, blinking back tears. "I didn't know how much I wanted her until right now." She sniffed and sobbed. "I don't want to lose her. I...

didn't realize I was so attached, and now, what if—" she choked on a cry.

"Amber." Lori stood up and walked over to the bed where Amber lay, grabbing her hand. "It's going to be okay."

"Your mother is right." Rick walked over and took Amber's other hand. "We've got you. And everything is all right."

But it wasn't all right. She had her parents, and they were here, and her family was together. Broken, but together. And that was all well and good but somehow, somewhere along the way, she'd learned to love the little Kidney Bean in her belly without even noticing it. And now...

"Amber Kittle." Dr. Angela Guittierez walked into the exam room, snapping on her own pair of rubber gloves. "How are we doing today? Lori, it's good to see you again."

"Hi, Doctor." Lori smiled. "This is my husband, er, ex, well..." She shook her head. "This is Rick, Amber's father."

"Pleasure." Rick shook the doctor's hand. "Sorry, we're just a little tense here, since the tech couldn't seem to find the heartbeat in the ultrasound."

Amber nodded, wiping away her last few tears and looking up at the tall, comforting doctor who'd guided her through this pregnancy so far. "I'm really scared, to be honest."

"I understand completely." Dr. Guittierez sat down on a rolling stool and scooted over to the side of the exam bed, pressing a couple of buttons on the ultrasound machine. "Let's not give in to that just yet, though, okay? These things do happen when the baby gets itself in a pretzel now and then."

Amber nodded, sucking in a breath, still holding both Mom and Dad's hands. She didn't care that she was almost thirty and about to be a single mom. She needed her parents.

The doctor squirted some more ice-cold gel onto Amber's stomach, but she could hardly feel it, she was so numb with fear.

Dr. Gutierrez began slowly moving the probe around again, narrowing her eyes as she focused on the machine and the screen next to them.

Seconds felt like hours, and Amber held her breath for every single one of them.

"Oh!" Dr. Guittierez perked up and smiled as she pressed the probe into the side of Amber's bump. "There it is. Listen."

As she moved it over a centimeter or two, the sound of a squishy, rapid thumping filled the room.

Lori gasped with joy. "I hear it!"

"See?" Rick reached down and ruffled Amber's hair. "All good."

"All good indeed." The doctor gave Amber an assuring nod. "That's a healthy heartbeat. Looks like your little girl was just turned around."

"Oh, oh my gosh." Relief washed over her like an ocean wave, and she laughed with joy, her heart light.

"She was just turned around," she repeated. "I'm so glad."

"That's right, my dear." The doctor took one more scan and peeked at the screen, letting them listen to the thumping for a few more blessed moments. "You've got a healthy baby, and you'll get to bring home some sonogram pictures of your little one."

Amber flopped her head back against the thin pillow on the bed, shutting her eyes and letting joy flood her. "She's healthy."

"She's healthy," Lori repeated, squeezing her hand and wiping a tear of her own.

Rick chuckled softly, stroking Amber's cheek. "Little girl is growing, huh?"

"Oh, yes." Dr. Guittierez reached over to the table next to them and pulled out a strip of black and white sonogram photos. "She is five point seven inches right now. Here you go."

Amber reached out and took the sonogram from the doctor, staring at the tiny baby curled up in each of the squares. She wasn't a kidney bean anymore, that was for sure. This little lady was a full-on grapefruit.

"Look." She held out the pictures for her parents to see.

"She's gorgeous," Lori cooed.

"Look at that nose." Rick pointed to one photo where the baby's face was visible. "She's got a great nose. A perfect nose. A nose for the ages."

The three of them laughed a lot and cried a bit more as Amber finished up with the doctor.

By the time they were walking out of the office, Amber was fully obsessed with the latest sonogram.

She hadn't met this little girl yet. Heck, she hadn't even named her. But in that moment, she was certain of one thing.

She'd do absolutely anything for her.

Chapter Eleven

Julie

"So if the stage is here..." Amber stepped back, motioning through the air with her finger in a large square. "We can put the speakers on either side. Would that work?"

Julie looked around the open gymnasium of the Cocoa Beach Community Center, which, in exactly seventy-two hours, would hopefully be bustling with fun and dancing at her campaign fundraiser.

But right now, it was cavernous and daunting, although Julie felt like she was in great hands with Amber. Her young campaign manager was clearly a pro and had been in particularly good spirits the past couple of days.

"Yeah, that sounds good." Julie placed her hands on her hips and walked around slowly, her black Converse sneakers squeaking on the gym floor. "I really hope this thing is a success."

"It will be." Amber glanced up from the iPad where she was jotting down notes, her smile beaming.

"Well, aren't you Little Miss Optimism?" Julie teased, sitting down on the edge of the first row of bleachers.

"I don't know." Amber shrugged and walked over to join her. "I have a really good feeling about the dance marathon. And the campaign in general. It's going to generate a lot of good press and..." Her voice trailed off.

Julie narrowed her gaze and searched Amber's face, sensing that there was more to her new sense of joy than "good press."

"And?" She arched a brow, waiting for more.

Amber turned to her, a smile pulling at her face. "Look." She reached into the purse on her shoulder and slid out a little rectangular piece of paper that Julie instantly recognized as a sonogram. "I got this a few days ago at my checkup. Meet my little no-name daughter to be."

"No." Julie pressed her hand to her heart and took the sonogram from Amber, admiring the visible features on the baby. "She's beautiful. Big!"

"Almost six inches," Amber said proudly, taking the treasured image back and slipping it into the side pocket of her purse.

"You're, uh..." Julie nudged her, smiling softly. "Coming around to the idea of motherhood a bit, huh?"

Amber glanced down, and nodded. "I finally realized how much it means to me. Just because it wasn't what I planned doesn't mean it isn't right."

Julie studied her, warmed by the sentiment. "Well said."

"But!" Amber stood back up, gesturing around the big, empty gym. "We've got to focus on this dance marathon. I'm thinking beverage cart over here..." She headed to the other side of the gym.

"And that's being arranged by the caterer?" Julie stood up to join her.

"Yup. All set up." Amber tapped the screen of her iPad. "And we can probably put the donation station right near there. Or closer to where the majority of spectators will be sitting. I think—"

"Hello, there." An unfamiliar male voice caught Julie's attention, and she turned to see a tall, lanky man in a button-down and khakis standing in the doorway of the gymnasium. "Mind if I come in and say hi?"

Julie squinted as she walked across the court to greet the stranger. As soon as she got closer, she realized exactly who she was looking it.

"Hi!" She put on a smile and held out a hand. "Julie Sweeney. You must be—"

"Trent Braddock." He flashed a charming grin and angled his head, making such direct eye contact with Julie she almost felt naked. "What a pleasure to finally meet you, Julie."

Trent Braddock had to be in his mid-forties, a few years younger than Julie. He was handsome in a way that was so polished and clean, it didn't feel real.

His dark brown hair was slicked back and his face was clean shaven. Even his eyebrows looked like they'd been groomed.

What was he doing here?

"You as well." Julie cleared her throat and stepped

aside, gesturing at Amber, who had joined them. "This is my campaign manager, Amber Kittle."

"Mr. Braddock." Amber shook his hand, giving him a tight smile.

"Sorry to just pop in on you like this." Trent leaned back, folding his arms over his chest. "I was just in one of the meeting rooms here at the community center and someone mentioned that you were in the gym. I figured it was about time I met my competition." He laughed in a way that was surprisingly...disarming. Maybe sincere, maybe flirtatious, maybe completely fake.

Impossible to tell.

"It *is* about time," Julie agreed. "I've heard a lot about you, I'm happy to finally put a face to the legendary name."

"Oh, please." He waved a dismissive hand. "I don't know about legendary."

"Around here you are."

"Well." He lifted a shoulder. "Small town."

"That it is. What kind of meeting were you having here, if you don't mind me asking? Hopefully not something I was supposed to do and didn't know about."

"No, no. Nothing like that." Trent flicked his hand. "I was just chatting with the library board. You know, improvement strategies, revitalization plans for the public library. Boring stuff."

Boring stuff that was going to get him elected.

From the corner of her eye, she could see Amber stiffen and glare at the man, silent.

"You know, just trying to help out the community. I

mean, hey, isn't that the ultimate goal in all of this?" He cocked his head. "It's so easy to get caught up in the politics of it all, but we really do just want to give back to the town that made us who we are, right?"

"Yes, I couldn't agree more." Julie grinned, her tension easing. "I grew up here."

"Mmm." He nodded, looking around. "So, what are you guys planning in this big empty gym?"

"Oh, a fundraiser!" Julie exclaimed. "We're planning a dance—"

"Thing," Amber interjected, cutting her off as she stepped forward and forced a smile. "Just a dance thing. It's not really fleshed out yet."

Not fleshed out? It was less than a week away.

But Julie picked up the cue instantly, adopting a much cooler posture. "Yeah, we're just...brainstorming."

"Gotcha." Trent nodded and grinned. "Well, it sounds awesome, whatever it is."

Julie gave a soft smile. "Hopefully it will be."

"Anyway." He looked at Amber, then back at Julie. "I'll go ahead and leave you ladies to it. I just figured I'd stop in and introduce myself."

Julie nodded. "I'm glad you did. It's good to meet you."

"You two as well. You know, to be perfectly honest with you?" He leaned close, speaking to Julie as if he'd known her for years. "The whole cutthroat, hardcore campaign thing...it's just not me. I know we're supposed to be 'enemies' and 'opponents,' but hey." He lifted his hands in a gesture of pure nonchalance. "It's small-town politics, not the presidency. I'd really like to be friends, and keep this all fun, if possible. It's for the good of Cocoa Beach, after all."

Julie felt like a weight had been lifted off of her shoulders. "I completely agree. I'm not interested in the cutthroat stuff, either."

"Wonderful." Trent smiled again, a grin that no doubt opened doors for him. Bedroom doors, boardroom doors, and fundraising doors. "So, we'll keep it clean and fair. I'd love to be friends, Julie. I'm sure we have a ton in common."

"I'd like that, too." She nodded, pushing some hair behind her ears. "I'm glad you see it that way."

"Absolutely." He stepped back, pressing his hands together. "All right. I'll be seeing you both around, then. Good to meet you."

"Bye, Trent. Have a good one." Julie waved.

He headed out of the gym and the double doors closed behind him with an echoing click of the latch.

Julie turned to Amber and arched a brow. "Not exactly in our friendliest mood today, are we?" she teased.

Amber curled her lip and crossed her arms over her chest, resting them on her pregnant belly. "First of all, it's not my job to be likable, it's yours. And you're very good at it."

"Why, thank you." Julie lifted her chin with playful pride.

"And second of all, never trust the competition. Especially our pal Slick, there."

Julie chuckled as they walked back over to the

bleachers to continue drawing out their dance marathon plans.

"He's a smooth talker, but seemed nice enough. Yes, we're technically opponents, but I certainly don't have anything against him personally. Besides, the whole town likes him. They can't all be wrong."

Amber gave a mirthless laugh and shook her head as they sat down on the first row of bleachers. "You mean a large number of people couldn't *possibly* fall for the fake charm and charisma of a slick, ruthless, no-good politician? Hah."

"Whoa." Julie drew back, raising her hands. "You *really* didn't like that guy."

Amber let out a breath, glancing down at her white sneakers as she shifted on the bench. "No, I just...well, I definitely got a bad vibe from Trent. He's...typical."

Julie made a face. "Just because he's running for a political office doesn't mean he's a phony. I mean, heck, I'm running, too, and I'm sure not a fake."

"Of course not." Amber lifted her gaze, and Julie instantly noticed that the light behind her eyes had significantly dimmed. "I just...I know his type. I'm very familiar with what he is, what he does, and what he stands for. Small-town mayor or president of the U.S. and everything in between, the political world is teeming with men like that. I can smell it from a mile away."

"Huh." Julie leaned back, pressing her palms into the wooden bleacher behind her as she thought about Amber's jaded attitude. "Well, you do have a lot more experience in this industry than I do, so I guess I can't argue. I just feel like he can't be *that* bad, right?"

The look Amber shot her said otherwise.

"Maybe I'm wrong," Julie said.

"And maybe I am, too. I'm a bit...cynical about this particular topic."

"Why is that?" Julie turned to face Amber, angling her head. "You've just seen a lot of corruption working on campaigns?"

Amber shut her eyes. "Enough to curl your hair."

"But this is so small-town. I mean, compared to the other elections you've worked on. I feel like we all just kind of believe in the good of the town, and—"

"Want to grab a cup of coffee?" Amber stood up abruptly. "I have a feeling it's gonna be a late night, and I saw a coffee station in the lobby of the rec center."

"Okay." Julie got up slowly, not sure what to make of this.

"Plus...I have a story to tell you."

"Wow." Julie stared at Amber, completely stunned and rattled by the saga she'd just heard. "So the whole one-night stand thing..."

"A lie," Amber said, sipping her coffee. "It's the story my mom and I came up with to explain the pregnancy and the lack of father. But it's not true. I'm actually not really one for casual things like that. I hate telling that lie, but as you now know, it's a lot better than the truth."

"Oh, Amber." Julie shook her head, leaning back in the plastic chair as she processed the trauma this poor girl had gone through.

They sat across from one another at a table in the lobby and check-in area of the community center, next to the coffee station and welcome desk.

Down the hall, there were dance studios and camp centers and sports areas, and the gym where they would hold the dance marathon was through the double doors to their left.

People were coming and going, kids and parents and employees and teachers, but Julie could hardly notice any of that. Her heart filled with sympathy for Amber, intensified by the fact that she'd had to lie to everyone because she was ashamed.

"You know," Julie said, stirring her coffee with a thin wooden stick. "You have absolutely nothing to be embarrassed about. That Michael guy played you. He lied to you, and cheated, and—"

"Yeah, with me." She lowered her voice, frowning. "He cheated with me. I'm the other woman, and I have to live with that shame."

"Amber, he was separated."

"Not divorced." She held up a finger. "Big difference between the two. My parents are separated, but they're not divorced. Not yet, anyway. And certainly neither one of them would even think about..." She screwed up her face. "Dating. It's wrong."

"He's a crappy guy, this Michael Garrison. He's a jerk. Believe me, Amber, you are not the first woman to get swept up by the magical spell of an older, successful, powerful man who promises to leave his wife for you. You shouldn't be so hard on yourself."

"I should have seen through his lines and lies."

"You were in love." Julie reached her hand out and gave a soft, gentle laugh. "It makes us do crazy things. Stupid things. Sometimes, it even gets us pregnant. And while we may feel in that moment that having a baby is going to be the end of life as we know it, it turns out to just be the beginning. It turns out to be the absolute best thing that could have happened."

Amber paused for a long time, biting her lip as she considered that. "Is that how you felt when you got pregnant with Bliss? Like your life was about to be ruined? From our last conversation about it, I figured you were overjoyed."

"Please. I was completely freaked out. I was living in a van playing gigs with my on again-off again boyfriend. He was not exactly *sober* a lot of the time." She flinched at the memories. "Bliss was a big, fat whoopsie."

Amber nodded, listening.

"My point is, I get it. I will never forget how horrified I was the day I picked up the phone to call my mom and dad and tell them I was pregnant. On the road, and not in a real relationship. I was…"

"Ashamed," Amber finished.

"Very much so."

"Were they mad at you?"

"No." Julie shook her head, feeling herself smile at the memory. "They were shocked, and a little disap-

pointed by my lifestyle, but they could never be mad
about a grandbaby. I think, if anything, they were way
more mad about the fact that I kept Bliss out on the road
and away from Cocoa Beach for so many years. But..."
She flicked a hand. "Water under the bridge."

"Yeah." Amber let out a sigh. "I'm definitely coming
around to all of it. And, honestly, it feels good to tell you
the real story. I guess I'm getting the secret out, one
Sweeney at a time."

"I can imagine. Secrets are heavy and exhausting."

Amber nodded. "No kidding. And you're just, I don't
know." She toyed with her paper coffee cup. "Non-judg-
mental. Since you went through something similar."

"Oh, Amber honey, I do not judge. And I respect
your privacy, so I can promise you that your secret is
safe."

"Thanks." Amber smiled. "Sam knows the truth, but
no one else in the family."

"You told Sam first?" Julie gasped, faking offense.
"I'm hurt."

"She overheard my mom and me talking about it
outside the cottage a couple of months ago," Amber
explained. "You're the first person I've told voluntarily.
Besides my dad."

Julie laughed, lifting her coffee in a pretend toast.
"Well, I'm honored. And happy to be here for you, and
for all of your single-mom questions and needs. I can't say
I did everything right, but my kid is my best friend, so I
like to think I had a little bit of success."

Amber smiled and leaned back in the plastic chair.

"At least now you understand my hatred for smooth-talking politicians that everyone adores."

"Oh, yes. It's visceral. But justified." Julie shrugged. "I guess Trent Braddock's true colors remain to be seen."

"That they do."

Julie and Amber sat for a while and talked, looking over the plans for the dance marathon again.

Afternoon rolled around, and slowly little kids with their parents started trickling into the community center for after-school classes and activities.

A few little girls in particular caught their eyes, jetting into the lobby in pink leotards and tutus, leaping all over creation and spinning in circles.

"Oh, the cuteness," Julie cooed at the group of dance students. "It hurts."

Amber watched the three girls playing around before their ballet class, practicing moves and dancing through the lobby, their giddy, girlish giggles filling the air.

Julie studied her face, watching the stars twinkle in Amber's eyes as she observed the girls, enchanted by their adorable sweetness and fun.

Julie finished off her coffee and reached her hand across the table, taking Amber's attention away from the ballet dancers. "Hey, Amber."

"Yeah?"

"You're going to be just fine."

She nodded, taking in a slow breath. "I know."

Chapter Twelve

Lori

"Feel the Earth pressing into your back as you center yourself at the end of today's practice," Lori said in a calm, peaceful voice as she slowly walked around her group of five women, all totally relaxed in *shavasana* after another wonderful class.

The sun beat down on the beach, and Lori fantasized about the cabana once again. Shade, comfort, and a dedicated space for her classes seemed like a dream come true. She believed in Julie's ability to make it happen. And even more so, she believed in her daughter. Amber could help Julie win this campaign, and that was a win for *everyone*.

"Now, stretch your arms up over your head and take one more big inhale, breathing in all of the positivity and growth we experienced this morning with the rising sun."

Lori stood in the center of her cluster of students, stretching her arms up over her head to mimic the movement they all did on their backs. "I want to thank you all again for opening your hearts with me today and aligning your bodies and minds in this practice." She stepped forward, back to her mat, which faced everyone else's.

"When you feel ready and comfortable, meet me in a seated pose."

The women all slowly sat up, looking rested and happy and relieved after the class. They had each shared a personal regret at the beginning of the practice, and Lori had talked through them one by one to help all five women address and begin to let go of those regrets.

As the orange glow of the morning sun shone on their faces, Lori could instantly tell she'd made a difference in their day. And it felt really, really good.

She sat down, crossed her legs and pressed her hands together at her heart center, bowing down and smiling. "*Namaste.*"

"*Namaste,*" the small group repeated in unison, thanking Lori for the class.

They started to mill about, gather their mats, and get ready to leave as Lori hugged a couple of the women and rolled up her mat.

"Thank you, Lori. That was absolutely amazing." Allison Foster, who had become a regular, beamed as she slung her mat underneath her arm.

"Thank you for being here." Lori smiled. "I'll see you next time."

She'd crouched down to slide her portable speaker back into her canvas tote bag when she saw the shadow of someone walking up to her on the sand.

Lori turned and shielded her eyes from the blinding sunlight.

"Rick?" She stood slowly, brushing the sand off of her knees. "What are you doing here?"

He angled his head, squinting against the sunlight as the soft breeze blew his hair around his face. "I was up early, and I was...curious."

Lori smiled, feeling her heart lift. She looked around to see that all five of her students had left, and she was alone with Rick on the beach. "Well, it's not much to see and my class is over, but this is where the cabana is going to be. Hopefully."

Rick leaned back, resting his hands on his hips as he gazed out at the picturesque horizon. "It's a heck of a spot, Lor. I'm happy for you."

"Thank you." Instinct told her to wrap her arms around him, but she had to remind herself that she couldn't do that anymore, even if it felt natural. "I'm proud of what I'm building with this yoga practice."

"You should be. When do you want to do those photographs? With this light, I could get some amazing shots."

"Yes, I would love that." Lori knew how talented he was with a camera, and she could tell from the look in his eyes that he was eager to photograph this spot.

Was he eager to photograph...her?

It wouldn't be the first time Rick had taken pictures of Lori, but it would be the first time in a long time. The thought made her heart race a little, even though she knew it would be strictly for her business.

"You know..." He wandered over to her mat, rolling it back out and sitting down. "I've never taken a yoga class."

"I remember." She crossed her arms. "You never wanted to come with me when I started going."

"You never really asked."

She opened her mouth to protest, but stopped herself. Maybe she hadn't asked. Maybe she had been so bogged down in work that yoga was her only outlet, and she'd never even bothered to invite her husband into that outlet with her.

She pushed away a wave of regret as she sat down on the sand across from him, meeting his familiar gaze.

"So, how does this all work?" He crossed his legs and folded his hands in front of him. "All the meditation and all of that?"

"Well..." Lori scooted a few inches forward on the sand, taking lotus pose and placing her hands gently on her knees. "My style of yoga is a bit different. I do a typical flow for the duration of the class—a *vinyasa*, usually. As we move, I introduce a topic of something that they might be carrying around, like anger or pain or, like today, regret. When flow is over and we've stretched out everything in all kinds of poses, the final section of the class is called *shavasana*, or corpse pose."

Rick snorted. "Morbid."

"Lay down." Lori turned and lay on her back, and Rick did the same. "Palms up, breathing in through your nose and out through your mouth."

"You just lay here? Like a dead guy?"

"Yes, hence the name."

He chuckled. "Well, if I'd known yoga involved napping I might have been more inclined."

"It's not napping." Lori turned her head to face him, smiling a little. "It's a meditative, relaxed state that comes naturally after a good practice. It's a way to decompress and process the mind-body alignment of the past hour or so."

Rick inhaled deeply, his chest rising and falling as he let out the breath.

"This is when my class becomes this sort of...open floor. I invite my students to share a certain thing about their lives or something on that topic I mentioned, or really anything that's on their hearts. They don't have to, and not everyone does. But generally, I've found that when one person speaks up, I can try to gently talk through that issue with them, and in the calm, meditative state that comes at the end of the yoga practice, people are very open to new thoughts and solutions."

"And lots of women just talk freely with strangers like that? About their personal problems?"

Lori laughed. "I was surprised, too. I certainly never planned on incorporating mental health counseling and wellness into an athletic class. But it happened sort of organically the first time, and kind of took off from there."

Rick listened, his eyes closed as he lay on her yoga mat. "Yoga therapy. How about that."

"Who would have thought?"

"You and your Midas touch." He opened his eyes, squinting in the brightness of the sunlight as he turned his head to meet her gaze. "I'm proud of you."

"Thanks, Rick."

"All right." He shut his eyes again and resituated himself on his back, shifting around until he was comfortable. "Let's do it, then."

"Huh?"

"Yoga therapy. Shoshanna or whatever it was called."

Lori cracked up. "*Shavasana*, and you can't just jump into it. Like I said, it happens organically because of the relaxed mental state after a yoga practice."

"Well, let's just try it anyway." Rick raised his hands and brought them together behind his head. "I'm pretty relaxed."

Lori rolled her eyes, unable to stifle her smile as she sat up and prepared to teach. "All right. As you lay still, feel every single muscle in your body totally relax, one at a time."

He took a noisy deep breath and shifted.

"Feel the sand underneath you and the sun on your skin..." Lori spoke slowly, closing her eyes and fighting the wave of emotion that seemed to keep crashing over her when it came to thoughts of Rick. "And as you breathe, inhale the positivity, the sunshine, the warmth. Exhale whatever you are holding on to that's weighing you down. Feel it leaving your body and your heart."

She sat still, watching Rick—who was taking this surprisingly seriously—let out a long exhale, his eyes shut and his body calm.

"So." Lori shifted her legs underneath her. "This is the part where I invite anyone who feels compelled to share something. Could be good or bad or neutral, just whatever might be lingering and taking up space in the heart and mind. Sometimes yoga practice can bring things to the surface, and this is a good chance to air them out. If you feel comfortable, of course," she added awkwardly.

"Yeah, I'd like to share." Rick spoke softly, continuing to lay motionless.

"Okay." Lori felt a smile pull as she inched closer to him. "What would you like to share, Rick?"

"You said today's class topic was regret?"

"More or less, yes."

"Well, I'm feeling a lot of regret." He turned his head, opening his eyes and instantly meeting hers.

Lori felt her heart skip, and she pressed her lips together and decided to let the moment become as honest and raw as it could. "Regret about what?"

"Leaving my wife." The words came out so quickly, so effortlessly.

Lori blinked back in shock at his blunt statement, and in that moment, had no idea how to feel or react or respond. But in keeping with her practice of yoga therapy, she tried to remove her emotions for the moment, and guide the conversation the way she would with any other patient or student.

She took in a shaky breath and dug for composure. "Why do you regret that?"

"Because I didn't know you were capable of change." He sat up now, looking at her face to face with emotion glinting in his eyes. "Maybe I underestimated you, or maybe my leaving turned everything upside down, but I had no idea it could be like this, Lor. I had no idea *you* could be like this."

Lori paused for a long time, his words hanging in the

air between the crashing waves and the squawks of seag-
ulls. "It was a wake-up call, Rick. A huge one. And then
add in Amber's unexpected pregnancy and the appear-
ance of the Sweeney family...Life all just changed at
once. And I guess I changed along with it."

"You're just..." He scooted closer, looking like he
wanted to place a hand on her but deciding not to.
"You're so calm now. You're so much happier. I feel like
you're back to how you were when we met, you know?
Early on. And it makes me miss you so much. And it
makes me wonder if...we could ever be how we were.
How things used to be."

Lori blinked back as the impact of the words hit her,
her heart thumping loud in her chest. "Rick, you...you
left."

"After months and years of trying to make it better,
yeah." He sat up straighter, his eyes fiery with passion. "I
was so lonely, Lori. I expressed that to you, and every
time it seemed like things might get better, work got in
the way."

She couldn't even try to deny that. "I know."

"But now, we're here." He glanced around. "In
paradise. About to be grandparents together. And it feels
like there's nothing in the way, at least nothing we can't
handle."

Lori swallowed, her whole body feeling shaky. This
was Richard Kittle, the only man she'd ever loved, the
man who broke her heart when he left. And yet, she
understood his reasons.

Was there hope for forever still? After all, no papers had been signed.

Maybe things really could change. Lori sure had.

She looked up at him, feeling a smile pull as the tension in her shoulders started to ease.

"How about this for starters?" she asked. "Would you like to be my dance partner at the fundraiser for Julie's campaign? You can see I need that cabana, so I've got to do everything in my power to help her win. Plus, she's my sister."

"Your dance partner for twenty-four straight hours?" His brows shot up.

"Yep. If we make it that long. I knew I'd participate, but I couldn't ask Amber to be my partner, since she can't be on her feet for twenty-four hours. Plus, she'll be running the event."

Rick stood up, then held out his hand to help Lori up to her feet. He kept his hand on hers, locking eyes. "Lori Ann Caparelli, it would be an honor to dance with you."

And suddenly, Lori was nineteen years old again, filled with hope and excitement and butterflies.

"Thank you, Rick," she whispered, squeezing his hand even though she wanted to throw her arms around him. "Thank you for...being honest."

Chapter Thirteen

Sam

S am would never usually have three cups of coffee at six p.m., but this particular Saturday night called for some craziness.

"Twenty-four straight hours of dancing arm in arm with my ex-boyfriend," Sam breathed, sipping her third cup of coffee next to Erica, Annie and Taylor on the bleachers. "What could go wrong?"

"It'll be fine." Annie smiled, her eyes gleaming.

"What about you?" Sam nudged her. "Where's your partner?"

"He will be here any minute." Annie grinned proudly. "And Riley, who is also participating in the mini-marathon for the kids."

"Oh, fun!" Taylor smiled. "It was a great idea on Julie and Amber's part to have a shorter option for the kiddos."

Erica nodded. "Absolutely. Jada's so excited."

All the women turned their attention to the back corner of the gym, where all the Sweeney cousins laughed and danced and got jazzed up on sugar and excitement for the dance marathon, and the idea of staying up all night.

Even the teenagers, Ben, Damien, and, of course,

Bliss, were full participants. Heck, half the town was here
to dance or spectate.

Sam looked around the community center gymnasium, amazed by how Julie was able to put together this
event in such a short time.

In addition to the wooden stage Ethan had built,
which was currently being set up by tech people to
hookup amps and speakers, there was ample décor. A
huge banner hung along the back wall and balloons and
streamers were scattered across the ceiling.

The whole place was teeming and buzzing with life,
and Julie was marching around with Amber, talking to
local journalists and smiling for pictures.

"Look at Jules," she said. "I hardly even recognize
her."

"I know, right?" Erica shook her head in disbelief and
smiled. "Julie the Rebel is Miss Cocoa Beach."

They laughed as they watched Julie answering interview questions as a photographer snapped a picture with
a big flash.

Amber clutched an iPad and gave orders to staff
members, before catching Sam's eye and smiling as she
walked over to the bleachers.

"Hey, Amber." Taylor stood up and gave her a hug.
"Everything looks awesome. You guys killed this."

Amber gave a nervous smile. "That remains to be
seen, but thank you." She glanced at Annie, Sam and
Erica. "And thank you all for being here, and bringing
your kids and husbands and boyfriends—"

"And ex-boyfriends," Sam teased, lifting up her finger.

Amber chuckled and gave her a sympathetic pout. "I appreciate it. Five minutes till go time, so enjoy sitting down while you still can!" She hustled off with a wave.

"Talk about coming into her own," Sam mused, jutting her chin at Amber.

"I know, it's amazing." Taylor lifted a shoulder and glanced at her phone. "Andre's here!" Her gaze locked on the double doors of the gym, where Andre Everett walked in wearing a floral button-down and khaki shorts.

He held his arms out wide and Taylor practically sprinted across the gymnasium to leap right into them.

Will glanced at Erica. "Why don't you ever greet me like that?"

Sam snorted.

"Trevor's here, too." Annie grinned widely and stood up.

Sam waved her off. "Go get your man."

As everyone started to take their spots on the floor, Sam caught Ethan's eye.

He'd been helping the volunteer staff set up all the electronics and haul the heavy gear in to prepare the stage. But it appeared like everything was ready to roll, and Sam was waiting for her dance partner.

"Hello, everyone." Amber tapped the microphone, standing up straight as the room fell silent. "I want to thank you all for coming out to the dance marathon fundraiser for our amazing future mayor of Cocoa Beach, Julie Sweeney!"

"Woo!" Sam cheered as the room echoed with applause.

As Amber continued the welcome speech and explained how the fundraiser worked, Ethan gently pushed his way through the crowd to get to Sam.

"Hi," Sam whispered.

"Hey." His eyes grazed over her for a brief second, and a smile spread on his face. "You look great."

"Thanks." She laughed softly. "I almost thought I was going to end up dancing alone."

He rolled his eyes at her. "I'm here. I was just helping out with the setup."

Amber transferred the mic to Julie, who made casual but heartfelt remarks thanking people and underscoring those "key messages" Amber kept drumming into her head.

Sam couldn't really focus on what Julie was saying. Something about education and teachers.

The only teacher she cared about was inches away, smelling like oak and good memories, and curling her toes with a crush. How on Earth was she going to get through the next twenty-four hours?

"And that's enough chatter," Julie said into the mic, whipping a guitar around her shoulder and starting to strum. "Let's dance! In three!"

Sam and Ethan locked eyes, and he awkwardly held his arms up for her to take them.

"Two!"

She placed a hand on his shoulder and her other hand in his palm, hoping he couldn't sense her jitters.

"One! Dance!"

Julie strummed a loud note on the guitar and the beat of a drum echoed through the gym as everyone took their partners.

"An energetic start." Sam laughed, swaying back and forth to the music with Ethan.

"I say we conserve our energy." He narrowed his gaze and eyed the rest of the dance floor. "Pace ourselves so we can outlast everyone."

"Oh, so you're in it to win it, huh?"

"Are you kidding?" He cocked his head and gave a playful smile. "I absolutely came here to win. Besides, see those kids over there?"

Sam turned her gaze to a rowdy group of teenagers who looked to be about Ben's age, laughing in the bleachers and snapping pictures on their iPhones. "Yeah?"

"They're betting and all wins go to the campaign. If they create a calculus problem about the number of hours and dance steps? Big extra credit."

"Wow. You were right. Teenagers really will pay money to watch their calculus teacher suffer."

He snorted, inching just close enough for Sam to get another whiff of that oaky cologne. "I'm not exactly suffering, Samantha."

A chill danced down her spine as they made their way across the floor, the room bouncing as everyone sang and danced to Julie's rendition of *Dreams* by Fleetwood Mac.

"Come on." Ethan guided her through the room. "Let's scope out the competition."

"Hey, you two." Annie grinned, dancing closely with Trevor as Riley bounced around below them. "Looking good." She gave Sam a way-too-noticeable wink.

Sam widened her gaze and smiled. "We're pacing ourselves. Going to win."

"We'll see about that." Trevor gave a joking smile. "Annie and I have some tricks up our sleeve. Plus, we've got a personal coffee runner."

"That's me!" Riley leapt around.

Sam laughed. "Have fun, guys."

They moved to the edge of the dance floor, getting a full view of the packed gym. "This is amazing," Sam said. "I'm so proud of Jules."

"It's incredible. I really hope she wins."

"I think this should help." Sam turned, meeting his deep blue gaze.

A few beats of silence reminded her of their awkward state of questionable friendship, but things right now didn't feel awkward. It felt natural. It felt right.

Sam couldn't help but wonder what in the world was going through his mind. He seemed relaxed enough, but how could he not be replaying their breakup and relationship in his head over and over again?

Because she sure was.

"Okay, Samantha Sweeney," Ethan said, giving her a little twirl as they moved back to the middle of the gym floor and nestled by Erica and Will, who had complete game faces on, of course. "We've got twenty-four hours to get through. How do you propose we pass the time?"

She angled her head and smiled, thinking. "Twenty-four hours is a long time."

Especially when you're spending it arm in arm with your ex, who you still have feelings for.

"Oh, come on." He lifted a shoulder, moving her around the floor as they swayed back and forth with the music. "It's not that long. We can do it."

"I hope so. Twenty-four hours...and it's been..." she glanced at the giant digital clock on the wall. "Six minutes. Great."

Ethan laughed. "Okay, think of it this way. How many times have you been through a twenty-four-hour period?"

She narrowed her gaze. "Are you asking me how many days I've been alive?"

"Basically, yeah."

"You're the math teacher." She flicked her fingers at him playfully.

"All right, fair enough. Let's see, you're forty-three, times three hundred and sixty five...fifteen thousand, six hundred and ninety five days."

"Whoa." Sam drew back, a smile pulling. "Impressive."

"I've got my talents," he teased. "But that's not entirely accurate, since you aren't forty-three on the nose."

"Let's pretend I am."

He chuckled. "Fine by me. So, more than fifteen

thousand, six hundred and ninety five times, you have gone through twenty-four hours. You can most certainly do it again."

"Right, but those are all filled with activities and life and sleeping! This is a full solid day of standing here with you, dancing, thinking, passing time..." She glanced up at him, meeting his deep blue gaze.

"Let's figure out how to pass the time, then." He gently swayed her arm up and down as they rocked on the dance floor.

"All right, what do you think we should do?" Sam looked around. "Rate people's dancing skills on a scale from one to ten?"

He snorted. "I was thinking something that's a little more...between us."

"Oh. Okay..."

"Let's start at the beginning."

"The beginning of what?"

"The beginning of those fifteen thousand-plus days." He cocked his head. "Tell me your earliest memory."

Sam tilted her head back and laughed, letting herself lean into his strong arm for a second as the music picked up over the speakers and the crowd hummed around them. "My earliest memory..." She smiled. "It's of my dad. I remember sitting on his lap Christmas morning, I must have been about five. I had just opened the gift I'd been dying for—a Cabbage Patch Doll."

"Oh, you were one of *those* kids," he said playfully, clicking his tongue.

"Absolutely. I remember it so clearly, clutching the

doll while my dad bounced me on his knee. John and Julie were running around with walkie talkies and Erica was only about two. It was such a happy moment. What about you, Ethan? What's your earliest memory?"

"I think it was walking to school in first grade. It was winter in Maryland, and I was so damn cold." He laughed, shrugging. "That's about the extent of the memory. Yours is much more sentimental."

Sam placed a hand on his shoulder. "I'm sure you've got some sentimental stories of your own. I want to hear them all."

"Well." Ethan arched a brow. "It's a good thing we've got twenty-four hours then, isn't it?"

Then, they got to talking. And talking, and talking, and talking some more.

She pictured Ethan as a little boy, those blue eyes filled with wonder and excitement, his affinity for working with his hands and doing math just starting to take form.

By the time Julie announced that they'd reached the two-hour mark, Sam and Ethan had fully and completely discussed their earliest childhood years.

"Two hours down, ladies and gentlemen! Keep dancing those hearts out and remember, you've got to stay on your feet!" Julie's voice between songs boomed through the gym.

Sam glanced over to the stage, where Julie held up her microphone and pointed at the giant digital clock on the wall behind her that was counting down from twenty-four hours.

Ethan gave her hand a squeeze as they swayed softly to Julie and Bliss's rendition of a Simon and Garfunkel song. "This is fun. What are we at, like, seven years old or so?"

Sam smiled and nodded, feeling comfort in his arms and in their conversation. "Let's keep going."

By hour six, they'd gotten all the way through high school. Ethan told Sam about how he was teased by the other guys on the soccer team for being in a mathlete in the off season, and Sam shared her cheerleading horror stories.

They laughed and talked and dove deeply into things she'd never known about him, things she wasn't sure that she would have ever had the chance to know without this fundraiser and their time glued together.

The only problem was, every passing moment was making her adore him more. And there was nothing Sam could do about that.

"How about a coffee break before we dig into the college years?" Ethan suggested, jutting his chin toward the coffee station in the corner of the gymnasium.

"Oh, boy. The college years." Sam shuddered, guiding him to the coffee. "I'm gonna need it in an IV to get through that particular era of memories."

After some chatting with the family and a steaming cup of joe, they made their way back to the dance floor, and Sam dove right in to her first day of freshman year of college.

As she told the story of meeting Max Parker, falling so hard for him she couldn't think straight, and then getting pregnant with Taylor, Ethan listened attentively.

Obviously, he already knew the majority of what had happened in Sam's marriage, but somehow this day-long marathon of togetherness brought everything into a new level of intimacy and detail.

Sam was fully leaning on Ethan as she recounted the day she stared at a positive pregnancy test in the bathroom of a college dorm. "I was shaking like a leaf. I couldn't even cry, because I couldn't even move."

Ethan let out a breath. "You must have been terrified."

"I was so overwhelmed. I knew right away that I wanted to marry him. Probably mostly out of fear."

He shut his eyes. "It all worked out the way it was meant to. But I'm so sorry for everything you went through with his cheating and..." He grimaced. "All of that."

"Slow down there, cowboy. We're still at sophomore year of college. We have much ground to cover before we get to the cheating. Plus, I believe it's your turn. Tell me about early college."

As Ethan shared stories of his mathematics major and his fraternity days, the minutes ticked by.

In what seemed like the blink of an eye, they'd passed the twelve-hour mark, and Sam and Ethan's memory lane road trip was deep into adulthood.

They took a break for pizza and assessed the gym. More than half the pairs on the dance floor had given up, and the group was starting to really thin out. Nineties pop music was playing through the speakers as Julie and Amber sat behind a laptop on the bleachers and whispered to each other.

"Staying strong, you two?" Sam asked her sister with a nudge as they moved past Erica and Will to take back their spot in the middle of the floor.

"Oh, yeah." Erica nodded. "We're just planning our future together. Starting with the win we're taking home in twelve hours."

Ethan angled his head and smiled at the couple. "I hope you two don't think you have a chance. I'd hate for you to be disappointed."

"Hah!" Erica snorted, giving him a playful challenge in her gaze. "I don't know if you know this about me, but I don't lose."

"It's true," Sam admitted. "She doesn't."

"Then we better figure out a tie breaker." Ethan tightened his embrace on Sam's hand and waist and stood up taller. "Because we're not going anywhere."

They laughed and moved away, watching as Annie and Trevor called it quits to take Riley home, as she'd fallen asleep on a blanket at the bottom of the bleachers.

Taylor and Andre were hanging in there, along with John and Imani and several other townspeople, who clearly had the same competitive streak as the Sweeneys.

"So." Ethan turned to Sam as they danced slowly. "Where were we?"

She cringed a little, knowing full well that their timeline had just about reached the point where Ethan met his first wife.

She decided it was best to tread lightly.

"I know things get a little personal around this time for you, right? A few years out of college was when you met..."

"Katie, yeah." He cleared his throat. "Hey, look, I told you the story of when I cheated on a test in third grade. Clearly, I'm not holding back today."

She smiled, a surge of relief and something that resembled hope shifting in her heart. "Okay, well, I'm all ears."

He took a breath and prepared to tell the story that Sam had spent the entirety of their relationship so desperately wishing he would open up about.

"I met Katie at school, actually." He ran his hand through his hair, then placed it back on Sam's waist, where it had been for nearly fourteen straight hours now. "She was an art teacher, a creative type. It was my fourth year teaching, and I was really starting to find my groove with AP calculus. My test scores were going up and I was really making a name for myself as a reputable AP teacher in the county. Katie was new. Not new to teaching, but new to Perryville."

Sam nodded, listening.

"She was pretty much that textbook art teacher. Kind of...eclectic, I guess. Artsy and interesting and wore all kinds of wacky outfits and hairdos. At first, she annoyed me to no end, but after a while she grew on me."

"I can't blame her," Sam quipped.

He flashed a smile. "Anyway, we started going out, and it just sort of worked. We clicked in a very 'opposites attract' sort of way. I was the analytic, logical realist, and she was the dreamer. We would restore old furniture together, and she taught me how to paint."

Sam tried to ignore the thread of jealousy that wormed through her chest at the image of Ethan young and in love with a beautiful, quirky art teacher. "It sounds like you two were really happy."

"We were, for a while." He glanced off, his eyes far away as he recounted these memories. "But things changed. We grew apart. After about ten years, our relationship was a bit strained and distant. We didn't like any of the same things, and I felt like she was starting to resent me."

Sam frowned. She couldn't imagine anyone resenting Ethan.

"Nothing divorce worthy, of course. I was determined to make it work, and I really cared about her. But then, the whole..." His expression darkened. "Thing happened, and she couldn't move past it. She couldn't even look me in the eyes."

Sam swallowed, remembering the shockingly unfair story of how a female student of Ethan's developed a crush on him and told the whole school that they'd kissed. Her lie ruined not only his small-town reputation and his job, but also his marriage.

Her heart tugged with sympathy. "Did she not believe you?"

"I think she wanted to believe me, but she had doubts." He bit his lip. "There was always this tiny part of her that thought I had a relationship with a student.

She couldn't shake it. And it tore us apart. When she finally asked for a divorce, I knew I needed to get far, far away from that town. Talk about small-town drama."

Sam gave a dry laugh. "I can't even imagine a scandal like that. It's just so unfair."

He shook his head. "It was a really rough time. For a while there, I wasn't sure if I'd get hired anywhere else. Of course, after some time, the girl took back her allegations and everything was cleared up, but rumors don't always disappear that easily. Neither do wounds in an already rocky marriage."

Sam took a deep breath, nodding as she processed this. She was stunned at how open he was being about all of it, how freely willing he was to share information that he'd kept under lock and key their entire relationship.

Maybe all they'd needed all along was twenty-four uninterrupted hours of talking.

"I'm so sorry, Ethan." Sam gave his hand a squeeze.

"Thanks. It's really okay. That was so many years ago. Once I moved here, I just decided I wanted it all to be in the past, you know? At the risk of sounding completely cliché, I wanted a fresh start."

"Right?" Sam scoffed. "I'm a walking fresh-start cliché, so I completely understand."

"Your turn, by the way." He grinned.

"Mine?" She leaned her head back. "Oh, gosh, where even are we? Mid-thirties? You know about my dumpster-fire marriage."

He lifted a shoulder. "Tell me stuff I don't know.

Stuff about when Taylor and Ben were little or how you decorated your first house."

"Oh, it was a masterpiece."

"I'll bet."

More hours ticked by, more couples gave up on the marathon, and more coffee was consumed.

When Sam emerged from her conversation with Ethan and looked at the giant clock, there were less than three hours left. And only three couples on the dance floor.

Taylor and Andre, Erica and Will, and Sam and Ethan.

"Home stretch now, baby!" Erica pumped a fist and downed what had to be her ninth cup of coffee.

Sam laughed and turned to Taylor. "Look at you two!"

"Feet...dying..." Taylor croaked, her entire body weight resting on Andre. "Won't...give...up..."

"It's true." Andre looked up. "She won't give up, despite my best attempts at convincing her."

"She might as well, because you're looking at the winners right here." Sam lifted her chin and playfully tapped Ethan's chest.

They moved back to the edge of the floor, and Sam's legs were feeling shaky and exhausted. Every muscle in her body was screaming to lay down, but she'd made it this far and, frankly, it had been wonderful.

"We're completely out of life history," Ethan said, resting his chin on the top of her head.

"I know so much about you now, I could pass an AP exam on the life of Ethan Price."

He laughed, holding her steady as he swayed a little himself.

"You finally opened up," she mumbled against his chest.

"What do you mean?"

Sam pulled away, looking up at him, feeling deliriously tired and dazed. "That was all I ever wanted. I just wanted you to take those walls down, to be real and raw and vulnerable with me."

He glanced away, his jaw clenching. "I know. It was... hard. But now we've had this time, and it was just so effortless. I didn't think I could ever feel that comfortable."

She shuddered. "Why didn't you try when we were together?"

"I guess...I always knew I was hiding something. It kept me from being completely open. But..."

"It's too late now," she finished.

He locked his gaze with hers, his brow flicking up. "Is it?"

The question woke her up, stirring in her heart.

Was it? This new side of Ethan was everything Sam had been missing when they'd been together. All of the openness and transparency and honesty about his past had filled in so many blanks and made her feel deeply close and connected to him.

What if it wasn't too late?

In a haze of exhaustion and the agony of standing for

an entire day, they stayed quiet for the next while. Not awkwardly quiet, though, just...peaceful.

Sam felt like her legs might give out at any moment, and she swore she nearly fell asleep standing up, resting all of her weight on him.

"Ten more minutes!" Julie's echoing voice startled her, bringing her out of whatever sleep state she was nearly in.

"Holy crap." Ethan chuckled. "We're almost done."

Sam turned around to see that Taylor and Andre had finally thrown in the towel, and were laying on blankets on the floor, laughing.

Erica and Will were stone-cold serious, laser focused on staying on their feet and doing whatever meager attempt could qualify as dancing for the next ten minutes.

"We've got to beat them." Sam tapped Ethan's arm.

"We're going to."

"Never!" Erica shouted, apparently overhearing them.

Sam laughed, shaking her head as tiredness crashed over her in waves.

"Since we're almost at the end, I've got one more major life question for you." Ethan looked down, gently running a finger over her cheek.

"Anything."

"What's your biggest regret?"

Sam's heart kicked up a bit as she pondered this. Maybe it was the sleepiness and the state of near confusion from how exhausted she was, but she simply didn't have the energy to be coy or clever.

"Losing you," she said bluntly. "Losing you is my biggest regret. I wish I never let you go."

Ethan stared at her for several beats, finally opening his mouth to say something.

Sam was wide awake now, anxiously awaiting his response.

"Sam, I—"

"That's time!" Julie shouted, clapping. "Woo! Looks like we have a tie."

Sam crumpled to the ground, her whole body buzzing and aching at the same time. She looked over and met Erica's gaze, and they both cracked up.

Ethan joined her on the ground, and she leaned her head on his shoulder.

Even confused, exhausted, and totally out of it, one thing was as clear as day to Sam in that moment. She was still completely crazy about Ethan, and after feeling him pour his heart and soul and history out to her, she wasn't sure she could live without him.

Chapter Fourteen

Amber

It had only been three days since their extremely successful and insanely fun dance marathon fundraiser, but the campaign left little room for downtime.

This evening was dedicated to hard-core canvassing, and Amber and Julie needed everyone to spread the word and gather votes in the upscale Cocoa Beach neighborhood of Riverside Palms.

Amber handed off stacks of fliers, handfuls of pens, and rolls of stickers to the gathering of Sweeneys that collected at the entrance to the development. "Okay, everyone ready?"

She looked around at the group who had graciously gathered after work and school—and staying up all night on Saturday for the dance marathon—to help out.

There they were, all in jeans or shorts and the *Julie For Mayor* T-shirts that they'd just gotten back from the printing company last week. Every one of them was smiling, ready, and enthusiastic.

Not for the first time, Amber let herself sink a little more in love with this group that would do anything under the sun for each other. Somehow, by a crazy twist of fate, she was a part of it.

That popular phrase "it takes a village" constantly popped into her mind with these people, and never seemed more appropriate.

It takes a village...a town...a family. It takes *this* family. *Her* family.

She slid her hand down to her growing baby bump and smiled to herself. Sometimes, it seemed like the wonders would never cease around here. And that just made her more confident that they could win.

"Okay." John stepped forward, his commanding voice and role as the patriarch garnering everyone's attention. "I vote we split up into pairs. Kids, go with your parents, of course. Imani and I can take Turtle Drive. Sam, you, Taylor, and Andre can hit Sandbar."

Amber agreed and as they sorted out the details and timeline, she made sure everyone was stacked up on merchandise and ready to convince voters to vote for Julie.

"Everyone ready to go?" she asked, half feeling like she should blow a whistle and start them off.

A chorus of, "Heck, yeah," echoed through the large family, accompanied with some thumbs-ups.

"Awesome. Let's go tell Cocoa Beach why they need Julie Sweeney as mayor!"

As they all dispersed, Amber and Lori headed down Driftwood, their allotted street. Amber felt a tinge of wooziness come over her, and she gripped her mom as she swayed on her feet.

"Hey, you okay?" Lori turned to her, holding her arm with a concerned look on her face.

"Yeah, yeah." Amber waved a hand. "I'm fine."

She had to be, because this was no time to let hormones or the family's infectious enthusiasm get to her. Canvassing was too critical in a small-town election.

"You sure?" Lori pressed a hand to Amber's forehead. "You look pale."

"I'm good, Mom, really," Amber insisted. "Just a little lightheaded. I'll eat something to settle my stomach when we get home. I'll be fine."

"Okay," Lori said, clearly not convinced.

Powering through, they reached the first house, a sprawling Spanish-style home with blue shutters and barrel tile roof. Armed with campaign gear and a speech that Amber had been preparing for days, they took the walkway to the front door.

After a couple of knocks, the glass front door swung open and an older man stood in the entry. "Can I help you?"

"Hi, there." Amber straightened her back and inched forward, ignoring how utterly awful she felt. "We're with the mayoral campaign of Julie Sweeney. Do you have a moment?"

"Oh, right." The guy nodded, frowning as he put the pieces together. "I forgot Pemberton is finally stepping down. All right, I'll listen."

"Great." Lori grinned, sneaking a glance at Amber.

"Thank you so much." Amber handed him a flier, but noticed her hand was shaking.

Why did she have to feel so terrible when she needed her energy more than ever?

"Now, I want to talk to you about Julie. I'm sure you're familiar with the Sweeney House Inn, yes?"

He nodded. "Yeah, that old one on the beach. They're redoing it."

"They sure are. The Sweeney family has deep, deep roots in Cocoa Beach, and..." She took a breath as a few imaginary stars flashed in her vision. "Their strong family values and powerful, influential history in this town makes their oldest daughter, Julie, a perfect candidate to..."

"Honey?" Lori whispered, her voice in hushed worry. "You okay?"

"I'm sorry." Amber laughed nervously and shook her head. "I'm just feeling a bit faint. It's so warm out, and..."

The man quickly offered to get her water, returned with a bottle, kindly took their flyers, and wished them well.

"He was nice," Amber said, sipping on water as they found their way to a bench meant for dogwalkers to rest along a grassy area.

"Sweetie, I'm worried."

"Don't be." Amber shook her head. "It's just the hormones and the fatigue. I think I'm still catching up from pulling an all-nighter at the dance marathon."

Lori shut her eyes. "I knew you shouldn't have stayed the whole time."

"I had to," Amber protested. "It was my fundraiser. And I'm fine. I'm just...not used to getting this wiped out.

My body is in a state of complete exhaustion. But it's canvassing day, and..."

"Amber." Lori placed her hands onto her daughter's, giving them a tight squeeze as she leveled her gaze. "I can canvass."

"Mom—"

"Please go home and get some rest. You're over-working yourself, and you've got to take care of you and that baby."

Amber opened her mouth to argue, but she simply couldn't. The dance marathon had taken it out of her, and as much as it pained her to admit, she was still recovering.

"How does Dottie have more energy than me?" she asked on a pathetic laugh.

"Because you're growing a person inside you." Lori reached an arm around and pulled Amber close. "I'm going to call your dad and ask him to come and get you, okay?"

Amber was sick at the thought of missing canvassing, but she did trust the Sweeney clan to do a good job with it. She had to, because right now, she had no choice.

Her eyelids felt like they were sticking together and every cell in her body cried out with exhaustion. "Okay. I'll go home."

"I can handle our street."

"All by yourself?" She looked up at Lori weakly.

"Of course! If anyone can attest to the greatness of the Sweeney family, it's me."

Amber definitely believed her mom could crush it at

this, especially with her inherent ability to talk to just about anyone.

Lori slid her phone into her purse after typing a message. "Your dad is on his way."

Amber nodded, rubbing her hand over her belly as she used the other to take a sip from the water bottle.

She was going to have to start thinking about a whole other person besides herself. Her needs, her health, her energy—or lack of it.

She wasn't just Amber anymore, and she hoped that when the day came to be a mom, she'd be truly ready.

⁂

"Thanks again for picking me up." Amber situated herself in the cozy corner of the sectional in their townhouse, positioning the cold washcloth that Rick had pressed onto her forehead.

"Of course, kiddo." He sat on the edge of the sofa, his brows furrowed with concern. "So, what happened? You were nearly asleep in the car, but you seem to have a bit more life now."

Amber nodded. "The wet washcloth helps."

"Always has." He smiled, and Amber noticed the familiar creases around his eyes didn't seem quite as pronounced as when he'd arrived.

He seemed happier. Lighter. She wondered if something had happened that lifted his spirits, or if he was just being classic Dad and putting on a happy face for Amber.

"You sure you're okay?" he asked.

"So much better." She shut her eyes and let out a sigh, sinking into the fluffy throw pillow underneath her heavy head. "I just had to get out of the heat. I'm exhausted. Still recovering from the dance marathon, I guess. God, I'm like a ninety-year-old."

"You're pregnant, A." He raised his brows sternly. "You've got to take care of yourself."

"I know," she said on an exhale. "You sound like Mom."

"Well, that's because we're right." He nodded down toward her stomach. "How's the little one doing?"

"Fine, I think." Amber placed a hand on her bump. "She was kicking earlier. Seems to have a lot of energy, probably because she's sucking up all of mine."

"Kids tend to do that, don't they?" Dad cracked, making Amber laugh.

"What can I do for her besides eat healthy and rest?" She adjusted her cool cloth. "I want to make sure she's, you know, doing all right in there."

Rick stood up slowly. "Well, there are mixed ideas on this, but I do know something that might be a way to bring the baby some good vibes."

Amber frowned and tilted her head. "What?"

"Hang on." Dad disappeared for a couple of minutes before returning with Mom's portable Bluetooth speaker, which he put on the coffee table where Amber had propped her feet. "When your mom was pregnant with you, we used to play you music."

"Ah, yes, womb music. I've read about it."

"We just called it early education."

Amber's heart tugged as she pictured the young, happy, in-love versions of her parents, both joyous about their baby girl. "I can't believe Mom went along with that. It seems so woo-woo for her."

"Are you kidding?" He blinked. "It was her idea."

"Huh."

"Here." He clicked the button on the speaker, and set it gently on the sofa next to Amber's side. "Let's start with a classic."

The first few familiar notes of *Stairway to Heaven* started to fill the air, and Amber instantly began to ache with nostalgia.

"Oh, Daddy." She pressed a hand to her heart. "This is what you'd always play in the car with me when I was little."

"Absolutely. Zeppelin for happy times, Pink Floyd for contemplative, and the Beatles when I wanted you to sleep. 'Cause..." He leaned in and started to whisper, but Amber held up her hand.

"They're slightly overrated, in my humble opinion," she said in a deep voice, imitating him.

"So you *do* listen to me." He laughed and shook his head. "A father is never sure."

"Every word, Dad." Amber reached out to take her father's hand as they listened to the comforting song that sounded like every morning of her childhood.

He'd always been there for her in a way that was impossible to describe. Sports, school, friends, even some boy drama, although his advice was never that spectacular. It was usually something along the lines of, *"You're too good for that lug nut, A."*

Dad had seen it all, and playing his old rock tunes was one of the earliest and best ways they'd bonded.

And now, they were bringing the new little girl into the circle, and Amber was flooded with emotions about it.

"Do you think she likes it?" Amber asked, smiling down at her belly.

"Are you kidding? She's a Kittle. And she's...*buying a stairway to heaven,*" he sang in perfect connection with the music.

Amber rested her head and closed her eyes, letting her mind run through a flashback reel of her thousands of memories to this music.

When he played *Let It Be*—the best of the Beatles, he always said—she suddenly recalled waking up in the middle of the night once when she was very small, and sneaking downstairs for a snack. This song had been playing softly on the stereo, and she peered into the kitchen from behind a wall, watching her mom and dad slow dance, kissing and each holding a glass of wine.

The memory shot an injection of emotion through her—wistful, bittersweet longing for those halcyon days, mixed with gratitude that she'd grown up in that happy cocoon...and an ache that such a special marriage had fallen apart.

She looked up at her Dad, who glanced away for a second as the song built up into the chorus, and she couldn't help but wonder if he was recalling the same exact memory.

"She kicked!" she said with a gasp, feeling that tiny little movement shift around on the edge of her tummy.

Dad turned his head, smiling wide. "A Beatles fan, huh? Okay, I can work with that. We'll have to build up to Rush and Metallica, but starting slow is good."

The baby kicked again, and Amber gestured for her dad to place his hand down and feel the subtle little movements.

His eyes instantly lit up, and seemed to fill a bit. "Wow. She likes the music."

"I think she really does!" Amber laughed, shaking her head with disbelief.

They sat and listened together, both humming with the melody, feeling the little kicks growing stronger and stronger. The baby definitely responded to the music, there was no question about that.

Amber caught her dad's gaze as Paul McCartney crooned, *"Mother Mary comes to me..."*

They sang along, patting her belly and suddenly, Amber bolted straight up with a soft gasp.

"What is it?" Dad asked, turning the music down as soon as he saw Amber's surge of excitement. "Are you okay?"

"I know her name."

"You do?"

"Mary." Amber looked down, gently caressing her stomach as she felt a tear of joy stinging in her eye. "This is Mary. That is the name I want to give my baby."

Her father smiled, his own eyes misting. "Mary. I love her already."

"So do I, Dad. So do I."

Chapter Fifteen

Julie

If running for mayor of a small beach town was this intense and exhausting, Julie shuddered to think what it was like to run for a massive, national political office position.

She'd been giving it absolutely everything she had, and still was down by a decent margin in the polls. Amber swore things would pick up since the dance marathon and their endless canvassing efforts, but Julie was worried.

She couldn't stand the idea that this could possibly be all for nothing.

"Next house, Mom?" Bliss asked cheerfully, looking down at the list on her phone, a stack of fliers tucked underneath her arm.

"On to the next, my girl." She slid her phone back into her pocket and started heading to the next house on the row with her daughter. "I was just checking in with Amber. She had to go home a little while ago. She wasn't feeling well."

"Is she okay?"

"Sounds like it, yeah. Pregnancy wipes you out sometimes."

Bliss looked up at her, her silky blond hair swaying gently in the breeze. "Did I wipe you out?"

"Only every single day of your life," she teased, wrapping an arm around Bliss's slender shoulders and planting a kiss on the top of her head.

They'd finished the ritzy neighborhood of Riverside Palms, and had moved on to canvassing in a nearby development called Hibiscus Point with older, smaller homes. Still beachy and charming, but not nearly as high-end.

Julie felt more comfortable in this kind of environment, anyway.

"I feel like these people have mostly been pretty easy to talk to. Do you think they'll all vote for you?" Bliss asked, sucking on a "Vote For Julie" lollipop.

Julie lifted a shoulder. "I have no idea. I mean, I'm putting my best foot forward and explaining why I think I'd be a great mayor, but it's hard to tell. Maybe they like me, or maybe they're just being nice."

"Yeah." Bliss wrinkled her nose. "Except for that old guy in 310. He wasn't being very nice when he slammed the door in our faces."

Julie nodded. "Comes with the territory, kid. Gotta have thick skin, right?"

Bliss whipped her phone back out, glanced at the screen and looked up at Julie hopefully. "Mom, Nicole is calling me. It's probably about the sleepover this weekend. Can I answer? It'll be quick, I promise!"

Julie laughed. "Go on, girl. Chat with your friend. I'll handle this next stop."

"You're the best!" Bliss lifted the phone up to her ear and skipped off. "Nikki? Girl, what's up?"

Julie smiled to herself as she reached the front door and gave it a knock, hoping for another friendly face who was willing to listen and, at the very least, take a free pen or two.

The house looked a bit tired and definitely needed some landscaping and a fresh coat of paint. There was an older beater of a car in the driveway, which gave Julie hope that someone was home.

After a few minutes, the door swung open with a creak, and a woman in the doorway managed a weak smile. "Hello."

She was thin and quite pretty, probably in her late thirties or early forties.

Julie instantly noticed the dark circles underneath her eyes and knotted strands of hair falling around her face.

What was her story?

"Hi, there. I'm so sorry to bother you," Julie said gently, sliding a flier out from the stack. "I'm running for mayor of Cocoa Beach, and I was just hoping I could chat with you for a couple minutes about your voting plans in the upcoming local elections."

The woman paused for a long second, turning her head to look down the hallway of the small house. "Okay, sure." She stepped outside and closed the door behind her, leaning against it.

Julie was surprised, given that this woman did not exactly look like she was up for the task of friendly conversation with a stranger, especially one who was trying to win her vote.

"First of all, hi." Julie reached out her hand. "I'm Julie Sweeney."

"Valerie Mitchell. Nice to meet you."

"I'll keep it brief, but I just was hoping to share my platform."

The woman nodded, but her smile seemed to quickly fade.

Might as well continue. "Well, you probably know my family, or at least the inn on A1A, Sweeney House. We have really deep roots in the area, and this town absolutely molded me into who I am. I feel that both my worldly experience as a touring musician and my hometown roots in this little city help me really understand not only this town, but people and their needs in a community."

"A touring musician?" The woman asked, a little absently, but hey. She was trying. "That's cool."

"Yeah, thank you." Julie grinned. "I was with several different bands all over the country for nearly twenty years."

She tucked a stand of light brown hair behind her ear and met Julie's gaze. "What brought you back to Cocoa Beach, then?"

"Actually, um..." She nodded toward Bliss, chatting on the phone out of earshot. "My daughter was...well, sick. And my entire family was here. Extended family, too. The whole shebang. And as much as I thought I was married to life on the road and the constant adventure, I needed support. Badly."

"So you came home?" she guessed.

"I did. And when I showed up, I knew I would get support, but what I didn't know was the incredible way that this town would rally around us and come together to get Bliss better." She glanced behind her shoulder, where Bliss was walking around the sidewalk, deep in an animated conversation with her best friend. "And that's why I'm running for office. To support people like myself and my daughter, who need that community. Anyway, I don't want to ramble, but..."

At the sight of Valerie's teary eyes, Julie's voice trailed off.

"Oh, no. I'm so sorry, I didn't mean to upset you." Julie inched forward. "Is everything okay?"

"I just..." Valerie wiped a tear and gave a weepy laugh, taking a deep breath to gather herself. "I'm so sorry, I don't usually do this in front of strangers. It's just that your story, it hit me. I...I have a son."

Julie smiled sweetly. "You do?"

"He's...he's sick." Valerie sniffled, shuddering on her exhale. "He's fourteen, and he's got leukemia."

Julie's heart sank hard and she drew back with the heavy impact of the other woman's words. "Oh, Valerie. I am so, so sorry for what you're going through. I'm all too familiar with that kind of hardship. It's unthinkable."

Valerie took a deep breath and wiped a tear from her cheek. "It's tough. We're hanging in there. We caught it early, thankfully, but it's tough."

"Bliss had kidney disease," Julie explained, momentarily forgetting that she was here to canvass for her mayoral campaign, aching with sympathy for this mother. "She was on dialysis for eight months."

"Oh, wow." Valerie looked past Julie and saw Bliss. "She's okay, now, though?"

Julie nodded. "My mother, actually, donated a kidney. She was the only match, and that stubborn old mule wouldn't let us keep looking."

Valerie managed a smile, pressing a hand to her chest. "That's a beautiful story. I'm happy your daughter is healthy. I just...It's so rare to meet a parent who can really relate to what I'm going through. They give sympathy and condolences and then just go on with their perfect, healthy lives."

"I know it." Julie shook her head. "I'd never felt more alone in my life. Until I came back here, and then I was so...surrounded. That's what made me fall so deeply in love with this town. So much so that, well, I'm running for mayor."

"I like that," Valerie said.

Julie reached her hand out and gently touched her arm. "Tell me about your son."

"Oh, wow. Where do I start? Parker is amazing. He's brilliant, and so funny." She laughed tearfully, shaking her head and smiling to herself. "He builds these worlds on his video game. *Minecraft*. Do you know it?"

Julie shrugs. "I've got a girl. I know TikTok and Taylor Swift."

"Well, Parker loves this game. At first I didn't want

him playing it so much, because it felt like he was always looking at a screen. But then one day he showed me what he was doing, and it's just amazing. I mean, he's creating entire cities on there, with architecture and people and economies." She laughed with wonder. "It's inspiring."

"He sounds incredible."

"He loves music, too. No clue where he got that gene, but he plays the piano like a natural."

"Hey, my kinda kid!" Julie exclaimed. "And you two are close, it sounds like?"

Valerie nodded, visibly fighting more tears. "Best friends. It's...just the two of us, so..."

"Oh." Julie pressed a hand to her chest, her heart aching with understanding. "Then you need family more than ever."

"No kidding. My ex-husband moved to Costa Rica with his new surfer girlfriend." She rolled her eyes. "Spare me."

"That's...ugh. Awful."

She gave a dry laugh. "It's tough, you know? Parker's treatment is actually looking hopeful, but it's so darn expensive. I'm a kindergarten teacher, so, you know. Not exactly rolling in cash. And I can't take time off to take care of him, because I so desperately need the money. If I requested a leave, it would have to be unpaid."

Julie blinked back with surprise and disgust. "It would?"

Valerie nodded. "Oh, yes. No paid leave for teachers aside from maternity, and even that is only eight weeks."

Julie felt like she probably should have known this

but hey, she was still learning. "Eight weeks? That's criminal."

"The pennies that they pay teachers aren't even making a dent in the medical bills, but it's better than having nothing." She wiped her cheeks again and stood up straight. "We're struggling."

"I bet you are. That system is completely unfair. I mean, the low wages are shocking and nearly unlivable, but you can't even get a paid leave for the medical care of your child?"

"Not here." She pressed her lips together.

Julie felt a fire ignite in her belly. She identified so deeply with this woman, she knew exactly what it was like to be helpless trying to get your child better from a serious, life-threatening illness. It was the hardest thing in the world. And then to have to go into deep debt on top of that? Horrifying.

As she watched dark clouds fill sweet Valerie's eyes, Julie knew she had to do something about this. She was staring face to face at the opportunity to actually help this woman, and many others. She could make a real difference in people's lives.

"Valerie." She took her hands and squeezed them tight. "When I'm mayor, I'm going to help you. I'm going to change the school board policy, I'm going to fight for higher wages, I'm going to get you a paid leave. You will have every person in charge of running this city supporting you and Parker. I promise."

Valerie held her gaze, her eyes filling again. "Wow. Julie...you've got my vote. I really, really hope you win."

"I'm going to win. I have to. Here." She dug through her bag and handed Valerie a handful of "Vote for Julie" pens. "Give them to all your teacher friends, neighbors, other parents at the school. Tell them I'm going to fight for them."

"I will." She clutched the pens and smiled, her eyes sparkling. "I believe in you, I really do. Thank you."

As Julie said goodbye to Valerie Mitchell and headed down the street to find Bliss, she knew this was no longer about a cabana, or Trent Braddock.

Forget a village. Valerie needed a *family* and that's what Cocoa Beach could be. A town that feels like family —and acted like one.

Clinging to that thought, she hustled toward Bliss, determined to soar.

Chapter Sixteen

Lori

Lori and Rick had always shared a love of getting up before the sun. It was one of the many ways they'd bonded during their dating years and throughout their marriage. The early hours of the morning, when those first slivers of light started to slip into the sky, that time belonged to them. The world was silent and sleeping, and Lori and Rick would share quiet laughs and deep ideas and many cups of coffee, feeling like the only two people on the planet.

Today took her right back to that, as the two of them set out for a sunrise photo shoot on the beach to promote Lori's yoga business and jazz up her website.

Being up at this hour was their happy place, their comfort zone. And somehow, even with all of the messy history and mistakes and pain, this early morning felt like so many others. It felt like home.

"Looks like it's going to be great lighting out here." Rick craned his neck to peer up at the sky as they got out of the car in the driveway of Sweeney House. "A few clouds to block the harsh sun, but a nice, soft glow."

"These Cocoa Beach sunrises are always spectacular." Lori shut the passenger-side door and sipped her coffee, unsure why she felt a little nervous.

Rick swung a small black camera bag over his shoulder and gestured around the side of the inn. "We're not trespassing, are we?"

Lori walked in front of him, leading the way. "All the beaches are public in Florida. But even if they weren't, this is technically my place of business, so I think I get twenty-four-seven access."

"Your place of business..." He repeated softly, a hint of disbelief in his tone. "Never thought I'd see the day."

Neither did she.

She felt a million miles away from her therapy office, where she rarely saw the sun and mostly wore work slacks and sweaters. Now, she was in a deep wine-colored long-sleeved Spandex top paired with matching athletic leggings. She wore a light jacket against the seaside wind on this January morning, and carried a yoga mat under one arm as she walked along the sandy path between the inn and the cottage.

Yep, a million miles away from her old life, yet standing right next to the man she used to be married to in that old life.

Stealing a glimpse at Rick, she noticed he fit right in to this new life. Tanned and fit in a blue T-shirt and khaki shorts, he was also barefoot on the beach, and that...was sexy.

"All right..." He unzipped his bag and pulled out the camera that Lori had bought him a few years ago as a birthday present.

It was a Canon EOS...something or other, and he'd completely flipped out when he opened it. She remembered the joy on his face, the total surprise and childish grin.She remembered the way he'd hugged her and kissed her and adored her, and she couldn't help but wonder if he could ever feel that way again.

Rick held up the camera to his eye. "We can't shoot until the sun starts to come up, obviously, but I think these are going to come out really nice."

"It's perfect that we came during sunrise." Lori unrolled her yoga mat onto the sand, spreading it out. "Since that's when I do my classes."

"Yeah, plus the lighting." Rick imitated a chef's kiss.

Lori laughed, hugging her jacket around her body and looking out at the horizon. She'd been out here during enough sunrises to know that once it started to light up the sky, the actual rising period only took a few short, but magnificent, minutes.

"We're getting close to sunrise."

Rick crouched down, holding the camera up and closing one eye as he turned it in several different directions. "I think I'm gonna use a zoom lens. It'll blur the background slightly, but keep the vibrance of the sunrise. Plus, it'll make you look like the feature model, which is what we want."

Lori could have sworn he winked at her, but it was too dark outside to be certain.

Before they knew it, the sky above the horizon was streaked with silver, and the first hint of orange glow was beginning to rise up into the clouds.

"Okay, let's get rolling." Rick knelt down, holding up the camera. "Give me some yoga, Lori Caparelli."

She laughed awkwardly, stepping out onto her mat. Suddenly, she had never done a yoga pose or been in front of a camera in her entire life. "Uh, what should I do?"

"Anything!" he encouraged, snapping some practice shots. "Poses, flows, whatever you call 'em. Think about what you want your website to look like, what pictures might work best."

"Uh..." She tugged her jacket tightly around her waist, shifting her weight.

She locked her gaze on the camera lens, which felt like a giant eye boring into her.

"Hurry, Lor, the light's getting good."

"I'm sorry." She laughed with embarrassment. "I don't...I can't think of anything. I feel like it'll look weird, and..." She pressed her palm to her forehead. "I'm being so silly."

"It's okay." He stood up and walked over to her, gently setting the camera on the edge of her yoga mat before leveling his gaze with hers. "Hey, look at me."

She smiled, feeling her cheeks burn with embarrassment, suddenly so camera shy. This was Rick, for crying out loud. He'd seen her deliver a baby and have food poisoning and cry until her eyes swelled up. This man knew her deeper than anyone on the planet ever had, and suddenly she was so aware of his eyes. She was so...nervous.

Why was she acting like a school girl?

"I know it's a little weird," he said in that soft but encouraging photographer's voice she'd heard him use with many clients and subjects. "But just channel that strength and power you use in yoga. That's what you want to convey to your potential students, right?"

"Strength and power." She nodded. "Yes."

"Okay." Rick backed up in the sand, returning to his semi-crouched position with the camera angled in front of his eyes, one of them squinted as he peered into the lens. "Give me power and strength."

Power and strength.

Lori opted for a tree pose, which was a challenge on the sand, but recognizable even to newbies, and one of her favorites. She heard the camera shutter as he snapped a few clicks.

"Nice, nice. Here comes the sunlight, keep moving around."

She bent down and assumed a downward facing dog, straightening her back and pressing back onto her heels. She was vaguely aware of her butt sticking up in the air, but this was a powerful and quintessential yoga pose, so, whatever.

"There you go," Rick said encouragingly. "Look at you."

Lori laughed, a shred of giddiness fluttering in her chest. Feeling her confidence rise, she lifted a leg and pushed all the way back into a standing split—an impressive pose, if she did say so herself.

"Whoa, okay." Rick whistled playfully as the camera clicked. "That one is...wow."

She laughed softly, standing back up and eyeing him. "You've gotten flexible."

"Thank you." She sat down on the mat to take a lotus pose and maybe some other floor poses from there. The sky was glowing with the tangerine sunrise, and the light warmed Lori's skin and heart.

"Lor." Rick lowered the camera and looked at her.

"Yeah?"

"Why don't we try some without the giant fleece jacket on?"

"Oh." Lori glanced down, having totally forgotten she'd worn an admittedly pretty ugly pullover. "Good call."

She pulled the jacket off over her head, and suddenly felt very exposed. The athletic top she'd worn showed a smidge of her stomach. She felt strong and fit, but still. She was fifty-five, and she didn't want to look silly.

"Maybe I should leave it on..."

"Uh, no." Rick snapped a picture she was definitely not ready for. "You should one hundred percent keep it off."

Was he...flirting with her?

She smiled, feeling the sun warm her skin as she slowly stretched her arms out into warrior two, bending her front knee and stretching out her other leg behind her.

Strong and powerful, Lori reminded herself as she lifted her chin and stared straight ahead, feeling the camera flashes as she breathed in and out slowly.

"Yes, these are great, Lor!" Rick moved into different spots, chasing all sorts of angles.

Lori shifted into a lunge, lifting her arms to the sky, arching her back. She felt her stomach exposed again in the slightly cropped outfit, but what did it matter? She felt great.

"Now turn to me." Rick said, stepping in front of her to get her face in the shot.

She smiled softly, keeping her gaze lifted and her stance powerful.

"You look..." He inched closer, taking in a soft breath. "Incredible. I mean...these are going to be great. You look...you're...great."

Lori laughed as she returned to a normal standing position and walked closer to him. "Thanks. And thanks for helping me come out of my shell."

They turned simultaneously to face the sunrise, which lit up the sky above the horizon and cast a soft orange glow onto the sand.

"Here." Rick stepped back a little, lifting the camera to his eye level again.

"Wait." She jumped back with a laugh. "I'm not ready."

He clicked the camera.

"Rick!" She shoved him playfully. "You're too close. All you're getting is my face."

"I know." He clicked the shutter again. "You're beautiful."

Her breath caught in her throat as a chill danced across her skin. "Rick..."

"Look at me." He held up the camera.

She rolled her eyes, but looked right at the lens, giving a soft smile as she heard the click echo when he snapped the photo.

Pulling the camera away, he studied the tiny preview screen, his face lighting up with a smile. "That's a gem."

"Oh, please." She waved a hand. "You're so close, you can see every wrinkle."

"Would you stop?" He set the camera down on her yoga mat, then leveled his gaze with hers. "You look amazing, Lor. In every way. You're radiant. You've got this...this glow that I haven't seen in years."

Lori felt her heart kick as she pushed some hair out of her face and drew nearer to her husband. "I do?"

"You do." He reached out and placed a hand on her cheek. "And I've missed it so much. I've missed you so much."

"I've missed you, too," the words slipped out in a breathless whisper, the confession shifting the world beneath her.

"You know..." He ran his thumb along her cheek. "You're still my favorite person to photograph."

"I am?"

He answered with a kiss, light and sweet, and everything else melted away into the orange sky and ocean.

Lori felt her head swim as she kissed her husband—the only man she'd ever loved. She hadn't realized how much she'd missed him, how she'd ached for his touch and his voice and his presence.

She'd missed the way he made her feel about herself

and the way he loved Amber and the comfort and joy of the family that she'd let fall apart.

As she stood there on the beach, lifted onto her tiptoes with her hands wrapped around the back of his neck, she knew one thing for sure.

Her marriage was far from over.

The fresh start she'd gotten in Cocoa Beach had flung her into this new chapter of life, one she'd been certain didn't involve him. But maybe it was time for them to have their own fresh start, too.

She'd spent so much time and energy trying to figure out how to move on from him and let him go that she hadn't even realized that was never what she wanted.

As they pulled apart, Lori kept her arms around him and her nose inches from his. "I'm sorry for everything. I'm so...so sorry. Do you think there's a chance we could—"

"Yes," he said, then kissed her again.

Chapter Seventeen

Sam

Everywhere Sam looked in the Sweeney House Inn, she saw bits and pieces of herself, her family, and her life. It definitely remained a true testament to the Sweeneys and their rich local history, but wow. What a difference some modern updates and renovations made.

The kitchen was just about finished, and the dining area was coming together one bleached wooden chair and sunshine tangerine cushion at a time.

"Mom, check it out!" Sam waved Dottie over as some workers hauled in more shipments of dining furniture.

"Oh, it's fantastic." Dottie clasped her hands together and beamed with joy. "And you were completely right about the floor. I'm so glad we kept the light wood."

"I had to fight you on the carpeting," Sam said on a playful laugh. "I don't fight you on much, but I felt strongly."

"Your instincts were spot on, as usual." Dottie reached her arm out and hugged Sam tightly. "It's all coming together, my dear!"

"It is." Sam took a deep breath and watched as her vision formed near completion before her very eyes. "I'm thinking we can start to look into setting a reopening date."

"Wonderful." Dottie smiled. "We'll be having wedding receptions in this very room by the end of the summer!"

"Small weddings," Sam interjected, raising a dubious brow at her idealistic mother. "But yes. We could be."

"Oh, I've always dreamed of hosting weddings. Tiny, intimate beach weddings, of course. But we've got just the space. And once the cabana is on the beach, it's just going to be magical."

"It really is," Sam agreed. "Like a magazine."

"Okay, I better run." Dottie glanced at her watch. "I'm picking Bliss up from school and then we're going to the record store in Cocoa Village. Julie is slammed prepping for the election, so I've been hanging out with Bliss a lot. Not that I mind spending time with my granddaughter. Or my old kidney."

Sam snorted. "Speaking of your granddaughters, Taylor is moving out next weekend."

"Oh, yes." Dottie nodded with a bittersweet sadness in her expression. "I knew the day would come. She's young and successful and in love. It's the natural step."

"It is." Sam sighed, pushing her hair back. "I know. And I'm so excited for her, plus I couldn't support that relationship more. He's so good to her."

"He's a gem, that's for certain."

"It's just so crazy seeing my baby all grown up."

Dottie folded her arms and flicked her brows up. "Well, how in the world do you think I feel?"

"Lucky." Sam kissed her mom's cheek. "I hope."

"The luckiest old lady around." Dottie hugged her one more time. "Okay, I'm off. Let me know if any problems arise with the furniture deliveries and whatnot."

Sam gave Dottie a wave as she headed through the lobby of the inn. "Will do. Love you, Mom!"

Dottie blew her a kiss and left Sweeney House, and Sam plopped down onto the loveseat in the back of the lobby. The sitting area had been totally finished with its upgrade, and it was wildly improved.

Five cozy blue sofas and chairs sat around in groupings with big coffee tables, all looking straight out through the huge, sliding glass windows at an unobstructed ocean view.

Sam stood up, admiring the picturesque beach scene, and turned to the left, where the cabana would be going up.

She could picture it so clearly, and couldn't wait for the day they broke ground on that project—the last finishing touch of improvement, the final thing that would make this inn the most—

Wait a second, was that Ethan? What the heck was he doing here?

Sam squinted to make sure she wasn't totally losing it and hallucinating, but her eyes did not deceive her. Ethan was out in the sand, hammering a nail into a huge plank of wood.

She looked harder, realizing there were many planks of wood, all being nailed together and laid down.

Sam yanked open one of the sliders and jogged over to him. "Hey, trespasser."

Ethan looked up from the ground, his smile lighting up as he met her gaze. "Hey, you."

"What are you doing?" She slowed to a stop, shielding her eyes from the blinding sunlight as she studied the huge, flat, and seriously well-crafted wooden deck.

"Laying the foundation," Ethan said nonchalantly, as if that was completely obvious and expected. "For the cabana."

She sucked in a breath, her heart catching in her throat. "Ethan, we don't even have the permitting yet."

"You'll get it." He looked up, a sparkle in his eye. "You do remember that I have a brother on the city council, don't you?"

Sam folded her arms. "Did you talk to him?"

"No, not yet. But I can if I have to." He smacked a nail in and leaned back to study his work. "Which I won't, because your sister is going to win the election and give you the permitting the day she takes office."

Sam smiled, warmed by his faith in her family and his unwavering support for both Sam and her loved ones. "Wow."

"What do you think?" He wiped some dust off of his jeans and stepped back to join Sam. "It's a bit bigger than we originally decided, but I talked to Lori and she agreed that bigger was better. I know it doesn't look like much yet, but that whole back wall is going to be shelves, cabinets, and cubbies. This front area will be open for yoga classes, and the rest of the time you can fit a lot of nice outdoor furniture here. And, since I know how you feel about curtains, hang 'em everywhere, all around the structure."

"It's...it's amazing." Sam shook her head with disbelief as she envisioned the massive cabana decorated with white sheer curtains billowing in the ocean breeze.

"Oh, and the bathroom." Ethan stepped up onto the wood and walked over to the back corner of the cabana. "I talked to the plumbing company you've got working on the inn, and they said we can do a half bath in the cabana, and an outdoor shower head around the back."

"Yes, I'm getting my half bath!"

"Yeah, it's gonna be great. You know, for Lori and her students, but also for inn guests who are out on the beach."

Sam walked closer to him, beaming. "It's fantastic. I wasn't sure at first that we would be able to make this cabana so elaborate, but it's all really coming together. You're...you're amazing. Thank you."

"Amazing, huh?" He dipped his head low, that familiar flirtation lifting the corner of his mouth.

"Yes." She nodded.

"Well, hold onto that thought, because 'amazing' might not be the word that comes to mind when I tell you this next part."

Sam frowned. "What is it?"

"Speaking of the cabana bathroom, I have to choose a toilet."

"Right."

"There's a huge home show in Orlando this week, and I could get a great deal on a really good, durable toilet that's well-suited for an outdoor bathroom."

Sam laughed, confused at why this would be an issue, and also amused at Ethan's dead-serious toilet talk. "Okay... sounds good to me."

"I need you to come with me," Ethan said bluntly, punctuating his sentence with a hopeful grin.

Sam, admittedly, did not hate the idea at all, but she also had no idea where things stood between them and wasn't sure a day trip with her ex was the best plan.

Then again, after the dance marathon, she felt closer to Ethan than ever before. Was that just a delirious all nighter where they passed the time by sharing life stories and memories and secrets? Or did it mean something?

"Okay." Sam pushed some hair behind her ears, searching his expression for clues. "Why is that?"

"Because." He shrugged. "You're the designer, Samantha. You've got an eye for what looks good and is trendy and modern and all of that. I work with hundred-year-old pieces of furniture, and raw wood. I don't trust myself to pick something that's completely perfect."

Sam laughed, drawing back with amusement. "You need my help choosing a toilet?"

"And sink." He lifted a shoulder, flashing that cheesy smile that was so annoyingly irresistible it made her heart tug.

Sam took a breath, turning to her side to glance at the calm, glassy ocean as the sound of the waves hummed through the air.

"All right, let's do it."

"You sure?" he asked, angling his head as he studied her for a moment. "I know things have been...a little..."

"It's fine." Sam swallowed. "You're right, I need to be there to pick out the bathroom pieces and finishings and all that."

"Okay, good." He exhaled. "I'm glad you agree. Are you free to head over there Thursday morning?"

"Free as a bird." Sam held up her hands. "Let's do it."

"I'll pick you up at eight."

"I'll expect a stop at Starbucks," she teased. "It's the tax for my design input and wonderful company."

Ethan laughed. "See you on Thursday, Samantha."

Sam said goodbye, unable to hide her smile. This little trip to Orlando could bring...a second chance or their love could be...in the toilet.

Laughing at that, she headed back to the inn, happier than she'd been in a long time.

"Cheers to my ladies." Annie held up her strawberry daquiri, her smile bright enough to light up the entire back deck of Sharky's Sea Shack.

"Cheers, girls." Sam held up her pina colada and clinked glasses with all of the women around the wooden high top.

Sam, Annie, Taylor, Imani, Erica, and Dottie had all finally found time to gather for a proper girls night at their go-to beach bar.

"I'm so happy we finally got to get together," Imani said, sipping from her straw. "I miss our girl time."

"I tried to get Lori here, but she's helping Amber and Julie on campaign things," Sam said. "But at least we all got here."

"Life is hectic." Erica laughed. "Wonderful and amazing, but hectic. I'm up to my elbows with this upcoming launch project. Plus, Jada's starting soccer."

"Aw." Sam grinned at her sister.

"Tell me about it," Imani agreed. "My three are as nonstop as ever, but I couldn't be happier."

"We are all so blessed." Dottie reached her hands out, touching Sam and Erica's arms as she smiled at everyone at the table.

They all chatted and caught up, enjoying frozen cocktails, soft live music, and the stunning ocean view as the sun set behind the clouds and the sky turned to dusk.

The conversation shifted to Annie, who gushed about her wonderful romance with Trevor and how much she adored little Riley.

"So, there's actually something I wanted to share with you all." Annie smiled so wide it looked like she was about to burst with happiness.

They all waited in anticipation.

"I am moving in with Trevor and Riley."

"Oh my gosh, Annie!" Sam exclaimed, pressing her hands to her heart. "That's wonderful news!"

"So exciting!" Taylor cooed.

"Thanks, guys. I know things are moving quickly, but it just feels so right. They're the family I've always dreamed of and have been missing my entire life. I don't want to waste another second, and neither does he."

Imani wiggled her ring finger. "Is there an engagement in the near future I'm sensing?"

Annie turned pink. "We have...discussed it. And, that is, uh, on the horizon."

"Oh!" Dottie clasped her hands together.

"I'm so beyond thrilled for you, Annie," Sam said lovingly. "No one is more deserving of love and joy."

"Thank you. And thank you all for your support." Annie looked around the table, her eyes shiny. "You guys are my sisters."

"Heck, yeah, we are." Erica lifted her cup again.

"Speaking of moving..." Taylor smiled and lifted her shoulder. "I get the keys to my new place next week."

Sam already knew that, of course, since she'd been helping Tay pack up her room at the cottage and get ready to move into her cool new one-bedroom apartment on Merritt Island. Sam had to constantly remind herself that it was just over the bridge, but not having her girl under the same roof was going to take some adjusting.

Still, she was thrilled for her new chapter and growing romance. She was thrilled for Annie moving toward becoming a stepmom and falling deeper in love. She was thrilled for all these amazing women that surrounded her.

Despite all the thrilled-ness, Sam couldn't help but feel a little blue by comparison. Her daughter and her best friend were in these joyful relationships and on exciting new journeys with men they adored.

Shouldn't that have been Ethan and Sam? She'd felt hopeful about things earlier, but now she wasn't so sure those hopes should be quite that high. Why was she lagging so far behind? She didn't even know where things stood between the two of them, and was stuck in this gray area of coy, flirtatious nothingness.

Could they ever get out of that?

"I guess it's my turn," Sam smiled softly.

"Yeah, Mom." Taylor gestured at her mother. "What's new with the inn and everything?"

"Well, everything is great at the inn, but I actually wanted to tell you guys about something that happened with Ethan today."

"Ooh." Erica shimmied her shoulders.

Imani raised a brow. "Do tell."

"I know it's small compared to falling in love and moving in together and, heck, we're still broken up." She laughed sheepishly. "But he asked me to go to Orlando with him. To...pick out a toilet. Romantic, I know."

Taylor gasped with a smile. "Aw, I think it's sweet."

"For the cabana bathroom?" Dottie asked.

"Yeah," Sam replied. "It's going to be the most incredible cabana in the state of Florida. He thinks I need to be there to pick out the finishings and the, well, toilet. There's a home show in Orlando, so we're driving over on Thursday." She took a deep sip of her pina colada, wiping a dab of whipped cream off her straw. "And that's the big, juicy update on my love life. Toilet shopping."

"Well, hey now," Annie said, tilting her head. "I think this might mean a lot more than you think it does."

Sam frowned. "I don't know, Annie. I don't want to read super deep into this thinking it means something and that there could be a chance for us when, at the end of the day, it was only ever about toilet shopping."

Erica arched a brow and leaned in. "I'm sorry, sister, but there is absolutely no way this is only about toilet shopping."

"I have to agree," Imani added. "It's a poorly masked excuse to spend a day with you."

"Facts." Taylor flicked her fingers.

"I don't know." Sam bit her lip and leaned back in the barstool, considering this. "Of course, that's what I want to think. But I'm afraid of getting my hopes up. He ended things with me, you know?"

Dottie stirred her drink. "And now it appears he's trying to start them back up."

Was he?

"Here's the question." Annie pressed her palms into the table. "What do you want out of all of this, Sam?"

"Well..." Sam sipped her drink again, glancing out at the ocean, which now glinted with moonlight on the waves. "I miss him. Badly. And after the way things went at the dance marathon, I know I'm not over him. Not even close. But I'm scared to get hopeful and get hurt again."

Taylor shook her head. "You can't stay in this in-between with him, Mom. It's time for a do or die."

"She's right." Erica waved her finger at Sam. "This day in Orlando needs to be an end all-be all moment."

Dottie nodded. "You're either doing it for real, the

whole shebang, serious, potentially lifelong commitment, or you're done. You have to decide, Sam. Your heart has been on the line for too long here, and I think it's time to, well, as your dear father would say...you-know-what or, excuse the on-the-money pun, get off the pot."

They all howled at the old Jay-ism, but Sam saw entirely too much truth in it. "You're right. You all are. I need an answer from Ethan."

"It's now or never, you know?" Imani shrugged. "Lay it all out there. Tell him what you want, and make it clear that he can't keep playing this on-and-off game with you."

Taylor nodded, pressing her lips together. "It's time, Mom. You deserve something real."

Sam let out a breath, finishing off the remains of her pina colada as she processed the wisdom and truth of her loved ones.

She needed to make a choice with Ethan. Either they were going to be together and be real, serious, and long-term committed, or they needed to be done for good.

And after this weekend, she'd have her answer.

Chapter Eighteen

Amber

A huge shipment of campaign merchandise and swag had been delivered to the cottage by mistake, since Julie had forgotten to update her shipping address, so Amber had gone there after dark to get it all.

She never thought she'd be comfortable just waltzing into the cottage the way all the Sweeneys did—no call, no doorbell, no knock. They just came and went as they pleased, taking food from the fridge and coffee from the pot.

The dynamic of the family had felt so foreign to her at first.

And yet, here she was, letting herself into the cottage with no real hesitation, knowing that she was now part of the group that had a sweeping, twenty-four-seven invitation to the family home. *Her* family...sort of.

"Hey, it's Amber!" she called out as she stepped inside. "Anyone home?"

Moonlight streamed in through the sliders in the living room, brightening the entire cottage, even at night. Amber took her time walking through the hallway, slowly scanning every family photo that covered that wall.

She enjoyed studying the pictures, though, running

her fingers along the frames as she smiled at the collage of memories and joy.

She was still an outsider, but this family had taken her in and cared about her now. Was she ready to truly be a part of something like this? Did they really want her around or were they all just being polite?

"We need to update that old wall." The voice startled Amber, and she whipped around to see Dottie coming down the staircase.

"Oh, hi, Dottie." Amber stepped away from the photo wall and smiled. "I'm sorry, I didn't know anyone was here."

"I was just doing some reorganizing." Dottie pushed back her gray curls. "With Taylor moving out next week, I'm getting my guest room back. Not that I want her to leave, of course, but the front room will be open and ready for whoever needs it next."

Amber smiled softly. "I'm sure some other long-lost Sweeney will blow into town and fill it right up."

"And I'd welcome them," she teased. "What brings you over here, then?"

"A package." Amber held her hands on her baby bump. "There should have been a big box that arrived here, full of campaign merchandise for Julie. It was shipped to the cottage by accident, I just came to grab it before tomorrow."

"Oh, that's what that was!" Dottie held up a finger and hustled down the hallway, motioning for Amber to follow her to the back bedroom where Sam stayed. "I put it in Sam's room to get it out of the way, I was going to call

Julie in the morning to see what she wanted me to do with it."

"Perfect." Amber walked into the quaint, beautifully decorated bedroom, her eyes falling on a large, heavy-looking cardboard box in the corner. She walked over to it and crouched down, grabbing the sides. "Thanks, Dottie. I'll just drag it out of here—"

"Actually, Amber." Dottie held her hands knotted together, smiling with a look of hope in her eyes. "There's something else I'd like to give you, if you're not in too much of a rush."

"Sure, of course." Amber stood up. "What is it?"

"Come." Dottie waved a hand and guided Amber all the way back to Taylor's room, which was on the opposite end of the downstairs, off the living room.

But the life had gone out of the room, which was now a collection of packed boxes and a few suitcases.

"I found this under the bed in here when Taylor and I were packing." Dottie slid over a big plastic bin and brushed a thick layer of dust off the lid.

They sat down side by side on the edge of the bed.

"What is it?" Amber asked.

Dottie just smiled, unclipping the plastic lid and sliding it off of the bin. Inside, it was filled with...

"Baby clothes," Dottie said softly.

Amber's heart folded as she slowly reached her hands into the bin, picking up a soft, pink onesie folded neatly on top. "Oh. Oh my...Dottie..."

"They're all Julie and Sam's, and I think some of Taylor's, actually." Dottie dug through the bin and pulled out several precious baby outfits, each more stinking adorable than the last.

"Oh, these are so cute." Amber held up a little white outfit for an infant, decorated with daisies. "They're in such good condition."

"I've kept them for so many years." Dottie smiled, turning to Amber with joy practically radiating from her. "I think passing down heirlooms and family memories is one of the most beautiful gifts we can give to our younger generations, and I wanted you to have these. For your baby girl."

Amber was speechless, and she couldn't quite identify why her eyes were starting to sting with tears. "Dottie, I can't...I can't accept these."

"Why on Earth not?" She blinked back.

"Because these clothes are..." She ran her fingers over the daisy-patterned outfit. "These are for your family. These should go to...to Taylor's daughter one day, or whoever is next. They should stay in the family."

"Amber, you look at me," Dottie said sternly. "You *are* in the family. Whether you like it or not, that's just how it is. These will go to Taylor's daughter one day, because you will give them to her. Just like we've always done with the mountains of baby clothes I accumulated while having four kids. Believe me, everyone has gotten their fair share. And these..." She pushed the bin toward Amber. "Are for you. And little baby..."

"Mary," Amber finished with a whisper. "I just decided."

"Mary." Dottie's eyes filled as she clutched her chest. "How beautiful."

"Thank you."

"And little Mary is going to be so loved and happy in the clothes worn by her great-aunties and cousins. Because they are her family. And they are yours, too."

Amber closed her eyes and drew in a slow, shuddering breath as emotions washed over her.

Why was this so hard for her to accept? Was she scared of getting attached, or did she just not know how to truly fit in?

"Honey, I guess what I'm trying to say is..." Dottie placed a hand on her leg. "You're stuck with us. So, embrace it. Take the baby clothes and let me be a great-grandma. Whoa! I haven't said that out loud yet. A *great*-grandma."

Amber blinked back tears and reached her arms out to give Dottie a hug. "The greatest great-grandma."

They pulled back and Dottie beamed lovingly at her, joy sparking in her eyes. A joy that Amber couldn't deny —this lady's love was real.

With a sigh, Amber picked up the daisy dress again, toying with the little lace details around the sleeves. "I guess I'm just scared."

"Of what?"

"Getting so attached to this amazing family," she admitted, the honesty tumbling out. "I'm scared of feeling like I'm not truly a part of it. It's always just been me and my parents. The cousins and aunts and uncles and the way everyone is so close and...it's wonderful."

She shook her head. "It's amazing. I'm just worried about getting too used to it all and then everyone suddenly realizing that I'm not *actually* in this family. It sounds stupid. My mom would pronounce it 'imposter syndrome' and teach me coping techniques."

"Imposter, im-shoster," Dottie asserted with a flick of her wrist. "You're one of us, okay?"

Amber nodded slowly.

"Take the baby clothes. Love them. Let them remind you that you have a family that loves you, all the time."

Amber let one tear fall from her eye and roll down her cheek, taking Dottie's hand and giving it a squeeze. "Thank you, Dottie."

"Oh, no." Dottie leaned in and kissed her cheek. "I only respond to great-grandma now."

They both laughed, and Amber stood, still holding the outfit close, gazing out at the moonlit sand, imagining sweet Mary dressed in daisies.

"Wow, Taylor had quite the view in this room," she mused, peering through the sliding glass door on the other side of the bed.

Even at night, the ocean glistened and the stars twinkled through the clear night sky.

"It never gets old, does it?" Dottie agreed.

Suddenly, as Amber watched the serene beach scene outside, she saw two figures walking along the shore, holding hands. Two familiar figures, she realized, recognizing the tall stature and smooth gait of the man and the tilt of the woman's head.

"Is that my dad?"

"Is it?" Dottie got up and looked through the sliding doors.

"And my mom," Amber said, watching the woman laugh and flip her long hair.

No question about it, those were her parents. Her separated parents who, right now, looked to be anything but.

"Well." Dottie chuckled. "Look what the tide brought in."

There was no way. There was simply no way that her parents were out there right now looking like a couple of lovestruck teenagers and...they were *kissing*!

Amber gasped, turning to Dottie. "Did you see that?"

"Oh, yes, I did." Dottie's eyes were glued to the scene outside. "Anything is possible, my dear Amber."

Her parents were back together. Or, at least, kissing on the beach at night.

"Yeah," she agreed, squeezing the soft cotton of the daisy outfit as she watched her mom and dad on a secret date. "Anything is."

Chapter Nineteen

Julie

"And for all of those reasons, plus my absolute love for this city and everyone in it, I truly believe I am the best candidate for mayor of Cocoa Beach, and it would be an honor to serve you. Thank you."

Applause erupted from the Cocoa Beach High School auditorium, which was surprisingly packed for the mayoral debate.

Julie let out a sigh of major relief as she savored the cheering and clapping, straightening her back and resting her hands on the podium in front of her.

She'd *crushed* that.

Her whole body buzzed with satisfaction and adrenaline and victory. The big debate had been one of the most daunting aspects of this election, but as soon as it started, Julie fell right into a rhythm.

Amber had prepped her so thoroughly, she answered every question like a pro, and even one-upped good old Trent Braddock on more than a few occasions.

Her burning desire to win this race only grew stronger when she saw how the locals responded to her and her mission. Her passion was genuine, and that seriously seemed to be coming across.

Julie was on a high, and more hopeful than ever.

"Yes, yes, yes!" Amber held both hands up for a high-five, bouncing on her toes as Julie walked off the stage to greet her. "You are an icon, Julie Sweeney. You totally dominated."

"It felt good." Julie let out a sigh and gave Amber a tight hug. "You're an amazing campaign manager and debate coach. I could not have done that without all of our practice questions and your preparation."

"Hey, we're a team." Amber nudged her. "Come on—your army of a family is all waiting to congratulate you."

Julie beamed. She'd been on bigger stages before, and had larger audiences cheering her on. But this was...different.

She'd been applauded for her music and her band, and that was great. But she'd never been appreciated and adored like this for her words and her mind and her heart.

This town understood her so deeply, and she was legitimately pumped to become mayor and give back to her community. This new stage of life felt so right, so perfect, Julie could hardly believe that everything was coming together so effortlessly.

"Oh my gosh, Mom!" Bliss leapt toward her, jumping in for a big hug and squealing with excitement. "That was so cool. You were totally badass up there."

"Was I?" Julie hugged her daughter and kissed the top of her head. "Thanks, sweetie. I feel pretty good about it."

"Uh, yeah! It was awesome. I got the whole thing on

video. I'm gonna edit it and post it on TikTok. You'll go viral."

"Viral? I don't know about that, but—"

"There she is!" John walked over to hug her, patting her back hard as he gave her shoulders a shake. "You were insane, Jules. You killed it."

"Thank you." She shook her head, laughing softly. "I just spoke my truth, and Amber helped me prepare a ton."

Amber waved a hand. "Please, stop giving me credit. You did that. You're actually, like, made for this."

"Well, I always knew I thrived being on stage," Julie joked. "I just never thought it would be for a political debate."

She made her rounds with the family, hugging them all, the entire group hyping her up and cheering her on.

"My Julianna." Dottie walked over, taking Julie's face in her hands and giving her a kiss on the cheek. "I have always been proud of you, and I am especially today."

"Thank you, Momma." Julie hugged her mom tightly, closing her eyes as she savored everything her life had become.

A year ago, she was living in a van, wishing her boyfriend would come back while she consoled their seriously sick teenage daughter. She had hardly any possessions to her name, and nothing that even closely resembled a root.

She'd been distant from her family for months, and spent the nights crying, desperate and alone.

It was hard to even remember those dark times, filled

with regrets and fear and unknowns. Because now she was here, surrounded by pillars of love and support, lifted up by the family and community that made her whole again.

She meant every word of her closing speech. It would be an honor to be mayor.

"Polls are in, Jules." Amber rushed over, frantically refreshing the screen of her iPad, which she rested on her pregnant belly.

"And?" Julie pressed.

Amber stayed silent and still while the screen loaded, her eyes quickly scanning it before she gasped dramatically. "You're up!"

"I'm up?" Julie's heart kicked. "By how much?"

"Four points." Amber shifted her gaze up toward Julie, her brown eyes dancing. "Julie...you're winning."

For the first time since she'd announced her candidacy, Julie was ahead in the polls.

"Holy cow," she whispered, pressing her hands against her head as though her brain could not compute this news. "I could actually, seriously win this thing."

"Ooh, look—speak of the devil." Sam elbowed her playfully as they all clustered in one of the aisles of the auditorium. "There's your competition."

Julie turned her gaze to see a very determined-looking Trent striding toward her family, boasting a massive smile that contradicted the frustration in his eyes.

"Give me one second." Julie stepped away from her family and walked over to Trent, meeting him behind a row of seats in the bottom level of the theater.

"Julianna." He held out his hand to give hers a notice-ably firm shake. "I have to say, you surprised me up there."

"Oh, well, thank you." Julie lifted a shoulder, trying to ignore the way his stare was piercing into her like two daggers. "You were very impressive, Trent. I was honestly so nervous. I've never debated before."

"I'm assuming you've seen that you gained some trac-tion in the polls today. Congratulations."

"Oh, thanks." She waved a dismissive hand.

Jay's voice echoed through Julie's mind. *Always take the high road, Jules. The view is a heck of a lot better up there.*

"But we all know the polls don't mean too much," she continued gently. "Anything could happen. And it really has been a great experience running alongside you, Trent. I know that no matter who wins, the town is in good hands."

"Right, yes." He pressed his lips together. "That's very true, Julie. But I just came over here to congratulate you." His brows flicked up with the slightest hint of condescension. "Well, you certainly know how to get the attention of a crowd."

Julie drew back, not quite sure what to make of that comment.

She decided to play it cool, and laughed casually. "Yeah, well, thanks to years of playing gigs all over creation, I guess. I'm comfortable in front of a crowd."

"Hmm." He nodded. "You do have quite the inter-esting past, from everything I've learned."

"Oh, you know. Just a wannabe rock star." She shrugged. "It's all behind me. Now I'm here, running for mayor of Cocoa Beach and debating you. Life is funny, huh?"

"Mm-hmm. Can you ever really escape the past, though?"

"Uh, I don't know. I think you can move on from mistakes and regrets and change your life. That's what I've done since moving here, and it's been wonderful."

"Well, yes, and that all sounds like sunshine and rainbows, but...at the end of the day, you are who you are, right? People don't *really* change. And you're a...how did you put it...*wannabe rock star*?"

Julie swallowed, anger slicing through her, making her hands nearly tremble.

It was clear that Trent was threatened by her success, and trying everything imaginable to get under her skin.

She wouldn't fall for it.

"Well, now I'm a wannabe mayor," she teased. "So we'll see how that plays out, right?"

"I supposed we will." He nodded, his gaze lingering on her for a few pressing seconds. "Watch out for that past, Julie. It can come back to bite you."

With that bizarre and unnerving comment, she said her goodbyes to weirdo Trent and resumed celebrating with the family.

He was just being a jerk and trying to freak her out and get in her head. Wasn't he? He was determined to make Julie doubt herself and question her ability to do this job.

She was so much more than her past. She'd grown and learned and changed drastically, and nothing Trent Braddock or anyone else could say would make her question herself.

He was terrified she would win. As well he should be.

Chapter Twenty

Lori

Lori was already running late to meet Rick for lunch when the phone rang. As she was reaching for her keys, she glanced at the number on the screen of her phone.

She didn't recognize the number, which had a 305 area code. Miami? She didn't know anyone there.

Assuming it was spam, she picked up her phone and slid the Answer button, holding it to her ear and fully expecting to hang up with a quick excuse.

"Hello?"

"Hey, there." A man's voice came through the call. "Is this Lori Caparelli?"

"Um, yes, this is her." She lowered her purse down onto the dining table and leaned against the edge of it. "Can I help you?"

"Hey, Lori. My name is David Farnsworth, I'm the director of strategic planning at Spring Valley Clinics. We're a network of in-patient rehabilitation centers for recovering addicts and psychiatric patients."

"Oh, yes, of course. I'm familiar with Spring Valley. Nice to meet you, David."

Lori had heard of the nationwide chain of psych clinics, but had never worked too closely with them or sent any patients there. Her practice was always primarily focused on marriage and family therapy. She didn't work much with cases of addiction or anything severe enough to involve an in-patient clinic.

But from what she'd heard, they did good work for many people in need and probably were looking for a reference or wanted her to speak at a conference.

"How can I help you, David?"

"Well, I hope you can, Lori," David continued. "I'm calling because we've had your name come up quite a bit in our strategic planning meetings lately, and I was really hoping to get a moment of your time."

"Um, okay." Lori glanced at the clock. She was seriously late, but Rick would understand. "How has my name come up?"

"Okay." The man cleared his throat. "To summarize, we've heard talk about this new program you've created, mixing yoga with talk therapy. Am I understanding that correctly?"

"Um, yes, I have sort of initiated a practice that's a hybrid of those two. It's not a regimented program or anything like that. It kind of happened organically when I started teaching yoga. I suppose I just couldn't keep my mouth shut," she added on a laugh. "And my yoga classes took on this element of talk therapy. People seem to respond very well to it, though."

"That's what I'm hearing. And, frankly, I'm not shocked. Yoga has already been proven in a multitude of studies to significantly improve serotonin levels and ease symptoms of depression, anxiety, even OCD."

Lori smiled. "It's a wonderful thing."

"And I can see why this hybrid you've invented has shown even more drastic results."

"Well...I haven't exactly measured any kind of results, drastic or otherwise. I just talk with people during the yoga class, and—

"Exactly. It's so much more relaxed and comfortable than sitting in an ice-cold office staring at a shrink, feeling like they're judging you."

Lori laughed at the man's bluntness. "I suppose that's been working in my favor."

"It certainly has, and I'll just go ahead and cut to the chase here, Lori."

What chase? She swallowed, her curiosity spiking. "Of course."

"We would like to hire you at Spring Valley as a full-time consultant to help us implement the practice of yoga therapy at every single one of our rehabilitation facilities across America."

Lori felt her jaw go slack. "You...excuse me? How have you even heard of me?"

"Our V-P of operations was on vacation in Cocoa Beach and took your sunrise yoga class. Not only did you work on the knots in her back, but the ones with her estranged father, as well."

Instantly, Lori remembered the woman who'd broken down after the session, talking about her emotionally unavailable father. She'd left with her mat in one hand,

and her phone in the other, about to call a man she hadn't spoken to in seven years.

And that led to...this.

"Lori, you've created something new in a space that is starved for fresh ideas and methods," he powered on with his pitch. "Just think of what your work could do for recovering addicts, or patients with severe depression. The concept of connecting physical movement with simultaneous talk therapy is utterly genius and we want Spring Valley to pioneer that subset of the mental health-care market."

"I... Wow." She laughed with disbelief, shaking her head as she paced around the little kitchen of the townhouse. "Thank you. I can't believe you want to bring this idea to your clinics."

"Every one of them across the country. We believe that a new method of therapy could open a lot of doors for better and more effective patient recovery, and our clinics are desperate for new ways to connect with and aid our patients. I'm sure you know as well as I do that psychiatric hospitals are not fun places to be."

Lori shuddered. "Of course not."

"We think this could breathe new life into our therapy methods. It could be groundbreaking, and we want you to lead the charge, training and recruiting and working on the marketing."

She could practically hear her heart thumping in her chest, so stunned by this interaction that her words stuck in her throat. "This is...this is such an incredible opportunity. I'm...wow. I'm shocked and honored."

"And on board, I hope," David said with a chuckle. "Because we want to get started on strategy planning right away. We'd like to hire yoga therapy instructors and train our staff to implement this program by the fall. Lori, this could be huge. It could help a lot of people, and, not to put too fine a point on it, we have earmarked a significant budget for this program and realize that the value you bring has a high price tag."

In other words, they were offering her a pile of cash. "This is just... Yeah. This is very unexpected, and I'm honored..."

"It would be a lot of work, but the majority could be done fully remote, so you wouldn't have to leave the comfort of your home. In a few rare situations, we may ask you to come to the office to meet with us, but we're headquartered in Miami, which is only about three hours south of you."

It sounded like a lot of work, a brand new undertaking when Lori had just finally started to slow down and put work on the backburner of her priorities.

But this...this opportunity was so massive and impactive. This could be huge. And she would love it. And, truthfully, she missed working a little bit.

"You certainly have thought of everything," she said on a laugh.

"We're really serious about making this deal, Lori." David exhaled. "But you know what? I'm going to leave you with that for now. I'm sure this has already been an overwhelming phone call."

"To say the least," she joked.

"So, take some time, think it over, process everything. I'm actually going to be heading up your way at the end of this week. I've got a new clinic opening in Jacksonville and I'm driving up there to help the recruiters get the staffing situation organized. Let's set up a time. I can stop in Cocoa Beach, since it's right on the way, and we can meet face to face. I'll go over your contract, salary, plans, timeline...all of it."

"O-okay. That sounds great, David. And thank you again. I mean, wow." She shook her head. "I never thought when I started doing little yoga classes on the beach it could ever turn into something like this."

"You have a gift, Lori Caparelli. You need to share it with the world."

She took a deep breath and shut her eyes.

"All right, I'll give you a buzz on Friday when I'm on my way upstate. We can grab lunch and iron out details. Sound good?"

"Yes, that, uh, that sounds good. I'll see you then."

"Nice chatting with you, Lori. Talk soon."

The phone call ended, leaving Lori with a mountain of thoughts and questions, but a new kind of excitement and possibility brewing in her heart.

Yes, she'd stopped working full-time as a therapist and had certainly enjoyed her slowed-down lifestyle recently. But this wouldn't be seeing patients...this was consulting. This could change lives, and help people, and—

Oh, dang it. She was so late.

Lori rushed out to her car, sent a quick apology text

to Rick, and sped down A1A toward Beachside Diner as fast as she could.

He would understand. As soon as she told him what held her up, he would get it completely. He had to.

"I am so sorry," Lori said breathlessly as she walked into the diner, spotting Rick alone at a booth in the back, holding a nearly empty mug of coffee.

"Wow, finally." He smiled, but his eyes looked hurt. "It's not like you to be late. Is everything okay?"

"Everything is...more than okay." She slid into the red leather seat of the booth, grinning widely and chomping at the bit to tell Rick the news.

"Wait, what do you mean?" He angled his head, smiling curiously. The hurt seemed to have already faded away. "What happened, Lor?"

"You're never going to believe this, but I got a phone call out of nowhere from this guy who works for strategic planning at Spring Valley Clinics."

He frowned. "The psych wards?"

"In-patient rehabilitation facilities," she corrected. "But yes. That Spring Valley. Their V-P of operations took my yoga class and—"

Rick's smile seemed to fade a little. "They want to hire you."

"Yes, but...not in the way you'd expect. They don't want me to be a therapist. They want to hire me as a consultant for the company, to help implement the concept of yoga therapy into their rehab centers for patients. Across the country! They want to, 'pioneer' was the word he used, the concept."

"Your concept."

"Which they will pay me handsomely to give to them, while I help hire, train, build a program, and...and..."

"And lose yourself in work again."

"No, no. As a consultant."

But he didn't look convinced.

"Yes, it would no doubt be a lot of work up front, and some travel, but David said I could do the majority of it remotely."

"Majority?"

"I might have to go to Miami here and there. You know, for meetings. But wow." She shook her head, knowing he'd come around to see how amazing it was any second. "I just can't believe my concept made it all the way to a company that big. I mean, it's crazy."

"It's not crazy," Rick said, sipping the rest of his coffee. "I'm not even the least bit surprised."

He also didn't *seem* the least bit excited for her, but she decided not to say that. "Why not? I mean, I'm shocked."

"Because, Lori. It's just what I've always said. Every single thing you lay your hands on turns to gold."

"Well, this is about more than money..." Her voice trailed off.

"I know that. Have you told Amber?"

Lori shook her head. "No. It just happened, and I haven't taken the job. I'd probably wait until the election is over before I even share this with her."

"Good call," he mumbled.

"Rick." She leveled her gaze with his, her excitement waning fast. "What's the matter? I mean, why aren't you happy about this? It could be huge for me and for these patients, and—"

"I know, Lori. I know it could be amazing and huge and profitable and impactful. And I know that hard work and long hours don't scare you. In fact, it's quite the opposite." He laughed dryly. "They excite you. I knew that you missed working too much, and it was only a matter of time before your desire to work took over again."

"Rick." She frowned, glaring at him as anger rose in her chest. "I didn't go seeking out this job opportunity. They called me out of nowhere. I—"

"I know that, Lor. You can't help it. I'm not blaming you, seriously. I just know what life is like with you when you're working like that. It's...lonely."

She swallowed her sadness.

"And, I don't know." He shook his head. "I thought things were really going to be different now—"

"They are different," Lori insisted.

"If anything, this consulting job is going to require *more* time and energy than your work as a therapist did."

She bit her lip, knowing full well he was probably right, and she couldn't argue that.

"I just...I knew it was too good to be true, Lori. I thought we could have this life of slowing down and relaxing and focusing on the family. I thought it was going to be a totally different chapter for us. But you're headed into the corporate world at full throttle, and..."

He put his napkin on the table. "I'm sorry. I just don't think I can handle it again."

"Rick, please." Lori reached for his hand. "Just hear me out."

"Lori, I love you."

"I love you, too."

"But you love working more," he said softly, his voice barely above a whisper. "And I spent so many years being second on your list of priorities. I can't do this again."

"It won't be like that."

"I have to go, Lor." He pushed up. "I...I can't go down that road again."

"So you're just going to walk out and leave...again?" She heard the pain in her voice, and saw it reflected in his eyes.

He blew out a sad breath. "I just need some time to think. This was too much false hope."

"It was...false?" She heard her voice crack.

"It was...not grounded in reality."

"What does that even mean?"

"That certain things about people don't change. You are not just a workaholic with a Midas touch, you are that person who can't *not* succeed. You thrive on opportunity and growth and changing lives. You'd slay a job like this Spring Valley thing. You'd dive in and shake things up and it will become...your whole world." He let out a sad sigh. "I just don't know if I want to take a backseat to that again."

"You won't." But even as she said the words, she realized that there was a lot of truth to what he was saying.

Since that phone call, all she'd done was mentally...plan and think and start to...dive in. Just as he'd said.

"You'll change lives and help people and probably put yoga therapy on the map," he said softly as he stood. "And that's what you should do, Lori. It's what you were born to do."

Was it? Or was she born to be his wife and Amber's mother and Mary's grandmother and a slightly eccentric former therapist who taught yoga on the beach?

"You're just going to leave?" she whispered.

"I need to go think. I'm not sure what I'm going to do. Except now, I'm going to...walk and take some pictures and think."

She watched through the blur of tears as he walked out of the restaurant and to his car in the parking lot.

Just like that, he was gone again. Melancholy déjà vu hit her like an eighteen-wheeler as she felt the familiar sense of emptiness creep up in her chest.

Maybe he was right. Maybe she hadn't changed. Maybe she never really could.

But now, he was leaving. And nothing else seemed to matter.

Chapter Twenty-one

Sam

S am turned around in the passenger seat of Ethan's truck to gaze out the back window and admire the toilet and sink in the truck bed, wide open for the world to see.

"We picked a good one, didn't we?"

"Oh, yeah." Ethan peered up through the windshield at some seriously foreboding dark grey storm clouds. "I wish they could have given us boxes, but no such luck when you buy off the trade show floor."

"No boxes, but a huge discount," she said, fighting a yawn from the exhausting day of travel and hours of walking through a packed home show. "And the cabana is going to be the best on the beach."

"I can't believe it's after six already," he said. "I'd really like to beat this storm."

"What's our ETA?" She glanced at the GPS on his phone, which was propped up in one of the cupholders on his console.

"Should be just about an hour, but I don't want to get stuck in flooding or a storm on the Bee Line. There's nowhere to run or hide on that road."

"True." Sam cringed, knowing the straight shot from

Orlando to the beach had long, long stretches with no exit and nothing but scrub and swamp on either side of the road.

As ominous as the black sky looked, Sam was grateful for an hour in the car with him. Despite being together all day, she'd never had the chance for her "now or never" moment.

In fact, the day had been filled with fun and laughter and shopping and opinions, but she never felt the moment was right to tackle the whole "relationship" conversation.

At this point, it felt like Sam and Ethan had been through so many ups and downs in such a short time, it was hard to dampen a happy, fun day together with serious conversation.

But she knew in her heart that her family was right. She had to figure out where this was going and get a definitive answer, before she got hurt yet again.

She deserved to know. She had a right to know where his head was at with everything, how he really felt about her, and where he saw this going.

Because she had to be real with herself. They were more than friends. More than exes. And yet, still, somehow not anything.

Sam hadn't realized quite how desperately she craved commitment from him until today. As they'd perused the rows of countertops and backsplashes and appliances, more for the fun of it than anything, she ached for something more. She found herself fantasizing about having a real partnership with him—building their own home, having a real life together. She wanted more than just this flirty on-and-off thing they couldn't seem to break out of.

It had felt like it was on the cusp of what she wanted before their breakup, when she brought up his past and it all backfired. But that seemed to have eased, and Ethan was more open about his past and his life than ever before.

Sam turned to him, studying his face and wondering what was going on inside his head.

"Can we…" She cleared her throat, shifting in the seat. "Talk?"

He turned to her, a smile pulling. "I'm guessing not about the weather."

Right as she opened her mouth to respond, the roar of a thunderclap followed by an instant flash of lightning startled her, and the skies opened up. Sheets of downpour dumped onto the windshield and the road in front of them, wrapping the world in a blur and forcing Ethan to slow the truck to a crawl.

"Or maybe we should talk about the weather," Sam gasped, her adrenaline spiking. "This is *bad*."

Forgetting the "do or die" conversation, she braced herself and focused on the road with him, as if paying attention could help them avoid hydroplaning.

"People are starting to pull off," Ethan said, raising his voice over the sound of the intense rain pounding on the roof.

"I know." Sam tried to see the shoulder, but it was nothing but sheets of water with dim yellow flashing hazard lights. "Should we get off? I think I saw an exit coming up."

"We might as well," Ethan replied, flicking his blinker on to slowly pull into the right lane. "I'm crawling anyway. We could just go and find somewhere safe to park, not on the side of this highway."

"Maybe get some food while we're at it," Sam suggested. *And have a talk about the future of our relationship,* but she decided to leave that part out.

"Definitely."

He drove in silence, concentrating on every foot until they were off the Bee Line and pulling onto a road where they could see the signs for a Holiday Inn and a Walmart. "We can wait it out here."

Sam nodded, watching the rain dump down onto the pavement in a drenching downpour familiar to Floridians, but not the many tourists on these roads.

He shut the car engine off, and suddenly the steady drumbeat of rain was the only sound, creating a tense, still silence between them.

"You, uh..." He turned to her, running a hand through his hair. "You wanted to talk?"

"Yes." Sam nodded and took a deep breath, unclipping her seat belt and shifting her whole body to face him. "Look, Ethan, I—"

A blinding bolt of lightning streaked through the sky, instantly followed by a crack of thunder so loud the car vibrated and shook.

"Oh my gosh!" Sam shrieked. "This is insane."

"It's really bad." Ethan looked forward, his eyes

landing on the Holiday Inn at the end of the parking lot. "It's not ending anytime soon, and it's only getting darker outside. I'm thinking maybe we should just check into this hotel and head home in the morning."

Surprise and, admittedly, a tingle of unexpected anticipation zipped up Sam's spine at the idea. Aside from the fact that she relished the thought of having uninterrupted hours with him to figure everything out, she was also getting pretty darn terrified sitting out here in this lightning storm. "Yeah, let's do it."

"Come on." Ethan turned on the ignition and drove the truck as close as possible to the entrance, which was set about twenty feet back. "We're going to get soaked. You want to wait in the car while I check in and offer my firstborn child for an umbrella?"

She laughed. "An umbrella? In this? Plus, I don't want to sit out here. I'm sticking with you," she said, getting a warm look in response.

"Good call, Samantha." He winked at her as he pulled into the closest parking spot. "On three?"

"On three," Sam agreed.

They both clutched the latches to open their car doors, and Sam watched the ocean of rain she was about to run through to get into the Holiday Inn.

"One." Ethan smiled at her. "Two. *Three*."

She flung her door open and leapt out of the car, and was instantly drenched.

Ethan rushed right over to her, wrapping his arm around her shoulders protectively and tucking her against him as they sprinted through the sloshing puddles.

She felt her hair sticking to her face and neck, her clothes completely saturated. She shuddered to think about what her makeup looked like, but now was not the time.

They ran into the lobby, dripping water all over the floor, laughing and clinging to each other.

"Hi." Ethan said as he breathlessly walked up to the front desk, shaking out his soaking wet hair. "Could we get two rooms for the night?"

Sam following behind him, wiping her hair off of her forehead and shivering in the blasting air conditioning.

"One second." The woman working the desk offered a sympathetic smile at Sam and Ethan's compromised state as she glanced down at the computer and typed rapidly. "Looks like...I've got one room left. King bed."

Ethan turned to her for an awkward beat of silence, and Sam stepped forward. "Um, is that all you have? You don't have two rooms or even a room with two beds, or..."

"I'm sorry." The woman shook her head. "There's a huge dance competition going on at the performing arts center in town, and a bunch of the dance teams got block rates here. We're nearly booked solid."

Sam tried not to laugh as she shook her head, feeling droplets of water dripping down her face. "It's fine," she said softly to Ethan. "We'll make do."

He turned back to the woman. "We'll take it."

Check-in took a few minutes, but once they got upstairs, Sam realized she had absolutely nothing with her other than her purse. "Wow. This is..." She walked into the generic-looking hotel room, dropping her purse onto the bed. "This has been quite the turn of events."

Ethan cocked his head, a smile playing on his lips. "No kidding."

"I don't have...anything." She laughed, throwing her hands into the air helplessly. "I don't have dry clothes or anything. And you don't, either. Also..." She shivered, crossing her arms. "I'm so cold. And so wet."

"Okay, how about this." He walked over to her, his hair still soaked and sticking to his forehead. It only made him cuter. "It's let up a little, so why don't I run over to that Walmart right next door, get us some dry clothes and snacks and whatever we might need to get through until tomorrow. You can just take a hot shower and relax. Okay?"

Sam felt like she should argue, offer to be the one to go to Walmart or at least go with him, but it was so wonderful to have someone selflessly care about her, she just smiled gratefully. "Okay. Thank you, Ethan."

"Of course." He flipped his keys in his hand. "I'll be right back."

Once she was alone, Sam peeled off her saturated T-shirt and jeans, hanging them on the towel rack before stepping into a scorching hot shower, savoring every moment.

Once she was clean and dry, she sat on the edge of the bed in a towel, her mind racing in circles about tonight.

Here they were, in a hotel, forced to share a bed for the night. The universe had handed her a golden opportunity in the form of a thunderstorm and a rom com cliche, and all she had to do was figure out how to make the most of it.

She wanted an answer from him. And she knew, without a doubt, she was going to leave this Holiday Inn either certain about him or heartbroken and done for good.

AFTER ETHAN HAD COME BACK with Easy Mac, chips and salsa, a package of Oreos, and some questionable choices of pajamas, he got in the shower and Sam changed.

Seriously? She had to laugh as she looked down at the outfit he'd picked for her. It was almost definitely from the teenage boy section, consisting of a Super Mario Bros. T-shirt and green plaid pajama pants.

"You're kidding, right?" she called into the bathroom once she heard the shower turn off.

"What do you mean?"

"You couldn't have looked in the women's section?" She cracked up as she walked over to the bathroom door.

"I was in a hurry." Ethan swung the door open, wearing a plain black T-shirt and grey sweatpants. "Besides, you look adorable."

Sam faked a curtsy. "I feel adorable."

With bowls of Easy Mac and a stack of Oreos, they sat side by side on the bed, laughing at their situation.

Sam knew...it was now or never.

"Okay," she finally said, lowering her little blue plastic bowl and taking a deep breath. "I do actually still need to talk to you."

"I'm just warning you," he teased. "I'm going to have a hard time taking you seriously in that outfit."

Sam laughed and shoved him playfully. "Well, you're going to have to try."

"Okay. What is it?"

"I need to know, Ethan." She locked eyes with him, her heart pounding.

"Need to know what?"

"What is really going on here? I mean, are we exes? Are we friends? Are we...still maybe going to be together someday?"

He drew back, clearly caught off guard by her blunt questioning, but he didn't dismiss it. "I understand. It's been confusing lately, and...unclear."

"Yeah." She scoffed. "Slightly."

Ethan sighed, leaning closer. He reached his hand out and tucked a strand of her hair behind her ear, his touch giving her a shiver.

Sam looked up at him. "What do you want? I mean, I know we broke up, and it seemed like that was for good. But then the dance marathon happened, and now this, and I've just gotten all of these mixed signals, and...I feel like it's kind of, well, keeping in the theme of today, do what needs to be done or...get off the pot. You know, the one in the back of your truck."

Ethan laughed, shaking his head. "Samantha... What do *you* want?"

She plucked at the hideous green plaid pants, her gaze fixed downward while she pondered the loaded question. "Honestly?"

"Yes. Please." He gently touched her chin, tilting her head up so their eyes met. "Tell me exactly what you want."

Oh, boy. Well, he'd asked.

"I want to be with you, but for real," she admitted. "No secrets, no hidden pasts, no glossing over things. I want to have a relationship with you that's genuine and deep and...long-term. I want commitment, not just fun. I want to do the whole, real, serious thing with you, Ethan. And I'm at the point where it has to either be that, or...nothing. If this isn't going to be a real commitment and a true relationship, then it can't be anything anymore. It's too hard for me."

She breathed out softly, letting her words hang in the air between them. Sam instantly felt a considerable weight lift off of her shoulders after dumping out her truth.

If he didn't want the same thing she did, that was fine. At least she was honest. At least she had the nerve to say how she really felt.

After an agonizingly long pause, Sam searched his face. "Please say something."

"I agree with you."

She blinked back. "You do?"

"Yes." Ethan nodded. "We can't keep dancing around our feelings anymore. It has to be all or nothing. And I know I had walls up before, but I can feel them coming down. With you."

She reached for his hands, her heart fluttering. "I can feel them coming down, too. And that's all I want, for you to let me in."

"I want to let you in."

She inched closer, touching her lips to his. "For real this time?"

"For...ever."

He kissed her softly, then with a passion that felt like fire. Sam smiled and Ethan laughed as he pulled her closer and ran his thumb across her cheek.

"Samantha," he whispered. "I love you. And I'm so sorry it's taken me this long to realize it, but I know now. I want to be with you, in every imaginable way. No more secrets, no more hidden pasts. I want the real deal."

She melted into his arms, feeling like she could actually float away on Cloud 9. "I love you, too."

Sam had never in her life been so thankful for a thunderstorm and a toilet convention.

Chapter Twenty-two

Amber

The election was now one day away, and Amber's heart slammed in her chest as her mind raced. The sun hadn't risen, but she was wide awake, wired and ready and staring at the ceiling fan.

She'd spent the past two hours willing herself to get some more sleep, for Mary's sake if nothing else. But sleep wouldn't come, and it had to be around five a.m., so that was a reasonable time to get up and start working on last-minute election prep.

Amber was so wrapped up in Julie's campaign, she'd hardly had time to seriously process the fact that her parents were seemingly back together, even though they hadn't told her that in any official capacity.

But the thought had her sitting up and smiling, even at this hour.

She'd gone so long feeling hopeless. She'd spent so many mornings hating her life the moment she opened her eyes. But now...everything was different. Everything was so much better, and Dottie was right. This place really did have some kind of magic.

Amber rubbed her eyes and reached onto her nightstand to take her phone off the charger and start getting ready for the day.

She gasped with surprise at the sight of her phone screen, which was flooded with notifications, more popping up by the second.

She squinted to read the words flying across the screen, her heart rate instantly picking up as a bad feeling stabbed her in her gut. This couldn't be good. This could not be good.

"Oh, my God." Amber shuddered, bringing her hand to her mouth as she stared at the photograph that had gone viral overnight, and the headline that went along with it.

"Mayoral candidate Julianna Sweeney's drug use caught on camera."

What? Julie didn't...

Adrenaline surged as she read the first paragraph and looked at the picture, which was ancient and grainy. But it was Julie, and she was puffing on a joint.

Looking like a twenty-something-year-old version of herself with long, long hair, too much eyeliner, and a really bad leather vest and a hideous crop top, the image showed Julie inhaling with the classic "three fingers up" pose, with two incredibly grungy-looking guys nearby, both perched on amplifiers, laughing.

Amber grunted noisily, throwing her hands in the air in symbolic resignation.

The day before the election. The freaking day before. This could ruin everything. Cocoa Beach was a whole-some town, and despite the fact that this picture had to be more than twenty years old, Amber didn't get the feeling this would help win votes around town.

She took a deep breath, trying to compose herself as she scrolled through the internet and local news to see how bad the damage was.

Instantly, a video of Trent Braddock popped up on her Twitter feed, his stupid, smug face talking to the camera.

"I mean, it's sad, really." He gave a snarly smile so fake it made Amber's blood boil. "I feel bad for Julie. Having a drug problem is not easy, and I just hope that she's recovered and gotten the help she needed."

"A *drug problem?*" Amber shrieked at her phone. "She smoked pot two decades ago when she was in a rock band, you moron!"

"And, as sad as it is to see that someone would resort to illegal drugs," Trent continued, "we have to ask ourselves, is this really a person we want running our wonderful city? I mean, is she going to be high on the job? We do have to ask these questions, unfortunately."

Amber shut her phone off and threw it on the bed, clenching her jaw as she gathered her thoughts.

Okay, all was not lost. *People aren't that dumb. They can certainly recognize that Julie was practically a kid in that photo.* She certainly never hid her past, but was proud of her musical career and years on the road.

Not to mention, medical marijuana had been legalized in Florida, so Amber could take that angle, too.

This could be saved, she decided. Trent Braddock was even more of a snake than Amber had originally thought, but she was certain she could find a way to help Julie take him down.

But first, she had to break the news. She threw on some clothes and sneakers as fast as she could, certain her "boss" was still asleep and had no idea any of this was happening.

She had to hear it from Amber, not from the news or, heaven forbid, Trent Braddock's pathetic interview.

Amber drove to Julie's loft quickly, which was easy, since there was nobody on the road. It was barely sunrise, and she spent the entire eight-and-a-half-minute drive planning how exactly she was going to talk Julie off the ledge.

Julie's confidence and self-assurance in this race was new and likely fragile, and Amber had a feeling this could totally destroy it.

She whipped into the first parking spot she saw at Julie's building and raced up the stairs to the third floor.

Sorry, Bliss, she thought to herself before knocking loudly several times on the door to their loft.

After about a minute, the door slowly opened, and Julie peered her head out, looking confused and half asleep.

"What is it? What's going on?" she asked, her voice groggy.

Thank goodness—she didn't know yet.

Amber jutted her chin toward the inside of the apartment. "You might want to make some coffee."

"Okay..." Julie narrowed her gaze, frowning with confusion as they went in and she started to brew a pot of coffee and slowly come to life. "Amber, I do love you, but there better be a good reason you're here at the crack of dawn."

Amber sucked in a breath, sitting down at their small, two-person dining table. "There is."

Julie joined her with two steaming mugs of coffee, rubbing her eyes and yawning as she sat across the table. "All right. I'm ready. What is it?"

Amber inhaled slowly, making an extra effort to keep her tone calm and collected. "Trent and his people got their hands on an old picture of you."

Julie's eyes widened and her breath caught in her throat. "What picture?"

Amber swallowed and slid her phone across the table to show Julie the screenshot she'd saved of the viral photo.

"Oh...oh, no." Julie picked up the phone slowly as her brain processed what had happened. "This was 1993 in Reno. I was nineteen, and playing in this band called Swords and Snakeskin with...these guys." She looked up at Amber, her brown eyes wide with fear. "And, yes, I'm smoking weed."

"I know, Jules." Amber slowly reached for her phone and took it back. "It's gone viral. Well, Cocoa Beach viral, which, in this case, is all that matters."

"Oh, God." Julie dropped her head into her hands, lacing her fingers through her messy black hair. "Amber, this is bad. This is really, really bad."

"I know it seems that way." Amber pressed her lips

together. "But I think we can salvage this campaign. I still think you can—"

"Oh, please." Julie picked her head up, her expression dark and defeated. "It's over, Amber. If this picture is out there, I'm done for. It's photographic evidence of me not only being a rebellious musician, but using drugs."

"It's almost thirty years old. People can understand—"

"It doesn't matter." Julie shook her head. "That's the image I have in this town, the reputation I've worked so hard to reverse. The only thing anyone here knew about Julie Sweeney was that I was a runaway rebel trying to make it as a rocker and living in a van. Just when they started to think maybe I could have changed, that picture comes out. And every single person who was considering voting for me will know that this..." She pointed at the phone screen. "This is who I really am. And it's all I'll ever be."

"Julie!" Amber exclaimed. "You know that's not true. You know you'd make a fantastic mayor, and smoking a joint in the Nineties doesn't change that fact one bit."

Julie dropped her head into her hands and huffed out a sigh. "You don't get it, Amber."

"I do get it, actually. We can spin this in your favor. We can use it to show your growth, to show how coming home to your family and the town helped you rebuild your life and—"

"What growth?" Julie slumped back in her seat, her eyes darkening. "Who was I kidding?" she whispered softly, shaking her head.

"What do you mean?"

"This." Julie gestured at the countertop, which was covered in "Vote for Julie" merchandise, T-shirts, yard signs, and fliers. "All of this. I mean, who was I trying to fool?"

"You weren't trying to fool anyone. You are more passionate about helping this town than any other campaign I've worked on. You're genuine."

"Amber." Julie swallowed. "That picture? That's who I am, and it's who I'll always be. Trent was right. People don't change, and you can never really escape your past."

"But you have changed, Julie!"

"I'm no mayor." She laughed mirthlessly. "I'm a retired wannabe rock star who lived hard and fast on the road until I had a child. And this race has been fun, but... it's time to get real. There are probably more damning pictures out there, and Trent Braddock will find and exploit every one. This is a waste of time. I need to drop out."

"No!" Amber stood up, pressing her palms into the table as she met Julie's defeated gaze. "Please, Jules. You can still do this."

"The election is tomorrow. It's over."

"It's not over." Amber walked around the table and took Julie's hand, giving it a squeeze. "Just listen to me for a second, okay?"

Julie lifted her gaze, her eyes misty.

"When Sam first started talking about Cocoa Beach having some sort of 'magic,' I physically couldn't roll my eyes hard enough. I was so down, so depressed, so alone and dejected and I couldn't stand the stupid idea that some sleepy beach town could somehow make my life better."

Julie chuckled softly and continued listening.

"But then, of course, you've seen the transformation that my mom and I have both had since we came down here. I mean, that was my rock bottom, and we didn't know where else to turn. And now? Look at us. Look at *you*. And Bliss!"

"Well, I can certainly relate to the rock-bottom feeling. This place saved my daughter's life, and it saved me, too."

"I know it did." Amber leaned against the countertop behind her. "Julie, you were a big part of that magic for me. Getting to know you, and seeing how incredibly close you and Bliss are...it really changed my entire outlook on becoming a single mom. You, and your family, and your love for this town...you are part of that magic, Jules. You're a massive reason why Cocoa Beach is as special as it is."

Julie took a deep breath, emotion in her eyes. "Thanks, Amber."

"You're so much more than a retired rocker. You're really an amazing person. You've helped me more than you know. You embody what the Sweeneys and what Cocoa Beach as a whole stands for and does for its people, and there is truly no one better suited to be mayor of this amazing little city."

Julie laughed dryly and waved a hand. "You're sweet, Amber. And I really appreciate that. But...Trent won with that picture. It wouldn't have taken much to topple my meager lead, and he found it."

"We don't know that. You just have to relate to them. I can write you up a speech for a press conference today with the local news, and we can spin this in a positive way."

"I don't know." Julie shook her head. "I feel like a fraud trying to do all of this, and I just know that when everyone saw that picture, they were thinking the same exact thing."

"Julie." Amber leaned forward, placing her hands on Julie's shoulders. "Please don't give up. I care more about this campaign than anything I've ever worked on, and that's because of how genuinely you deserve this position. How much good you could do."

"I'm not qualified. I was never qualified to—"

"Yes, you are. Please, just trust me, okay? I'm going to call Regina at *Florida Today* and set up a press conference in the afternoon. I'll write up notes for you. Please."

"Amber, I don't know—"

"Think about it." Amber grabbed her purse and slung it over her shoulder, pointing a finger at Julie as she backpedaled toward the front door. "I'm going to get this ball rolling, okay? Promise me you'll think about it."

"I..." Julie huffed out a sigh. "Okay."

"Okay." Amber smiled. "Chin up. We got this. We're in it together, right?"

She nodded weakly.

"I'll call you." Amber opened the front door and started to step out.

"Amber, wait."

She whipped back around and looked at Julie. "Yeah?"

"You're, um..." Julie smiled wistfully, beaming a little as she looked back at Amber. "You're going to be an amazing mom."

Emotion swelled in her chest. "Thank you."

For the first time since the moment she'd found out she was having a baby, Amber was actually certain that was true.

By the time Amber pulled back into the driveway of the townhouse she shared with her mom, she was feeling hopeful.

Obviously, the pot picture had thrown an enormous monkey wrench into what was shaping up to be a possible win in this election, but Amber had dealt with scandal before.

She knew how to play this into a positive thing, and she was itching to sit down at her computer and start drafting up a heartfelt, raw, emotional statement for Julie to make that afternoon.

Yes, smoking marijuana was a bad, bad look. But if she could help Julie convey the message of growth and change, and relate it back to how Cocoa Beach saved her from that world and forgave her for her mistakes, she just might be able to pull it off.

Amber whipped into the driveway, and instantly

noticed that Dad's car was there. Why was dad over here so early? Possibly a sneaky rendezvous with Mom?

The thought was equal parts exciting and icky, but it made Amber smile to herself as she hopped out of her car and walked up to the front door.

But...no. Mom would be at yoga right now; she had a class this morning. Maybe dad was here to see Amber.

"Hey, Pops. You here?" Amber called as she walked into the townhouse, beelining for her bedroom to get started.

"Amber, hi." Dad stood up from the couch in the living room, and with one look at his face, Amber could instantly tell something was very wrong. "Mom told me the door code, so I just sort of popped in. I wanted to talk to you..."

"I'm guessing you saw the pot picture," she said quickly, holding her hands up as she walked toward him. "Believe me, I freaked out at first. But I think I have a good plan to handle it, as long as Julie can—"

"Pot picture?" He frowned.

He didn't know? Then why was he here and why did he look so...upset?

"Uh, yeah. A photo leaked of Julie smoking a joint at a rock concert when she was nineteen, and it's all over the local election coverage and social media and all that. Like I said, I'm handling it, but it definitely threw us."

"Oh, shoot, kid." He walked over and placed a hand on Amber's arm. "I'm so sorry. How stressful right before the election."

Amber nodded. "The timing is less than ideal, that's for sure."

"And poor Julie." He shook his head. "As if she's the only person in the world who made mistakes and dumb decisions as a teenager."

"Seriously." Amber scoffed. "But you know how it is with politics. From the presidency all the way down to small-town mayors, those candidates are under a microscope and nothing is off limits. The question is how you deal with it, and I've got a plan."

Rick smiled, beaming with pride as he looked at Amber. "Now that I believe, A."

"So, what are you doing here so early, anyway?" Amber glanced at the oven clock in the kitchen. It wasn't even seven o'clock. "Not that I'm not happy to see you," she teased.

Her dad didn't crack a smile. "I'm actually, um..." He cleared his throat. "I'm here to say goodbye, Amber."

Amber blinked back, shock and confusion smacking her like a slap in the face. "You're leaving? Why? Is there a job you have to go to, or—"

"No, I'm..." He sighed and shook his head. "I'm going home. To Raleigh."

"You are?" she whispered the question. "But what about Mom? Aren't you guys, like, I don't know, a thing?"

He gave a soft laugh. "I don't think we're 'a thing' anymore, Amber. Mom hasn't told you yet, but she received a pretty massive offer to be a full-time consultant for a healthcare company. They want to implement her method of yoga therapy in a nationwide network of rehab clinics."

Amber's jaw fell slack. "Holy cow."

"And while I'm truly thrilled for her and I think it's going to be an amazing project, I've been thinking about how that might work. And, honestly, it won't."

"What do you mean?"

"Honey, I can't take ten more years of being in the background of her life. I wanted things to be different this time around, and I really thought they could be, but not with this job. It's going to be long hours, travel, meetings, tons of work. And your mom, well...she just loves that life, Amber. She can't stay away from it, it's who she is. And I don't want her to have to change herself or compromise or give up on something just so she and I can be together. It's not fair to her."

Amber swallowed, drawing back as she processed this overload of stunning new information. "And she's definitely going to do it? You're sure? She never even mentioned it to me."

"I can't see her turning this down. She'll fill you in on everything after the election, and I'm so sorry to put this on your plate right now, I really am. I just didn't want to lie to you, and I wanted to make sure you understood that my leaving has absolutely nothing to do with you."

"But..." Amber felt emotion choke her for a second. "We were going to be a family again. I thought that we were..."

"I'm so sorry, Amber." Rick wrapped an arm around her shoulders and hugged her tightly. "I just don't think it's meant to work out between your mom and me. She's got so much drive and ambition and...I love that about her. I do. I just miss her so much, and I can't go back to being pushed away all the time for work. That was a really lonely marriage for me."

"I know." Amber nodded, sniffling. "I know, and I really just want you both to be happy."

"All any of us want is for everyone to be happy." He kissed the top of her head. "We are a family, A. We always will be a family. I'll come back here when the baby's born and you can bring her up to Raleigh to see Grandpa Rick."

Even as she nodded, she wanted to scream, "No!" That wasn't what she wanted.

But this was her parents' life, and it was their decision. She wasn't privy to their personal conversations, and she hadn't known how serious this reunion really was.

She wiped a tear as she pressed her face into her dad's chest, just like she always did when she was little. "I miss you already."

"You have to promise me, though." He pulled away and looked at her. "You have to promise me that you will keep taking care of yourself, you won't fall back into that slump."

"I promise." Amber sucked in a breath.

"And no more secrets." He held out his pinky.

Amber interlaced her pinky with his, smiling at the gesture he'd always used to make promises with Amber growing up. "No more secrets," she repeated.

"Now, go write a killer speech for Julie and save that election, okay?"

"Okay." Amber hugged her dad one more time, trying to tamp down the thick lump of sadness that sat in her throat.

She understood, but it hurt. Badly.

"I'll call you, kiddo."

Amber nodded. "You're going right now?"

"I'm going to head back over to my Airbnb and finish getting the last of my stuff. But after that, yeah. I better get on the road."

They walked over to the front door, hugged again for a long moment, and then said one final goodbye.

"I'll call you on my drive, okay?" he shouted over his shoulder as he opened up the driver's-side door of the car.

"Okay. Bye, Daddy." Amber forced a smile onto her face.

"Love you, kid."

"Love you."

After one more wave, she went back into the town-house and shut the front door behind her, leaning against it and crumpling to the floor with a sob.

Amber had not realized until just now how happy the idea of her family being whole again had made her. Seeing her parents kiss on the beach wasn't just fun and exciting, it was real hope for her.

And now...it was all gone. And she wasn't mad at her mom for getting an amazing job offer or her dad for leaving. She understood completely where they both came from, and had no desire to take a side.

She was just...broken. Maybe it had been silly to think they could be some kind of happy family again, but she'd thought it. She'd let herself get so wrapped up in the hope and the optimism and the magic, that she'd lost touch with reality.

The reality was, her parents were separated, and they were staying that way.

With a heavy heart and a few more tears, she got up and dragged herself down the hall and into her bedroom, opening her laptop with a deep breath.

She couldn't save her parents' marriage, but darn it, she could save this election.

Chapter Twenty-three

Julie

Embarrassment, shame, defeat, and a heaping pile of regret pressed down on Julie's chest like a thousand-pound weight as she stepped out of the car to meet Amber and the local news crew outside of the community center.

She'd managed to drop Bliss off at school, after briefing her on the whole photo situation, of course. Lovely and understanding as ever, her daughter was certainly old enough to know what sort of things went on at concerts and in that lifestyle.

Julie was grateful all over again that she'd decided to take Bliss away from all of that and get her to Cocoa Beach, where she had a stable family and home.

She'd worked hard to try and rebuild her reputation and her life, but there was no escaping her past mistakes. After spending way too long staring at that horrific old photograph, Julie was drowning in a sea of sadness and self-doubt.

She might have changed, but with only one day to convince the voters of Cocoa Beach, she knew this election was over. Her past was a big part of her life, and she didn't really want to stand on her head begging people to believe she'd grown. She knew she had, and her family knew.

That was all that really mattered.

"Thank God you're here." Amber rushed over to her, iPad in her hand, sheer determination on her face.

"Hey, girl."

It killed Julie to know how badly she was about to let Amber down. She knew how much this campaign had meant to her, and Julie was so deeply touched by how much effort and energy and passion Amber had put forward.

They'd bonded and grown and learned together, but Julie knew what she had to do today at this press conference.

She couldn't continue playing dress-up as this happy, perfect Cocoa Beach mom with the flawless family and a love for the town.

Her truth was out now. Her past, her reality, her life. Everyone would see right through her and know that she was not destined to be the mayor of anything.

"Okay, let's go over these notes. Quick." Amber frantically waved her over to a bench next to the building.

"Amber..." Julie sighed, following her as they moved past a camera crew setting up to record and air the conference on the local news.

"Look." Amber handed Julie the tablet. "I wrote out all of your major talking points, your intro speech, and your closing statements. These are just listed in bullets, because I don't want you reading something word for word. This has to come from your heart, and I know that it can. I know how badly you want this, and how much you truly deserve it."

Julie felt tears stinging behind her eyes as her mind flashed to the dreadful picture. She didn't deserve this. She'd run away from this town. She'd turned her back on it for a rebellious, impulsive life filled with bad decisions.

"Amber, I don't know if I can do this."

"Yes, you can." Amber locked eyes with Julie, taking her hands and squeezing them. "You can do this. Speak from your heart, because all of the answers are in there. All you have to do is be your authentic self, and people will love you. They can overlook a mistake, they can forgive it. You're a symbol of growth and change, Julie. You're the perfect example of the magic and community that this town has to offer, and what it can do for its people. Talk about how Cocoa Beach saved Bliss, and how it saved you, too."

Julie so wished she could do that. But in her gut, she knew what she had to do. She didn't have the heart to hurt Amber right now, so she just nodded. "Okay."

"Okay?" Amber smiled and pointed down at the screen. "Good. Now, remember, you want to focus in on the idea of growth, so you can—"

"Julie, you ready?" Regina Carrington, a journalist for the local paper, *Florida Today*, walked over to them and smiled. "We're all set up for print and accompanying video that will run on our site."

Julie glanced at Amber, who gave a reassuring nod and a big thumbs-up. "We're ready, Regina."

After a quick introduction, the camera was rolling,

the microphones were on, and the press conference was completely set up and ready to go in front of the entrance to the Cocoa Beach Community Center.

A few local publications and one TV news outlet had joined to watch, record, and ask questions for their articles, so the crowd in the parking lot was a bit bigger than Julie had imagined.

The old pot picture sparked some interest, she guessed. Well, people love a good political scandal. Julie just never thought in a million years she'd find herself in the center of one.

"Hello, Cocoa Beach." Julie leaned into the microphone as a couple of cameras flashed from the gathering of people in front of her. "I just want to start by saying—"

"Julie! Julie!" A man's voice blurted out from the crowd, "Is it true that you struggled with a drug addiction while raising your daughter?"

"I...*what?*" Julie spat out the word, so offended and horrified by the question she nearly fell to the ground. "Absolutely not. I would never—"

"Julie, how do you explain to local teenagers that drugs are dangerous when you yourself have used them?" a woman called out.

"I made a mistake, it was a long time ago." Julie gritted her teeth, searching the parking lot for Amber.

When she finally found her, Amber mouthed, "*Change. Growth.*"

Sorry, Amber, Julie thought. *I can't recover from this one.*

Nerves, anxiety, and flat-out anger coursed through

Julie's veins as she looked around, her gaze darting from one reporter to the next. Her heart slammed and her hands grabbed the podium.

"I'm dropping out!" she yelled.

That silenced the crowd in an instant.

"I'm stepping out of the race," Julie said, her voice lower and calmer this time.

In the distance, she could see Amber drop her face into her hands and shake her head. A stab of sympathy hit Julie's gut, but she was doing what she had to do.

"You're all right," Julie said, letting out a breath. "I did use marijuana recreationally in the Nineties. I was a touring musician, messed around with the wrong crowds, and I frankly didn't know any better. I'll also add that I was nineteen years old, but it doesn't matter. I made a mistake."

She swallowed, watched every set of eyes fixed on her, gathering confidence to continue.

"In fact, I've made many, many mistakes. I left home when I shouldn't have, and I hurt my family in the process. I turned my back on the wonderful, beautiful town that raised me, and I didn't come home until it was out of pure desperation. I had hit rock bottom when I drove back into Cocoa Beach, and, truthfully, I never in a million years expected to be welcomed, forgiven, and surrounded by love and support the way that I have been."

Amber was standing to the side, watching Julie. She looked miserably sad.

"The girl that you all see in that photo...that is me.

That's who I was, and there are many things about that girl that I'm not totally proud of. But to be honest, I wouldn't change a thing about my life or my past. It brought me my baby and best friend, and it brought me home to this town and my family. And when I came home that rock-bottom day, I realized that Cocoa Beach and the people of this community are the very thing that my life had been missing for thirty years. Heck, I loved being back so much I ran for mayor."

Soft laughter echoed through the group of people as a few more camera flashes went off in front of Julie.

"And this campaign has been incredibly rewarding and fun, and I'm beyond grateful to have had this opportunity. But...the doubt and fears that people have about me are sadly correct, and I can't stand up here and deny that or pretend to be someone I'm not. I did make that mistake a long time ago, and I do come from a past that isn't nearly as shiny and perfect as my opponent's."

She paused for a moment, taking a breath, squaring her shoulders as she continued, "I was a runaway and a wannabe rock star and, well, a bit of a hippie. My incredible campaign manager told me to be my authentic self up here, so...there it is. That's as real as it gets."

She held her arms out and laughed dryly, hearing a few more chuckles and murmurs in the crowd.

"That is who I am, and I get it if that's not the right person to be your mayor. I don't have the qualifications, the experience, or the squeaky clean history of Trent Braddock. He's going to do an amazing job as mayor, and I'm...I'm out of the race. Thank you."

A slew of questions and flashes and microphones held out toward her face bombarded Julie as she tried to sneak away from the podium and get out of the crowd.

She held up an arm to try to shove away some of the attention as she pushed past the reporters and found Amber behind the side wall of the community center.

"I'm sorry." She reached out to hug her.

Amber looked up at Julie, her eyes rimmed with red and her cheeks wet with tears.

Ache and sympathy and sadness rocked Julie as she saw the broken expression on the girl's face. "Amber, I know how much this meant to you. I just had to do what was right. I'm not cut out for this. I'm not—"

"You actually were, Julie."

"I didn't have half the qualifications of Trent, and all the—"

"Forget the qualifications!" Amber exclaimed, the crack in her voice breaking Julie's heart. "And forget how much it meant to me. This isn't about me. This is about the fact that you were born to do this, and you could make a real difference for people."

Julie sighed, disappointment pressing down on her shoulder so hard she could barely stand up. "I'm sorry, Amber."

"It's okay." Amber sighed as Julie held her arm out for a hug.

"Please don't be mad at me."

She laughed dryly. "I'm not mad, Jules. I guess if that's what felt right in your heart, then you did the right thing."

Julie couldn't seem to discern what felt right in her heart today. The leaking of that old picture had thrown her for such an emotional loop, everything in her mind felt muddy and confusing and dim.

Still, the disappointment written all over her niece's face crushed her almost as much as the leaked picture had.

"Let's get the heck out of here." Amber nodded around to the back parking lot of the community center, where she had parked her car.

They ducked back there to avoid any more questions from reporters.

Julie's heart hurt. Her eyes stung. Her throat tightened and she finally let herself cry the moment she slid into the passenger seat of Amber's car.

"You know..." Julie sniffed, leaning her head against the window. "There have been times in my life where I've been homeless, lost, booed off stage, with not a single dollar to my name. And yet, I've never felt like more of a failure than I do right now."

"Julie," Amber sighed, shaking her head. "I wish you didn't drop out, but you're not a failure."

"So how does this work? Do they pull my name from the ballots?"

"Technically..." Amber glanced at her. "It's too late to officially drop out, because the ballots have been prepared and printed. The withdrawal deadline passed, so...you're still in the race. *Technically*. But after that press conference aired, I'm sure most people will...you know..." Her voice trailed off.

"Right. Well, that's for the best."

Amber clearly didn't agree, but just sighed. "Want to get some coffee or something?"

Julie shook her head. "Let's just head back to the cottage. I'm gonna have to explain all of this to the family. I'm sure Sam and Dottie will be there."

"All right, cottage it is."

Julie knew she had to talk to her family. She knew they'd make her feel better, as they so often did.

But truthfully, what she wanted most in the whole world was to go home, curl up, and disappear for a while.

Chapter Twenty-four

Lori

This was good. This was a good thing. This was going to be a big change, and not necessarily what she'd planned for, but it was all part of the new chapter of Lori's life. It was positive and new and exciting.

So why was she sitting in this hotel restaurant with a giant pit in her stomach so massive it felt like it could swallow her whole?

Lori took a deep breath, tapping her fingers on the glass tabletop as the waiter came by to refill the water she'd nervously sucked down.

David Farnsworth would be walking through the lobby of this Hilton and into the restaurant any moment now, armed with paperwork and a pen and the power to change the course of Lori's entire life in seconds.

Why wasn't she happy? Why did she feel nothing but fear and dread?

Work *excited* Lori. Work was the thing that kept her going, that drove her and all of her decisions. And this new consulting position could be massively impactful, bringing her into a whole new industry and potentially spreading her ideas to patients all over the country.

She should be giddy with glee and hopeful about this new future.

But all Lori felt was heavy sadness.

Of course, Rick's reaction had been a kick in the gut. He'd leave, she was certain. And with him went any hope of rekindling their relationship. She hadn't begged and pleaded with him to stay, because, frankly, he was right. About everything.

A buzz on her phone startled her out of her thoughts, and she glanced at it to see who was texting. Possibly David to say he was running late, although it was still eight minutes before the time they'd agreed to meet. Lori was just perpetually early.

She drew back with surprise to see a message from Rick.

I talked to Amber and have decided to pack up and head home. Leaving in a few. Wish we could have said goodbye.

Her breath caught in her throat as she swallowed a wave of emotion. Lori began typing a message in response, but before she could finish it, a clean-cut man who looked to be in his mid-thirties walked up to her with a wide smile and an extended hand.

"Lori Caparelli?"

"Oh!" She quickly clicked off her phone screen and stood up, reaching her hand out to shake his. "Yes, that's me. You must be David."

"It's a pleasure." He smiled and sat down at the table across from her, wasting no time before pulling out a file folder and an iPad. "So. How are we feeling about this consulting opportunity?"

"Well..." She toyed with the condensation on her water glass, unsure why the question seemed so much more difficult to answer than it should have been. "I feel, you know, good. It's a lot to take in, and I definitely need some more information before committing to anything, but...yeah. I'm excited."

Yikes. That was not even close to convincing.

"Good." David flicked his brows up, clearly trying to read her. "As far as details, I've got all the info for you right here." He tapped some keys on the iPad and turned it around so the screen was facing Lori.

She leaned in to read the pages of fine print and information on the online document when her phone buzzed again. "Sorry," she said with a gentle smile.

"No worries." David waved a hand.

Lori picked up her phone and quickly read another message from Rick, which had just come in.

Come on, Lor. Please just say something. I get that you're busy, but I'm having a tough time here, and it hurts that you won't even respond after everything.

Lori swallowed, an uncomfortable shiver making its way up her spine.

"Everything all right?" David asked.

"Oh, yes, yes." She shut her phone off and flipped it over so the screen was facing down on the table. "Sorry. I'm all ears."

"Okay." He smiled, pointing a finger to the list of bullet points on the first page of her consulting contract.

"So, if you look here, the contract lists expectations regarding hours and travel, conferences, specific descriptions of the work involved..."

Lori scanned the words on the screen, her mind racing rapidly as she tried to make sense of everything and take it all in.

Flying to cities all over the country to train clinical staff in the concept of yoga therapy...working on year-round curriculums, programs, and therapy systems for individualized patient needs as well as creating a company-wide standard practice... searching for study opportunities to conduct extensive research on the effectiveness of the methods...

"Wow." Lori choked on an awkward laugh. "This is... a lot."

"It's no part-time gig, that's for sure." David lifted a shoulder. "But...we know you're the woman for the job. We've done our research on your former practice and actually spoke to some of your colleagues in North Carolina. We know your work ethic Lori, and that paired with your innovative concepts could be quite profitable. And help a lot of people."

She winced at the word "profitable" but played it off. "Well, I appreciate that. I've never strayed away from hard work before."

So why would now be any different? A few months ago, Lori would be jumping for joy at an opportunity like this. She'd already be shopping for new business suits.

"And..." David reached across the table, scrolling through a few pages of the contract on the tablet screen.

"Because it would be a ton of work, Spring Valley will be compensating you in a way we believe is fair." His finger slid to a number in the corner of the screen.

"Oh, my..." Lori blinked back, staring at the jaw-dropping salary. "That's a...a lot more than most yoga instructors make."

He laughed. "We are well aware that you are so, so much more than that. Your reputation in mental healthcare is outstanding. So, you will be compensated accordingly. This is a huge job, I'm not going to lie. It will take an enormous amount of time and travel, but your kids are raised, right? You have the time, correct?"

Yes, her daughter was raised...but her granddaughter wasn't.

And, yes, she had the time for this job, but not anyone else...who mattered.

Still, she stared at that number, which was higher than her biggest years as a private practice therapist. As she did, her phone vibrated again. Then again, and again after that.

"Sorry." She held up a finger and picked up her phone.

David looked slightly annoyed this time, but Lori was more interested in the messages coming in from Rick.

I really thought you had changed, Lori.

I wanted this to work so badly. Telling Amber absolutely sucked, and I really wish we could have had the chance to talk about it.

"Lori?" David sounded irritated now.

"I..." Her eyes stayed fixed on the phone. "I just need

one moment. I—"

"Are you having second thoughts? Because I can assure you, this is a once-in-a-lifetime opportunity," David said sternly, pushing the iPad closer to her. "I suggest you read through this and—"

"I'm sorry. Can you just hang on for one second?" She held up a finger again as she read another message from Rick.

All right, Lor. I won't keep bugging you. I wish you the best of luck with everything, I'm hitting the road.

David cleared his throat. "Lori, I just need you to go ahead and sign this. We'd really like to get started as soon as possible."

Lori felt her heart racing in her chest, and suddenly the thought of Rick getting on I-95 and driving all the way back up to North Carolina was making her physically sick.

No, he can't go, she thought. *I can't let him go.*

"Um...I..." She stammered, trying to steady herself but her adrenaline only pumped harder.

"Here." David grabbed the iPad and flicked through the contract, then shoved it back to her with a dotted line on the screen. "Just sign this, and we can send a copy of everything over by email. We'll iron out all the details at your initial meeting with corporate in Miami next week."

Miami next week? Her head was spinning.

"David, I'm so sorry." Lori looked at the dotted line, the echoes of the job and the money and the intensity of it all bouncing through her brain.

She tried to take a steadying, calming breath, which

was what she would tell her patients to do.

She could hear her own voice in a therapy session:

In a moment of conflict or panic or unforeseen stress and anxiety, take a breath from the diaphragm, calm the senses by closing the eyes, and focus on the dilemma at hand. All things can be processed slowly and methodically, once the initial extremes of reactive emotion have passed.

She looked at David, at her phone, at the iPad, her gaze frantically darting around as quickly as her mind.

Screw the deep breathing. She had to go.

"I'm sorry." She stood up abruptly, her whole body buzzing. "I can't sign that."

"What?" David sounded disgusted. "Are you kidding? Lori, please, I'm begging you to rethink this. This opportunity is enormous, and you would be growing our company exponentially. We need your expertise to profit from—"

"Respectfully, David, I..." She swallowed, holding her chin high. "I do not care."

"Excuse me?"

"I don't care about your company or your profits. I'm not interested in your fancy conferences or that juicy salary. You are more than welcome to implement yoga into your rehab practices. I don't have a patent on it, and I don't want one."

"Lori, there's a misunderstanding here." He folded his hands together, clearly digging for patience. "We need you to head this up, and—"

"I'm about to be a grandmother," she said quickly,

grabbing her purse from the back of the chair and swinging it over her shoulder. "And I teach yoga classes in the mornings at the beach. Aside from that, I am... retired." She nodded. "And I intend to stay that way."

"Lori." David stood up.

"If you'll excuse me, David, I have to go." She marched out of the restaurant and into the Hilton lobby.

The life of putting work first was behind her. All she could do now was look forward, embrace change, and stop the man she loved from getting on that highway.

The second she was in her car, she whipped out of the Hilton parking lot and called Rick.

He answered on the second ring. "Lori," he said, sounding surprised. "Hey. Look, I'm sorry I bombarded you with messages. I just—"

"Where are you?" she blurted out. No time for small talk.

"Huh?"

"Where are you, Rick? Right now. Did you leave yet?" She pulled out of the parking lot, turning right onto A1A, since she knew there was a good chance Rick was north of where she was.

"I'm, uh, I'm at Wawa, actually. Filling up on gas."

"Which Wawa?"

"Uh...off of A1A and Shepard Street. I'm about to get on the highway. I just wanted to get gas and a coffee. Lori, what's—"

"Don't move." She smashed her foot on the gas and sped north on A1A.

"What?"

"Just stay at the Wawa, okay?"

"Is everything all right, Lori? You sound panicked."

"Everything is fine. Well, it's not, but it will be." She merged into the left lane and passed three cars all in a row. "Just stay at Wawa."

"I will stay at Wawa, but you know, if you want to talk, we can talk on the phone while I'm driving back up to North Carolina."

"No," she said sharply. "I don't want to talk on the phone. Just...stay put."

"Staying put."

Lori hung up the phone and set it in the cupholder, continuing up A1A.

In her high-speed drive to Wawa to potentially and hopefully save her marriage, Lori felt a thousand times more excited than she ever did about work or the consulting job.

Rick was her heart, not some fancy corporate position or ritzy salary. Her family was what mattered, and Lori wasn't about to waste another single second of her life putting anything before the people she loved the most.

Finally, she reached the turn for Shepard Street, and saw the big, bright red Wawa sign calling to her like the North Star.

Pulling into the parking lot, Lori spotted Rick standing next to his car.

She parked at the pump next to him and got out, her heart pounding as she ran up to him. "Rick."

"Lori, hey. What's going on? Are you—"

Before he could finish his question, she threw her

arms around him and kissed him. Blessedly, he kissed her back, and all of her fears and worries melted away, right there in the parking lot of a gas station.

"Lori." He laughed, shaking his head with shock as they pulled apart.

"I turned down the Spring Valley job."

His eyes widened. "You what? No, Lor. I never meant for you to do that. I know how important that was to you, and—"

"It wasn't." She shook her head, feeling as free and light as the birds fluttering through the blue sky above them. "It wasn't important to me. You are. I want a life with you. A calm, peaceful, slower life. Here. With you and Amber and our new grandbaby, Mary. I don't want to hustle and grind anymore, Rick. I want to teach my yoga classes at Sweeney House, and spend the rest of my life with my best friend in the entire world." She reached down and grabbed his hand, giving it a tight squeeze. "I want to make up for all the years I wasn't there for you and Amber. I want this to be our next chapter."

He stared at her, blinking with surprise as he gave a laugh of disbelief. "Lori, are...are you sure about this? I don't want you to regret walking away from Spring Valley."

"Rick, the only thing I would regret is letting you get on that highway and drive away from me." She inched closer. "I'm not letting you go again."

He leveled his gaze, relief and joy lighting up his expression. "I love you so much, Lori Caparelli. And I love this town. And your new family."

She rose up onto her toes and kissed him again, wrapping her arms around his neck. "So...you're happy to stay here, right? Because I'm kind of in love with this place."

"Are you kidding?" He glanced around. "Beach life with you? And Amber? And Baby Mary? This is all I've ever wanted, Lor."

She hugged him tightly, melting into his chest as peace and happiness warmed her like the Florida sun on her skin. "Me, too."

This was home. *He* was home.

"Did you see Julie's press conference this morning?" Rick asked, a worried look on his face.

"Yes, I saw," Lori answered with a sigh. "I haven't seen Amber, but I'm sure she's wrecked."

"Well..." He kissed her forehead. "At least we have some good news for her. Hopefully, we can brighten up her bad day."

Lori smiled. "I think we can."

"We should start house hunting," Rick suggested. "There's no room for me in the townhouse."

She shoved him playfully. "There is room for you, but I agree. We're really doing this, then? Putting roots down here, in Cocoa Beach?"

"Leaving this place is the absolute last thing I want to do," he said. "I realized that today."

She nodded. "Me, too. This is home now."

Lori had felt a lot of success and victories and accomplishments in her life, but the Wawa parking lot reunion had to be the greatest of them all.

Chapter Twenty-five

Sam

Sam woke up knowing, without any shadow of a doubt, that she was in love. She could smell it in her coffee and hear it in the morning songs of the birds. She could feel it in the quiet breeze as she walked over to the inn, the whispers of wind reminding her of the night she and Ethan shared, the promises they'd made.

Sam was overcome with a sense of peace, a feeling of calm about Ethan that she'd never had before. She was no longer mentally bouncing around questions or stressing about unknowns. She was not worried about their future or his past.

Everything had leapt forward to a whole new level in her heart and mind, and Sam truly felt invincible.

But despite her overwhelming joy, today was going to be stressful and hard for her loved ones.

It was election day. And election day was certainly not shaping up to be the wildly happy occasion for celebration that Sam had assumed it was going to be. After spending the better part of last night talking to a deflated and depressed Julie, no one had particularly high hopes for the outcome of today's mayoral race.

That didn't stop Ethan from sending her a text at the

ripe hour of six a.m. to announce that he was coming over
before he had to be at school teaching to work on the
cabana—the one they didn't have permitted, and probably never would.

Whoops.

That would all figure itself out. Sam's energy last
night had been entirely focused on Julie, who was heartbroken and crushed over having to announce her withdrawal from the mayoral race. She'd found out, however,
that she couldn't actually withdraw this late in the game,
but she'd said to the whole town that she was dropping
out, so...that was that.

Dottie, Sam, Erica, Lori, and Imani had all rallied
around Julie when she and Amber had come to the
cottage after the press conference. Julie's heartbreak and
shattered confidence was the object of all of their attention, and rightfully so, but it meant that Sam never had
the chance to fill anyone in on her unexpected overnight
with Ethan.

That was okay. She'd tell them when the time was
right, when the election had passed. For now, it felt like a
sweet little secret, and she held it close to her heart and
smiled like a kid every time she thought about him.

Speaking of Ethan, he'd be at the inn any minute.

Sam was grateful he was coming so early in the morning, since it would be just the two of them for a little
while. She paced around the silent lobby, taking in every
detail of the work and time she and Dottie had been
putting in for the last several months.

The dining room was finished. The curtains were

hung, the tables were set, the kitchen was ready. Every single suite in the ten-bedroom inn had gone through a complete overhaul, and the fingerprints of Dottie's nostalgia, Sam's eye for design, and Ethan's touch with woodworking were all over every room.

She walked down the hallway, peeking into the open doors of the suites. Down to the decorations and the bedding, they were perfect, each with their own unique personality and style, brought together by the threads of antiques and rich history that Dottie and Jay had infused into this place.

Pride, joy, and fulfillment radiated from Sam as she admired the beautiful, finished inn. All that was left were the absolute last touches—and, of course, the cabana.

Speaking of that, it was just about 6 o'clock.

Sam wrapped her soft, gray cardigan around her waist and walked back down the hallway of Sweeney House, peeking out through the sliders to see if Ethan had arrived.

Sure enough, he was out there, setting up for whatever the next steps in building the cabana were.

She wasn't certain if the bathroom would get done before the roof or how that would work. All Sam knew was that she was excited to pick out the most fabulous white sheer curtains that money could buy and watch them billow in the ocean breeze after Ethan hung them up.

Holding a cup of coffee in her hand, she leaned against the glass, admiring him and taking in the sight of the man she loved most in the place she loved most. It was beautiful, and she stayed still and quiet as she watched.

Ethan was bent over the foundation of the cabana, his back facing the inn. It looked like he was messing with something, maybe a loose nail in one of the wood panels.

Sam knew she should probably just go out there, but she decided to watch from the windows for a second more.

He stood up, backing away and tossing something out of his hands.

What was that?

Sam squinted, leaning closer to see what he was doing on the cabana.

There were little red dots all over the wooden ground. Were those...rose petals?

Sam's heart leapt into her throat as she grasped the handle of the sliding glass door and shoved it open, walking out onto the sand, which was cool and soft and squished between her toes.

"Hey!" she called to Ethan, waving.

"Oh, Samantha!" He looked startled by her arrival. A bit nervous, even, as he scratched his neck and smiled widely. "I didn't think you were here yet."

"I came over early." She stepped closer. "Used the morning to pace around the inn and take in all of its fabulosity and perfection."

"As you should." He glanced behind him nervously at the floor of the cabana, which was definitely covered in flower petals.

What was going on here?

"What are you doing?" Sam asked softly, nodding toward the cabana behind him.

"I'm, uh..." He turned around, scratching the back of his neck a bit awkwardly as he smiled at her. He reached out and grabbed her hand, gently pulling her onto the wooden platform. "Come here."

"Okay." She set her coffee down on the edge of the cabana and walked with him, her heart fluttering. "Ethan, what are you—"

"Samantha." He took both of her hands in his, his gaze locked on her with certainty and love and admiration.

She felt her pulse quicken as she glanced down at the rose petals, then back up at him, noticing the wide smile pulling at his cheeks. "Ethan..."

Birds sang as they flew through the early morning sky, which was streaked with an orange and white glow. The ocean next to them was calm, soft waves lapping up onto the sand.

The world was still and quiet and peaceful, but Sam's whole body felt like it was on fire as she drew closer to the man she loved.

"I think you know that I love you," he said, pulling her near with a gentle tug on her hands.

"I love you, too," she whispered, her mind racing. "What on Earth are you doing with those flower petals?" She gave a giddy laugh.

"From the moment I first laid eyes on you, I knew you were going to change my life completely. I was freaked out by it at first, because I knew how powerful our connection was going to be." He swallowed, tucking a strand of her hair behind her ear. "I wanted to just jump in and take the leap with you, but I was scared, honestly."

Sam nodded.

"We've both had bad marriages in the past, and we both had wounds that needed to heal. But Sam...I feel like we're healed now. We're ready, or at least I know that I am. I'm ready for all of it, with you. You were right, in the hotel. I don't want casual. I want to be committed to you for the rest of my life."

She felt herself gasp a little as she realized that this was, in fact, happening right now.

"It is now or never. So, I'm not wasting any more time. I'm not wasting another day not living completely for you."

Sam took in a breath, nerves and excitement prickling up her spine.

Ethan drew back, exhaling before he slowly lowered himself to one knee, pulling a little black box out of his back pocket.

"Oh, my gosh," Sam whispered breathlessly, shaking with joy and shock as her hands flew to her mouth.

"Samantha Sweeney...I want you to be my wife. I want to spend every day loving you, laughing with you, serving you in every way I can." He paused, that sweet, familiar smile lighting up his blue eyes. "Will you marry me?"

"Yes!" She answered without even thinking about it. There was no question, no doubt, no hesitation. "Yes, oh my gosh, a thousand times yes."

She dropped down and threw her arms around him, kissing him as they laughed together and the world seemed to stop turning just for them.

He opened the box, revealing a stunning gold ring that didn't look like any engagement ring Sam had ever seen before. The delicate gold setting wrapped around a glimmering diamond.

Wow, it was gorgeous. Sam could hardly catch her breath as he gently slid it onto her quivering finger. "Ethan, it's...it's so beautiful." She held it up to the sunlight and admired it.

"I'm glad you like it." He kissed her hand and pulled her close. "I, uh, I made it."

She laughed with shock, her heart nearly folding in half. "You *made* this? A diamond ring?"

"Yes. Actually, it's not as hard as you would think. I already had the tools to forge the gold setting, and I just placed the diamond in it."

She pressed her left hand to her heart, feeling tears of joy and love springing from her eyes as everything started to hit her all at once.

"I love it so much. I love *you* so much." She pressed her lips to his as they laughed and kissed, still sitting on the deck of the partially built cabana.

"I just figured, you know, you've had the traditional diamond ring thing before." He shrugged. "I wanted to do something special."

"It's incredible," Sam said on a contented sigh. "But... Ethan, we only had that conversation a few days ago. When did you have time to forge a diamond ring?"

He glanced off at the horizon, pressing his lips together. "I...I made it a while ago."

Sam felt her throat tighten. "You did?" she croaked out, emotion nearly choking her.

Ethan nodded, turning back to face her as the ocean breeze gently blew his sandy blond hair around his face. "Early on, actually. When we first started dating. Back when Ben was still my student and you were still very much off-limits."

Her jaw loosened. "You're kidding."

"I guess I just had a good feeling. I didn't know if I'd ever give it to you, but...I think part of me knew I needed it."

"Ethan. That's...incredible." Sam felt a tear fall down her cheek as he wrapped his arms around her, holding her close as they watched the ocean gently sway. She glanced down at the flowers again and laughed. "I feel like I'm on the finale of The Bachelor or something. In the best way."

"I know it's cheesy." He shrugged. "I just wanted you to feel special."

She couldn't help but think of where she was a year ago. Broken, betrayed, alone, and completely lost. Her relationship with her family had been strained, and her world had been shattered. Sam didn't know what home was or how to get there.

And now, she was here. Engaged to the love of her life, outside the inn she'd rebuilt with her beloved mother. Taylor was thriving, Ben was blossoming. Sam's world was finally, finally at peace.

This place saved her. This man healed her. The inn gave her purpose and passion, and her family gave her support.

Sam held her hand out and giggled like a giddy little kid at the sparkling diamond on her left ring finger.

"You're stuck with me." She turned to Ethan, kissing him softly.

"It's an honor and a privilege."

She rested her head on his strong shoulder, sighing with joy and comfort. "Whoever said you can't go home again was dead wrong. Going home was the best thing I ever did."

Chapter Twenty-six

Julie

"We meet again, my familiar friends." Julie glared at the pint of Ben & Jerry's Cherry Garcia in her hand, digging the spoon into the top and savoring a delicious bite of creamy, fruity sweetness.

Cherry Garcia had been Julie's comfort food of choice for as long as she could remember, and there was no better time to break out the big guns than tonight. Election night.

At this very moment, votes were being counted, and they were probably only minutes away from announcing the next mayor of Cocoa Beach.

Julie's phone was off, her TV was off, and the black sequined dress that she and Bliss had picked out for this occasion was shoved deep into the back of her closet. Julie needed no reminders of her glaring failure.

With all electronics and sources of news cut off, she didn't have much to do besides strum her guitar, eat her ice cream, and be sad and miserable.

So, that's exactly what she was doing. Bliss had gone to a friend's house after soccer practice, and even though Julie was bummed that she wouldn't have her best buddy to wallow with, she couldn't help but be overjoyed by how social and well-adjusted Bliss had become at school.

Besides, Julie should spend tonight alone. She was the one who wrecked everything and destroyed her own chances of actually doing something worthwhile with her life. She should have known Trent Braddock would go for the jugular. Amber didn't trust him, and boy, she'd been right about that.

"If I could go back in time...I think I just might..." She sang softly, strumming a C chord on her acoustic between bites of ice cream. *"Change my bad decisions. I'd try to make it right...give that girl a real home. But I was just so selfish... I just had to roam."*

This song was turning out kind of dumb, Julie thought to herself, rolling her eyes as she went for another bite.

Giving up on songwriting, she leaned her guitar up against the coffee table and slumped back on the couch. Maybe she'd cave and watch TV, just try to avoid the news at all costs.

As Julie was reaching for the remote, the front door of the apartment swung wide open, and a breathless Bliss came flying in. "Mom! Mom! Did you see?"

"See what?" Julie sat up, setting her ice cream on the table and studying her daughter with concern. "Honey, are you okay?"

"I ran here," Bliss explained as she caught her breath, still wearing her Surfside Sharks Soccer Team practice uniform. "I ran here because I knew you'd have your phone off. I had a good feeling there'd be Cherry Garcia involved, too. But...Mom."

"What?"

"You won."

"Ha-ha." Julie flicked her hand, frowning at Bliss. "A bit too soon, don't you think?"

"I'm not kidding." Bliss marched forward, aggressively thrusting an iPhone into Julie's face.

Julie sat up as she squinted to read the headline of a Tweet on Bliss's phone screen. The tweet was from the *Florida Today* news account and the headline read:

"Cocoa Beach: *Julie Sweeney shocks Florida with mayoral victory after dropping out of race.*"

"What the..." Julie grabbed the phone, reading the words over and over again. "This can't be right... There's no way that..."

"It is right." Bliss snatched the phone back and pulled up five more tweets, each of them from verified local news accounts confirming Julie as the winner.

"But I..." Julie could barely breathe, her head swimming as if she was living in a dream, expecting to be woken up any second. "I dropped out."

"You heard Amber." Bliss shrugged. "Technically, it was too late to withdraw, so you were still on the ballot, and people could vote for you. And vote they did!" She squealed with joy. "You won, Mommy! You're the new mayor!"

How was this possible? People still voted for her even after they saw the pot picture?

"Look at this interview." Bliss handed her the phone and clicked on it to start a video.

The video showed a woman outside of the community center with an "I voted" sticker on her shirt. "I cast my vote today for Julie Sweeney!" The woman, who had to be in her mid-eighties, proudly asserted with a wide grin. "So what if she had a little bit of fun back in the day? That woman is real and she cares, and that's what we need in this community."

Julie's eyes stung as she swiped through the local coverage, which had more interviews with voters, all echoing the same praises.

"Now." Bliss tapped the screen. "Search, 'Julie Sweeney Cocoa Beach.' See what people are tweeting."

Julie, speechless and stunned and nearly frozen, followed her daughter's instructions. A slew of tweets filled her screen after she searched her name, and Julie scanned through them all.

"Cocoa Beach needs a genuine person with a good heart, who isn't afraid to own up to her mistakes! #VoteForJulie"

"Let's go Julie! The Sweeney family has given back to Cocoa Beach for decades, and you can tell that Julie wants to continue that legacy. I'm gonna #VoteForJulie"

"#VoteForJulie y'all...Trent is a fake!"

"Holy cow, Bliss." Julie lowered the phone with a shaking hand, unable to contain her laugh of total disbelief. "People voted for me. I won!"

"Yes. You did." Bliss reached out and smoothed Julie's knotted hair. "Now, can you put the Cherry Garcia away and get that fabulous black dress on? You've got to make a speech!"

JULIE WAS RIDING the highest high of her life after her mayoral acceptance speech at City Hall. The place was swarmed with reporters, locals, board members... everyone had come out to see Julie accept her win.

The speech was mostly improvised, with a little help from Amber, who had strung something together when she saw the shocking news of Julie's win, and sped to City Hall to get prepped.

The last couple of hours had been a blur—a surreal, cloudy, dreamy blur. Julie was floating, indescribably overwhelmed with surprise and joy and the validation she so desperately needed.

"Julie girl." Dottie was the first to hug her after the speech, and the entire family followed quickly after.

Bliss clung to her side, snapping selfies and laughing joyfully.

The whole Sweeney and Company clan swarmed the lobby of City Hall, and Julie was swamped with attention, love, and support.

"Jules, I am so proud of you." Erica squeezed her.

"My twin sister." John chuckled and ruffled Julie's hair. "You deserve this."

"You really do," Imani agreed, beaming. "We love you."

"We all love you!" Annie blew her a kiss, side by side with her man, Trevor, and her sweet little soon-to-be stepdaughter.

"Oh, my goodness." Julie shook her head, admiring the giant group of people she loved more than anything in the world. She couldn't believe there had ever been a time she didn't want to be with them. "I'm just so overwhelmed, and so grateful."

"We love you, Aunt Jules!" Taylor cheered. "We're so proud."

"Thanks, Tay. I couldn't have done this without all of you. But especially..." She turned, her gaze falling on Amber. "You."

Amber smiled and walked over to hug Julie. "It's been a blast."

"I am so darn thankful that this year has brought me not only another sister..." She winked at Lori, who grinned back. "But another niece. I love you, Amber."

"Julie," Amber cooed, her eyes misty. "Thank you. I love you, too. You're going to be an amazing mayor."

"You know..." Julie took a deep breath, lifting her chin high. "I actually think I am."

"We need pictures!" Imani shouted, waving a hand. "We all want pics on Julie's election win."

"Step right up, one at a time," Julie said playfully, moving to the side to make room for anyone who wanted a photo.

"I'll go first." Sam stepped forward, and Julie noticed that Ethan was there, too, glued to Sam's side.

Guess they're back together. Julie decided she'd have to get the full scoop later.

"Come here, sister." Julie held her arm out to bring Sam in for a hug and then pose next to her for Imani's iPhone.

As soon as Sam lifted her arm to hug Julie, she noticed something new and different and quite sparkly on her left ring finger.

"Um..." Julie dramatically grabbed her hand, gasping with shock. "Excuse me, but what is this?"

Sam could hardly contain her beaming smile. "It's, um..." She glanced at Ethan, who smiled back and winked at her. "I didn't want to steal your moment, Jules."

"Are you freaking kidding me?" Julie shook Sam's hand aggressively, laughing with joy and surprise for her sister. "You guys are..."

"Engaged." Sam held up her hand and turned to the whole family. "I really didn't want to make tonight about me. It's Julie's moment. We were going to wait until tomorrow to tell everyone, but—"

"Oh, my gosh, will you stop?" Julie grabbed Sam's shoulders and squeezed her in a hug, her heart bursting with happiness for her dear Sam.

Everyone burst into cheers and exclamations of joy, celebrating Sam and Ethan now alongside Julie.

Even Ben was over the moon for his mom and his

former math teacher, which everyone got a huge kick out of.

Dottie hugged Ethan for a long time and whispered something to him, no doubt a golden nugget of some sort of Jay Sweeney wisdom.

Bliss took pictures and videos, John, Erica, and Will all congratulated the couple and Taylor dove right into wedding planning excitement, Andre laughing by her side.

"I'm sorry, Jules," Sam whispered to her when the whole family was occupied in the buzz of commotion and conversation. "I really didn't want to steal your moment."

"You have got to stop with that." Julie rolled her eyes at her younger sister. "You are getting married, Sam. That's incredible. Tonight is both of our moments, and we can celebrate it together." She pulled her in for hug. "I love you, my girl."

"I love you, too, Jules."

"Oh!" Julie clapped her hands together, getting everyone's attention and quieting the loud bunch of family and friends that took up the entire City Hall lobby. "I'd like to hereby announce my first act as mayor of Cocoa Beach."

Everyone listened with soft laughter as they turned to Julie.

"I am officially granting the lovely and fabulous owners of the Sweeney House Inn full permission to build the cabana of their dreams on the beach! I'll put it in writing tomorrow."

"Thank God," Ethan said on a laugh. "Because it's already half built."

"And..." Sam held up a finger. "It's already been home to its first marriage proposal."

Dottie brightened. "The first of many, we hope."

As they all laughed and talked, Julie made her way through the group, soaking up every moment.

She'd come a long, long way from that lost girl who ran away from home in the hopes of achieving some big, wild dream.

Little did Julie know her real dream was right here, under her nose, the entire time.

Chapter Twenty-seven

Taylor

One Month Later

March 6th? How could it possibly be March 6th? As Taylor Parker stared at the monthly calendar on her laptop screen, quickly realizing that something important was very, very late. A week and a half at least.

She flopped down on her bed, staring at the soft pink curtains she and Mom had put up in her new apartment, watching them gently sway with the movement of the ceiling fan.

Her mind spun in circles, with one glaring question lighting up Taylor's brain like a neon sign.

Could she be pregnant?

Yes, she supposed she could. Accidents happened, and she and Andre were serious and committed and in love. It was unlikely, and would certainly make for a big fat shocker, but...it was possible.

"Okay. Holy crap. Okay." Taylor sat up, closing her laptop and hugging her knees to her chest. She drew in a slow, quivering breath, trying to prevent herself from completely freaking out.

Andre had gone to Austin for a few days to help

launch a new Blackhawk Brewing location there, and Taylor quickly decided this conversation wasn't one to have over FaceTime.

Not that she knew anything yet. She didn't, and her cycle could be late for a wide variety of reasons. Still, the more she panicked and Googled and worried, the more it started to seem to make sense.

She had been feeling a bit lightheaded lately, and hadn't she been a little nauseous the other day? She'd blamed it on hunger and a busy day at work, but...

"Oh, man," she whispered to herself. This was getting real.

Since she didn't want to call Andre and completely and totally freak him out while he was working in Texas, she called her other go-to person.

After one ring, the phone clicked with an answer.

"Hello, my girl!" Sam said cheerfully. "You lonely with your man gone on a business trip?"

"Well, yes, but..." Taylor swallowed, nerves and anxiety prickling up her spine as she shifted the phone to the other ear. "I sort of have a problem, Mom."

"What's wrong, honey? What is it?"

"I, um..." Taylor sucked in a breath. "I'm late. Like, over a week late. And I've been feeling kind of nauseous and a bit dizzy and I'm kind of mildly having a complete panic attack, because—"

"Oh, my gosh," Sam said with a gasp. "Holy cow, Tay."

"Yeah."

"Do you think you could be pregnant? I mean, it is...a possibility?"

Taylor winced, a bit embarrassed, but...come on. She was almost twenty-five and Mom knew how serious she was with Andre. "Yes, it is," she admitted.

"Well...you better take a test then. I mean, you can't start worrying until you take a test, you know? And if it's positive then, well, we will start planning for a massive life change."

An earth-shattering life change. Taylor shuddered. She was not ready. Not even remotely. But...if she had to adapt, she would.

"Can you come over?" she asked, panic in her voice.

"Of course, Tay. I'll stop at CVS and pick up a pack of pregnancy tests. I'll bring them over and be with you the whole time, okay?"

Taylor nodded, squeezing her eyes shut as tears stung behind them. This couldn't be real. This was so not supposed to happen right now. "Okay."

Taylor spent the next seventeen minutes pacing around the house, mostly trying to imagine how Andre would react if the test turned out to be positive. She'd have to wait until he got back from Austin because, again, not a phone conversation.

But that would give her plenty of time to gather her thoughts and make a game plan, and, honestly, she couldn't really picture Andre being upset.

Shocked, definitely. Terrified, probably. But the giddy kind of terrified. The kind that was causing all the butterflies in her stomach right now. They already knew this was a long and lasting relationship—maybe forever. Probably forever. If there was a baby, it would be forever.

After several deep breaths and another half mile pacing around her one-bedroom apartment, Mom finally knocked lightly.

Taylor swung her front door open and collapsed into her mother's arms. "I feel like that took forever."

"Well, it's late, hon. There wasn't much open. I had to drive all the way to the CVS over on the mainland, because it's open twenty-four hours."

Taylor groaned, pressing her hair back off of her forehead, and shutting the front door as Sam walked in.

"Place is really coming together," Sam said with a smile. "It's so you and, oh, is that a new lamp?"

"Mom, I love you, but this is *so* not the time to talk decor." She grabbed the white plastic bag from her mother's hand.

Sam relinquished it with a frown. "Tay, I know you're worried—"

"Worried? I'm low-key dying, Mom! Andre and I haven't even been together that long, and I live in a one-bedroom, and I have so much traveling and working and stuff I want to do before I become a mom. Andre and I need more time and I'm not ready for this and—"

"Taylor." Sam leveled her gaze, placing a hand on each of Taylor's shoulders to steady her. "It's going to be okay. You're going to be okay."

Taylor felt like she could cry or faint or throw up. Yikes. Throw up, because she was *pregnant*.

"Just sit down for a second, okay?" Sam took her hand and guided her over to the couch in the living room that they'd picked out together a few weeks ago.

Taylor nodded, sitting down and hugging a throw pillow to her chest. "When you first got pregnant with Ben and me, like, really early on, what did you feel?"

Sam's eyes flashed, and an odd expression that Taylor couldn't quite read came across her face. "I, uh, I was a bit nauseous. And dizzy."

"Oh, gosh. I've been nauseous and dizzy." Taylor pressed her lips together. "Like, when you stood up quickly, did it feel like the room was spinning?"

Sam inhaled sharply, glancing away. "Yes, it...did. That was definitely an early pregnancy symptom for me."

"Oh, man." Taylor dropped her head into her hands.

For a moment, her mother was quiet, and Taylor looked up, seeing how pale Sam was. Of course she was upset, trying to put on a "we'll figure it out" face when she knew as well as Taylor that this was...unsettling. Shocking and scary and life-altering.

"Headaches?" Sam asked, the question tentative as if she already knew the answer and how bad it was.

"All day today," Taylor said.

Sam let out a soft moan as if the realness of it hit her, too. Of course she wasn't ready to be a grandmother at forty-three! And she'd hate for Taylor to give up everything to be a mother, like Sam had.

On a worried sigh, her mother pointed to the plastic shopping bag from CVS. "Go take the test, honey. You want to know either way, right?"

Taylor nodded, peeking inside the bag. "How many did you get?"

"A few. In case we don't believe the first one." Mom smiled, reaching for her hand and giving it a squeeze. "I'll be right here, okay?"

"Okay."

With shaking hands, Taylor took the whole bag into the bathroom and quickly briefed herself on the instructions, although she'd seen enough movies to know how to do this.

After taking the test, she washed her hands, and waited for a result that could completely alter the course of her life, staring into the mirror.

She certainly didn't look like a mom. But that was probably how Amber felt at first, and now she was so excited for her baby. But Taylor wasn't even close to ready, and as wonderful and supportive as Andre was, there was no way he'd be ready, either.

"Everything okay, Tay?" Sam called from outside the bathroom door.

Taylor picked up the stick, her hands quivering as one very distinctive pink line formed. Only...one.

"One line is negative right?" she asked, relief washing over her.

"Yes, but the second one can be faint."

Taylor opened the door and showed her mom the pregnancy test.

Sam leaned in and squinted at it, shaking her head. "Nope, that's definitely negative. You're good, honey, just a late period."

"Should I take another one?"

"Nah," Sam said. "I was worried it...well. No. Negative is negative. You'll have your period in the next half hour, if I know anything about women's bodies."

"Oh, thank goodness." Taylor dropped the stick into the waste basket and threw her arms around her mom. "I wasn't ready. I want that one day, and I want it with him, but...I wasn't ready."

"I know, baby." Sam hugged her tightly, resting her chin on Taylor's shoulder. "I'm glad it was negative. You have a lot of life to live, both you and Andre. When the time is right, it'll happen, and you'll know."

Taylor pulled back, sniffing as a few tears of joy and relief fell from her eyes. "Oh, wow, I was so worried. I feel silly for freaking out now, but I'm glad I know!"

"Yeah." Sam pressed her lips together. "It's always better to know."

"Well, now that you're here and I'm lonely, I believe we have some *Love Is Blind* to catch up on. Shall we break out some celebratory, 'I'm not pregnant' junk food and binge watch?" Taylor bounced into the kitchen to scavenge her pantry for any of Mom's favorite snacks.

"Yeah, sure," Sam said softly.

"Why the gaping lack of enthusiasm?" Taylor turned around to see her mom still lingering in the hallway near the bathroom. "Oh, you want to go home to Ethan your fiancé," Taylor sang the word. "I get it, I've been replaced. It's cool," she teased, her mood soaring with the relief over the good news.

"No, no, Tay. Of course I want to hang with you.

Gimme a sec to use the bathroom and you get *Love Is Blind* ready to roll. And snacks. I'll just..." She pointed at the bathroom. "One minute."

Taylor laughed softly. Dang, Mom was seriously dazed by that scare. "Okay," she called as the door closed behind Sam.

Humming and doing a little "woohoo, I'm not pregnant" dance, Taylor grabbed some potato chips, a bag of Twizzlers, and Hershey's Kisses, arranging them all on a big plate before clicking on the TV and opening Netflix.

She heard the bathroom door open and turned around to face the hallway. "Which episode were we on again? I can't remember if—"

"Uh, Taylor." Mom's voice was barely audible.

"Yeah?" Taylor walked down the hallway to find her mom. "What's wrong?"

Sam's hands were behind her back, and her face was ghost white. "Your test was definitely negative."

"Yeah..." Taylor frowned, angling her head with confusion. "I know."

"But..." Sam slowly held up another white stick, the other one that had come in the package. It had two unmistakable pink parallel lines on it. "Mine wasn't."

Chills cascaded down her back as Taylor felt her whole body go numb. "What?" she breathed. "You're..."

"Pregnant." Sam inhaled shakily, looking like she was teetering between laughter and tears. "I'm pregnant."

For a moment, neither one could speak. They just stared at each other, silent and stunned, and then folded into a hug, both of them releasing a sob. Happiness? Horror? Shock or delight?

Or maybe they just both realized that life was about to take another major change.

*Want to know what's next in store for the Sweeney Family? Look out for book seven, **Cocoa Beach Bride** Sign up for my newsletter to get the latest on new releases and more, at www.ceceliascott.com.*

The Sweeney House Series

The Sweeney House is a landmark inn on the shores of Cocoa Beach, built and owned by the same family for decades. After the unexpected passing of their beloved patriarch, Jay, this family must come together like never before. They may have lost their leader, but the Sweeneys are made of strong stuff. Together on the island paradise where they grew up, this family meets every challenge with hope, humor, and heart, bathed in sunshine and the unconditional love they learned from their father.

About the Author

Cecelia Scott is an author of light, bright women's fiction that explores family dynamics, heartfelt romance, and the emotional challenges that women face at all ages and stages of life. Her debut series, Sweeney House, is set on the shores of Cocoa Beach, where she lived for more than twenty years. Her books capture the salt, sand, and spectacular skies of the area and reflect her firm belief that life deserves a happy ending, with enough drama and surprises to keep it interesting. Cece currently resides in north Florida with her husband and beloved kitty. When she's not writing, you'll find her at the beach, usually with a good book.